ADVA

"If you're looking for a mystery with intrigue, heart, a finely drawn setting and relatable characters finding their way through tragic circumstances, Fatal Harvest is for you. Brenda Chapman knows how to tell a story and is, quite frankly, one of the most readable Canadian mystery writers of our time."

- **Anthony Bidulka**, author of *Going to Beautiful*, Crime Writers of Canada 2023 Best Crime Novel

"This was hugely readable and compelling. And there are enough dangling threads regarding the principal characters to make Book 4 a must!"

- **Susan Rothery**, Editor

PRAISE FOR WHEN LAST SEEN

"… compelling characters, an interesting plot and a conclusion that one does not see coming."

– *Glebe Report*

"...wows with well-crafted tension and original characters. In a genteel Ottawa neighborhood, ...Literary sleight-of-hand comes naturally to Chapman, and the culprit could be one of many poker-faced or temperamental suspects as in any worthy mystery-thriller. A tryst with an escort, a traumatizing roofie, a naive vigilante, and plenty of delectable surprises make *When Last Seen* a treat for mystery readers."

-*BookLife*

FATAL HARVEST

A HUNTER AND TATE MYSTERY

BRENDA CHAPMAN

Brenda Chapman

IVY BAY PRESS

Title: Fatal Harvest / Brenda Chapman

Names: Chapman, Brenda, 1955 – author

Description: Series statement: A Hunter and Tate mystery - #3 Edited by Allister Thompson. Cover Design by Laura Boyle Published by Ivy Bay Press, First Edition May 2024

ISBN Trade Paperback: 978-0-9784284-9-5; ISBN ePub: 978-9784284-7-1

For Ted, as always

"Then must you speak
Of one that loved not wisely but too well."

- Shakespeare, Othello

CHAPTER 1

A shaft of sunlight flashed off the front windshield of the vehicle parked nearly out of sight behind the woodpile. Matt would have missed seeing the sliver of light if he hadn't turned his head at the exact split-second when the sun broke through the darkening sky and refracted off the glass. From this distance, he couldn't make out if it was a car or a truck tucked in behind the stacked logs. He slowly surveyed the shadowy perimeter of the property before his eyes landed on the front bumper of the vehicle, only partially visible from where he'd stopped. He swung his gaze across the space until it landed on the door of the old white farmhouse, open and swaying in the gusty September breeze. Devina hadn't gotten around to turning on the porch light, and darkness filled the deepest corners of the wrap-around veranda. The sun was moments away from disappearing altogether behind the row of pines at the edge of the fenced-in back yard.

Matt slid off his bike, wondering who had come visiting on a Saturday. Something didn't feel right. It had to be a stranger, if they'd entered by the front door. Everyone else knew to go around the back, push open the screen door, and step directly into the kitchen where a pot of coffee always sat warming on the stovetop with fresh baking on the counter to go with it. Devina hadn't mentioned that she and Stu were expecting company before he set off with his fishing pole soon after sunrise. He'd been in a hurry to leave, his friend Jimmy leaning on his bike handlebars at the bottom of the driveway as Matt waved goodbye to Devina. Strangers rarely found their way to this place in the country; most who dropped by were neighbours, and they always parked at the top of the laneway nearer to the front door.

He set his fishing rod and the small cooler containing three perch and a rock bass on the grass while he squatted next to the row of sumacs and pondered what to do. The last of the mosquitoes swarming in the dusk landed on his arms, and he absentmindedly swatted them away while he thought. Devina had told him to be back before dark, and he'd cut it close. He hated to worry her. He rose from his crouch and stared toward the house as the front door swung all the way open and someone stood for a moment in what was left of the waning light, a dark shadow that Matt only caught a glimpse of before he ducked down behind the bushes. From his hiding place, he heard the person clatter down the front steps and the crunch of gravel as they hurried across the yard. A door opened and slammed shut, and an engine revved a few seconds later.

Matt crouched farther into the bushes and pulled his bike closer as the sound of the vehicle drew nearer. He tucked his head and stayed in place until the engine sped past. He glanced up in time to watch the red taillights reach the end of the lane and turn right onto the highway in the direction of Ashton. He watched a moment longer to be sure the driver wasn't coming back before standing and gathering up the rod and cooler. He wasn't sure what instinct had made him hide and felt foolish immediately afterward. Stu would swat him on the side of the head and laugh when he told him. Devina would say that he was right to listen to his instincts.

He wheeled his bike around to the side of the house and rested it against the water barrel. The back-porch light was off as well, and he fumbled with the doorknob before stepping inside the hallway. Devina had asked Stu to put the outdoor lights on motion sensors, but he hadn't gotten around to it. Seemed the more Devina nagged at Stu to do something, the longer he took to do the chore. He was stubborn that way, almost like he was pushing her to see how long before she got upset. Any time Matt had been late before, she'd always made sure to have the yard well lit. He was surprised she'd forgotten this time as dusk crept in and swallowed up the light.

The kitchen was in darkness, but a yellowish glow spilled into the hallway from the living room. Devina and Stu usually watched television in the evenings, but he couldn't hear it and figured the visitor had broken their routine. He set the cooler on the counter and padded on stocking feet across the kitchen floor, stopping in the doorway to listen.

"Devina?" he called, hesitant to interrupt if she and Stu were talking about something important. "Sorry I'm late, but I got four fish." He took a step and paused.

Why hadn't she answered? Were they planning the birthday surprise they'd been hinting at all week? "Turning twelve is a big deal," she'd said only that morning as she forced him to eat a bowl of cereal before he set out. "We need to make Tuesday's celebration one for the history books."

Had the man dropped off a present? Could it be the puppy he'd been asking for? He'd never believed he'd be allowed to have one, and his heart leapt at the thought of a rescue dog. Now *that* would be a gift to remember. He was smiling as he stepped into the living room, and later he'd think of it as the final moment of happiness — the last second before he saw Devina and Stu lying still on the floor with their eyes open and blood soaked through their shirts and pooled around them like spreading crimson puddles, the smell thick in his nose and mouth. He could tell by their empty expressions and stillness that they were gone. He had to force himself not to rush over and wrap his arms around them and tuck his head into their necks. He wanted to beg them to come back to him but stayed where he was. Any closer and he'd be stepping in their blood. He knew that would be a mistake.

A lamp was turned on beside the couch, and Stu was on his back next to the window, in front of the ledge of geraniums and African violets that Devina called her babies. Stu liked to tease her about all the attention she showered on them instead of him, but Matt counted three times when he'd showed up with a new pot of blooms for her collection after driving to town. Devina was some distance away at the entrance to the dining room, lying on her back with her eyes wide open, staring at the ceiling. Her right hand rested on the shaft of a rifle. It looked like Stu's gun that he kept in an umbrella holder in the back hallway. It was always unloaded, and the ammo was in an unlocked box screwed into the wall above the stand. "Not exactly legal, but if I'm going to have half a chance at killing off the wildlife predators, I can't be searching around for a key." Even now, Matt could hear Stu's gruff voice in his head. Matt wiped his eyes and tried to swallow the sobs that filled his throat. He stood there as the minutes ticked past, rooted in place, unable to process what he was seeing.

Devina's grandfather clock struck the hour, jolting Matt out of his trance. He moaned and stared wildly around the room. There was no time to grieve or do something he couldn't take back. This house was no longer a safe place to be. He took gulping breaths to calm himself and cast one long, last look at the two people he'd come to love and would never see again before turning to run down the hallway, stopping to slip into his sneakers. He left the light off and entered his bedroom directly off the kitchen, a storage space Devina had converted for his use. His eyes quickly adjusted to the darkness, and he crossed the floor, bending to yank out the pack that he kept wedged in the gap between the dresser and his bed. His wallet and few possessions from before he'd arrived almost four months ago were already inside. Devina had left laundry folded on his dresser earlier that day, and he stuffed the clothes into his half-filled backpack. His hands trembled as he slid the buckles into their slots before slinging the satchel onto his back. Grief overwhelmed him for a moment, and he dropped into a crouch and covered his eyes. A sob ripped up from his throat, and he fought to hold it in.

Forcing himself to his feet, he started walking toward

the bedroom door, wondering if he should chance finding Stu or Devina's cell phone to call the police, when the sound of tires on gravel froze him in place. As he stood trembling, a car door slammed, and a few seconds later a single set of footsteps trod up the front steps. Whoever it was paused for a moment, likely listening for noises carrying through the night air, before they knocked lightly and the door creaked open. Had the person returned for him? If it were a neighbour or friend, surely they'd have used the back door. They'd have called out.

Matt turned and searched for a hiding place in the shadows. He'd be cornered in here, nowhere safe that the person wouldn't easily find him. He'd be spotted if he moved into the hallway to exit by the back door. His mother's face rose through the panic, and he imagined her next to him, encouraging him to get away. He could almost hear her voice in the room: *Matty, you know what to do.* He closed his eyes and took a deep breath. The footsteps stopped at the entrance to the living room, and Matt forced himself to shake off the paralyzing fear. He slowly backed away while keeping his eyes focused on the half-closed bedroom door.

CHAPTER 2

Liam Hunter took a couple of practice swings before stepping up to the plate. Night had fallen since they started playing, but floodlights kept the ball diamond well lit. He raised the bat and faced the pitcher, trying to get a read on the coming throw. He was aware of Tony standing on first base, chatting with the opposition, totally unprepared to run. They needed him to score in order to tie the game. Liam swung and missed a slider that arced across the plate and out of reach before he glanced toward the stands. Ella Tate sat on the bottom tier, speaking into her cell phone. She caught his eye and gave a thumbs-up before he turned back to the plate just as the pitcher threw a fastball that narrowly missed his head. *Shit, Liam, concentrate*, he ordered himself. He connected with the next pitch, a curveball that hung over the plate, hitting it on the narrow part of the bat just above his hands. The ball popped right, landing squarely in the first baseman's glove. He easily tagged Tony, who'd taken three or four steps toward second with no chance of making it back. The double play ended the game, their second loss that day. They'd done well the afternoon before to make the Sunday playoffs but had dropped into the B category after losing the semifinal that morning. Their luck had run out with one last swing of Liam's bat.

Tony jogged across the field toward Liam. "Tough one, Detective."

Liam rested the bat on his shoulder. "Goes that way some days."

"Guess I should have waited to see if they caught your pop-up before making a dash."

"No, it was my fault for not getting all of it. You never had a chance."

They both turned and began walking toward the stands. Liam watched Ella tuck away her phone and bend to check on Lena, who was sleeping in her stroller. He was still surprised to see how Ella had taken to caring for her friend Finn's baby, now ten months old. She'd never struck him as the motherly type, but then he didn't know her all that well. Adele, Finn's wife and Lena's mother, had taken off almost two months before, leaving him a single dad with no idea whether or not their separation was permanent. Tony had readjusted his work schedule to spend time caring for Lena while Finn worked long hours to keep his gym afloat and pay for a nanny during the week. Tony and Ella spelled him off during the weekends.

"How's our sleeping beauty?" Tony asked, bending over the carriage.

"Out like a light." Ella's smile slid over Liam and landed on Stefan Pomeroy, who stepped past him to get to her. Pomeroy wrapped an arm around Ella's waist.

"Tough one, Hunter," Pomeroy said. "We'll get 'em next time."

"I have no doubt."

"Coming for a beer?"

Liam looked from Pomeroy to Ella and shook his head. "It's been a long day, and I have a stack of paperwork to tackle tomorrow morning. I'll need fresh eyes." He liked to think he saw disappointment in Ella's expression, but that was likely a stretch. She seemed happy with his colleague from patrol.

"I'm taking Lena home. You go for a beer, Ella." Tony grabbed onto the stroller and started walking away before she could protest. Ella shook her head and sighed. "I planned to take Lena home and work on a podcast," she said to nobody in particular.

"Nice change of plans then." Pomeroy moved his arm from around her waist and draped it across her shoulders. "I'll drive you home afterwards."

"Well, just one beer then. I have video to edit." Her voice was on the grumpy side, but she looked into Pomeroy's face and smiled.

"Catch you later." Liam waved before turning and walking away. He reached the bleachers and dragged his equipment bag from under the bottom row, stuffing in his glove and bat. He chatted for a bit with two of the guys on his team who worked in the traffic division before saying goodnight and taking his leave. It was a cool evening for early September, and he inhaled the sweet scent of grass and clover as he strolled to his car. The leaves had barely begun changing colour, although it would turn cold overnight, just not below zero. He leaned back and looked at the stars, pinpoints of light in the blackness overhead. There was a big old universe out there. Maybe it was time to think about a trip to change things up. He'd accumulated a lot of overtime and had wanted to visit Europe one day. There was nothing in his workload that wouldn't keep a few weeks, and he'd come back refreshed, with a better perspective.

Tony was waiting for him in the parking lot and followed Liam to his car. He'd already strapped Lena into her seat and left the back door of his own car open to keep an eye on her. She looked angelic in the glow from the streetlight. Liam hoped that her mother Adele's desertion wouldn't leave any lasting scars. Lena certainly had a circle of people who loved her.

"Ella's like an antisocial turtle," Tony said. "I have to prod her out of her shell or she'd spend all her time upstairs in her garret, podcasting and pounding out articles for *The Capital*. Are you really going home, Detective?"

"I am. It's ten o'clock, and I'm beat." Liam opened the trunk and slid in his equipment bag. He had no desire to talk about Ella with Tony.

"Yours isn't exactly life in the fast lane or anywhere approaching the speed limit, for that matter, Detective. You're too young to pack it in this early."

"I'm not another turtle you need to prod out of its shell, Tony." Liam gave him a sideways grin before shoving the bag deeper into the trunk. Still, Tony lingered, his expression that of a man with something on his mind. "Do you need help with something, mate?" Liam asked.

Tony squinted at Liam and frowned. "Nothing I can't fix. Well, see you anon, Detective."

"Yeah, catch you on the flip side." Liam slammed

the trunk shut and watched Tony saunter back to his car. He never knew what was going on in Tony's head, but whatever it was would emerge eventually. Tony was not a man who kept his own counsel for long.

Liam took the Carling on-ramp toward Kanata and had almost reached the exit to his neighbourhood when the cell phone rang in his pocket. He let it go to voice-mail while he drove and waited until he could safely pull over before checking the caller. The name of his staff sergeant, Julie Quade, popped up on the screen, and his pulse quickened. She never contacted him on his time off, especially this late at night, unless something big was brewing. He hit redial and she answered immediately.

"Sorry to interrupt your Sunday evening. We've got a double homicide near Ashton, in the outer fringe of the Ottawa district. I'll text you the address. Rosie Thorburn will meet you there."

"Any details about what happened?"

"A neighbour called it in. He said the victims are the married homeowners. A boy was living with them, but he's missing." Quade paused. "I'm on standby if we need to put out an AMBER Alert. I'll be waiting for your call after you check out the scene and get the names of the victims. The neighbour who called it in was in shock and could barely tell the 911 operator his own name, let alone theirs. Hunter?"

"Yeah, Quade?"

"Find out about the kid."

"I'm on my way. I'll call when I know."

He hung up and opened Quade's text a few seconds later, quickly punching the address into his GPS. All thoughts of a holiday were pushed aside as he steered

back onto the roadway. Two dead and a boy missing… Was the kid a victim or the killer? Neither option
gave any relief as he sped through the night toward the
crime scene.

CHAPTER 3

Detective Rosie Thorburn welcomed the phone call that interrupted the argument she and her live-in boyfriend, Brad Gregoire, were having about their future together. The confrontation had started on the drive home from their friends' house, where they'd eaten a Sunday roast beef dinner followed by two games of euchre. Brad had accused her of being distant since her near-death experience while on duty in July — he suggested she'd stopped seeing the police psych too soon. She'd responded by asking if he thought they should take a break, an angry leap to keep him from knowing how close he'd come to the truth. It was a relief to find herself on the way to a crime scene with the possibility of working through the night. Getting immersed in a murder case would stop the mess of emotions going on inside her, maybe quell the panic that threatened without warning at random times of the day or night.

The address Quade had recited took her to a farm just outside of Ashton, a village of two hundred people straddling the Ottawa region's boundary line, located about half an hour southwest of the city. The homicides were this side of the line, or they'd be in a different jurisdiction and handled by another police service. She merged onto Highway 417, driving until she reached exit 145 toward Carleton Place. The off-ramp fed into Highway 7, which she followed until she saw the exit toward Ashton Station Road. It was a typical country highway, one lane in either direction, cutting through farmland with set-back homes, the occasional porch light glowing through the blackness. She rolled down the windows and inhaled the ripe scents of harvest and loamy, end-of-summer soil. Crickets sang in the grass, and the twang of cicadas periodically pierced the night air. Driving out of the city calmed her as she mentally prepared for the crime scene, but the sense of peace disappeared as she neared the town limits. Her heart rate quickened and sweat beaded on her forehead, even though the night air was cool. She loosened her hands, squeezing the wheel in a death grip, and ordered herself to relax.

You are not walking into a trap. Hunter is on his way.

She slowed to scan house numbers and names on mailboxes. Her GPS told her the place she was searching for was on the right, but she had missed the driveway on the first pass. She pulled a three-sixty and drove back into the laneway, seeing trees and bushes lining the entrance to the property and extending up an incline. Ten seconds in, she saw the house lit up in the distance, emergency vehicles wedged next to each other, red and blue lights strobing through the darkness. A uniformed officer she'd never seen before directed her to drive onto the lawn next to a shed. She turned off the engine and inspected the vehicles, seeing no sign of Hunter's car. She took a moment to send him a text before stepping outside. She should have taken a longer route to give him time to arrive ahead of her. This was her first murder scene, and she didn't want to show her inexperience. A cop she recognized from training waved at her from near the front door to the house, and she made her way toward him while trying to remember his name. It came to her as she stopped a few feet away.

"Hey, Carlos. What have we got?"

"A couple in their fifties shot at close range, one in the chest, not sure about the other. She's a mess." His milk-chocolate eyes fixed on her, and she remembered having found him attractive during those months in class. He'd rarely volunteered answers yet always knew the correct response when asked. "They were in the living room," he added when the silence lengthened, and Rosie told herself to get a grip on her scattered thoughts and focus. Perhaps she could learn something insightful to tell Hunter when he arrived. She pulled a notebook and pen from her jacket pocket.

"Names?"

"Stu and Devina Petrie. They've lived in the house the past five years, although Devina grew up here."

Rosie jotted down the details and looked up at him. "Who found them?"

"The guys waiting over there." Carlos pointed at two men in plaid jackets and jeans leaning against a truck. Both had beards and wore baseball caps. "They'd come to pick up Stu to play darts at the Ashton Pub around 9:00 p.m. Apparently the Petries kept the back door to the house unlocked, so the taller one," Carlos pointed, "named Lanny Dooley, entered and called out for Stu.

When he didn't appear, Lanny wandered down the hall and into the living room, where he found the bodies. By the looks of it, the couple has been dead nearly twenty-four hours."

She squinted at the men. "Has anyone taken their statement?"

"Not fully. That's why they're waiting around. There's one more thing."

The drop in his voice alerted her that the one more thing was not good. "What's that?"

"An eleven-year-old boy has been staying here the past three to four months, and nobody knows where he is. Apparently, he turns twelve Tuesday." Carlos checked his watch. "About twenty-six hours from now."

"Jesus." She tried to see past the two men, beyond the lights set up around the yard. "Are the deceased his grandparents?"

"No idea."

"Did you catch the boy's name?"

"No, but those two can tell you."

"Is this a working farm?"

"Used to be a bigger operation. They own a couple of acres and grow corn and veg, but that's it now. They also keep chickens and sell the eggs. Calvin Frisk, the second man who found them, said they sold their cattle and a chunk of land to him a couple of years ago. His farm abuts theirs."

They both turned toward the driveway at the sound of tires crunching on gravel. Headlights caught them for a moment before the vehicle stopped and the lights went out. Rosie was relieved to see Hunter step out of the car. He walked directly toward her and Carlos. He was wearing a baseball uniform and appeared tired.

"Evening." He nodded at them both. His eyes studied the exterior of the house and then moved to take in the yard. He nodded in the direction of the two neighbours by the truck. "They the ones called it in?"

"They are." Rosie glanced at Carlos to make sure he was okay with her taking the lead before quickly telling Hunter what she'd learned so far. He listened without moving until she was done.

"Rosie, get their statements and then join me inside. You'll need to put on the white suit. Forensics will have some in a box somewhere close by."

"See you around," Carlos said. He was still watching her when she chanced a look back. She'd never dated anybody but Brad and wasn't sure how she felt about his interest — if it even was interest.

"Gentlemen," she said as she drew up to the two men. She had her notebook and pen ready. "I understand you called in the deaths. I'm here to take your statements. Could I have your names, please?"

The taller of the two spoke for both of them. "I'm Lanny Dooley, and this is Calvin Frisk. We both have farms in the area."

"Tell me what happened when you got here."

The two exchanged glances, and Lanny continued speaking in a deep, pleasing voice. "Calvin stayed in the truck, and I went to get Stu. Usually, he'd be waiting outside, so we were a bit surprised when he wasn't. The house was quiet and felt empty, but I went looking for him anyway. At first, I couldn't believe my eyes." His voice cracked, and he wiped a hand across his face. "Couldn't get my head around it." He rubbed his forehead and choked back tears.

Calvin cleared his throat and spit on the ground. "I

heard Lanny yell all the way from out here and got myself inside the back door right quick. Lanny met me in the kitchen. He was white as a sheet and told me Devina and Stu were both dead in the living room. Shot. I went and looked 'cause it seemed so ... so crazy. Don't know how long I stood there, trying to process what I was seeing, but then I heard Lanny on the phone calling 911. We were both in shock. Still are, I guess." He tried to laugh, but the sound was more of a strangled gasping for air.

Rosie bowed her head so as not to show these two men any weakness. She hadn't been this close to death before and its impact on those left to grieve. Before she could ask her next question, Lanny resumed speaking.

"The boy, Matt Clark, isn't here. I ... I went upstairs to look for him after I couldn't find him downstairs. His bedroom's on the main floor, and there's not much in it. Looks like most of his clothes are gone. No sign of the boy."

"Do you know if Matt is related to Stu and Devina?"

The men exchanged looks. Lanny spoke again. "Not sure, but I think they took him in as a favour. Stu didn't talk about him much except to say that somebody who knew Devina asked her to look after him for a few months."

"Do you know the name of this person?"

Both men shook their heads. "Someone from Devina's chequered past, I guess," Calvin said. "Stu just shrugged off my questions about the kid as if it was no big deal whenever I asked."

"I don't know," Lanny added. "Taking in someone

else's boy for an indeterminate length of time even if they are family seems like a mighty big favour."

Rosie tried to think about what else Hunter would want to know. "Were Stu or Devina worried about something? Had anybody threatened them that you know of?"

"Nothing comes to mind. You notice anything, Lanny?"

Lanny was quiet for a moment, seeming to struggle to keep his voice steady. "Nope. Stu and Devina were laid-back. Well liked."

"She grew up here but moved away after high school. They took over the farm about five years ago from Devina's dad and fit right into the community." Calvin stopped talking, and Lanny put an arm across his shoulders.

"I don't like to ask, but were they involved in anything that could have led to violence?"

"You mean like drugs?" Calvin laughed. "Nah, they weren't into that anymore. Weed is legal, so that couldn't be the issue. Stu liked his beer, but he wasn't a big drinker by any stretch. Say, do you mind if we call it a night? We can give you our contact information if you have more questions. This has been a lot."

Rosie nodded. She could see both men were barely holding on. "I'll take your phone numbers and addresses, and we'll be back in touch. You've been a big help." She wanted to offer words of comfort, but they nodded and turned away before she could think of the right thing to say.

CHAPTER 4

Coroner Brigette Green met Liam at the entrance to the living room. The harsh, metallic smell of blood and death preceded her. "This is a bad one, Hunter. Both shot at close range. By the way they're positioned, I think Stu was killed first, but that's only an observation at this stage. He took a shot near his heart." Green's grim expression spoke volumes, more than she would ever put into words. Liam wasn't put off by her terseness, her way of keeping herself removed from feelings that would get in the way of her work. He'd learned ways to distance his emotions as well.

He made a preliminary scan of the floor around the bodies. "Any idea of the weapon?"

"Well there's that rifle lying next to the woman, Devina. She appears to have been holding it unless the scene has been staged. I'll remove the cartridges and get ballistics involved to ascertain if that's the murder weapon."

She looked back at the bodies, now being

photographed by one officer while two others methodically carried out their search. All were dressed in hooded white suits with slip-on coverings over their shoes. Liam had donned a suit before stepping inside the house. Every light was on, illuminating the corners of the room. Brigette stood silently for a moment, studying the woman. "By the bruising and scratches on Devina's hand and arms, it looks to me as if she struggled. Forensics found a bullet lodged in the wall above the window, so the gun was fired from the vicinity of where she was standing."

"So Devina walks through the dining room and encounters this person with the gun. She would have come up from behind. The person kills Stu on the other side of the room, or it might have been the noise of the shooting that brought her running. She tries to take the gun away, and it goes off—"

"Or Devina might have had the gun, and this person took it from her, but she got a shot off first. I'd say the gun was then used to kill her and Stu, although that doesn't explain why she's holding on to it, unless someone placed it there afterwards in an attempt to mislead us. Or there might be another weapon that the killer took with them. Forensics should be able to give us a clearer picture."

Liam made a fuller examination of the room before zeroing in on the bodies. The couple were in their mid-fifties, both in decent physical shape, attractive. The woman had long grey hair plaited in a side braid and wore a patchwork vest now soaked in blood. The man was tall, over six feet, Liam guessed. He was wearing faded jeans, a plaid shirt, and Doc Martens. His grey hair was pulled back in a ponytail, and his thick beard had been neatly trimmed. They would not have imagined their lives ending today. Liam forced himself not to follow that train of thought and to instead focus on solving the case before him. "I know you can't say, exactly, but any estimate on the time of death?"

She raised her eyes to his and gave the briefest of smiles. "As you say, I can't make a firm determination, but likely late afternoon or early evening yesterday by the state of rigor mortis. Dead twenty-four to thirty hours is my best guess."

They moved deeper into the room, and Liam tried to make sense of what he was seeing. Devina lay near the dining room entrance, and Stu was a distance away in the living room. Had the killer come into the house and surprised the couple or knocked at the door and they'd let the person in? Did they know their killer, or was it a stranger? Had Devina run for the gun because they were threatened by this person's presence? More pressing, where was the boy who'd been living with them? Could he be the one who struggled with Devina and turned the gun on them both? The idea seemed unlikely without evidence, and he didn't voice the thought. An intruder was the more probable scenario, or the one he'd consider for now, keeping the boy's involvement on the back burner.

"Has there been any indication of a struggle or blood found in another part of the house?" he asked. "We have word that a boy was living with them." The couch was positioned to his right, facing wall-to-wall bookcases and a wide-screen television mounted above a wood-burning fireplace. A recliner and coffee table, lamps, faded paisley area rug — the room was cozy and lived-in. He sensed the home had been happy, welcoming. *Why this couple?*

"No, the violence is limited to this room, from our first examination. There's no sign of the boy." She shook her head and continued as if reading his thoughts. "Why this older couple in a farmhouse in the middle of nowhere? I understand they moved here five years ago and were fully integrated into the community. Devina Petrie grew up in this house and inherited the land from her father." She turned toward the door as if the subject had wearied her. "I'll schedule the autopsy right after two other urgent ones on my plate. I want you to catch the bastard, Hunter." She nodded curtly at Rosie Thorburn as she passed her on the way into the hallway. Thorburn stopped next to him, her eyes wide, surveying the room and flitting across the bodies. Liam could hear her intake of breath and watched the colour drain from her face.

"First time?" he asked.

She closed her eyes and nodded. "It's not like on television. The smell…"

"Focus on the scene and remember why we're here. These people are counting on us to figure out what happened and who did this to them."

She opened her eyes and straightened her shoulders. "I'm fine."

Liam studied her as she walked toward the bodies. Things didn't add up, especially finding out today that she'd never seen a dead body before. She'd been hired by Kurt Auger in Toronto, and they'd arrived as a pair, recruited by Staff Sergeant Greta Warner, who currently was off on medical leave. Why would Auger bring along an untested, inexperienced officer and make her a detective, a plum position in Homicide and Major Crimes that cops with years of experience angled to get? Auger was married, with two kids. It wouldn't be the first time a cop in a position of power had an affair with a younger recruit. The optics were definitely not good.

"Any sign of Matt Clark?" Thorburn interrupted his contemplation of her relationship with Auger. She was squatting next to the female victim but had pivoted on the balls of her feet to look up at him.

"Is that the boy's name?"

"It is. Lanny Dooley and Calvin Frisk, the neighbours who found them, confirmed that these two are indeed Stu and Devina Petrie as Carlos reported. They also named Matt Clark but weren't certain if he's a relative or the son of a friend. Devina grew up here, apparently, and left after high school, only returning five years ago. Lanny and Calvin said they don't know much about those intervening years, although Calvin said the Petries didn't appear to be involved in anything illegal since moving to this farm. However, I got the impression from the way he spoke that Devina and Stu were once into illicit drugs."

Liam wondered whether her assessment would hold up under further investigation. Was this a freakish crime of passion or a preplanned hit? Perhaps the prepubescent boy sent to the country to give his parents a break had gone berserk and picked up the rifle. It was too early to know. He waited for Thorburn to finish her examination of the bodies before suggesting they look through the rest of the rooms. He was pleased to see the colour had returned to her face, and she appeared to be taking in as much of the scene as she could, her eyes scanning while her mind filed away details for later.

They walked down the hall and stopped in the doorway to the kitchen. The smell of burnt coffee filled the space, and he spied an empty, blackened pot sitting on the counter. "Lucky that didn't catch fire," Liam said, scanning the rest of the countertop. Dishes had been left to dry in a rack, and half a bundt cake sat under a glass dome. A fishy smell rose up from a small cooler sitting on the counter near the stove. "I don't see anything out of place."

"It's hard to tell if something was taken." Thorburn took a slow look around before continuing down the short hallway to the small room on the right. "This must have been Matt's bedroom," she called over her shoulder. "It's utilitarian at best. They appear to have cobbled the space together for his visit."

He followed her into the cramped quarters that had likely been used for storage at one time. Thorburn was already going through the dresser drawers, wearing gloves so as not to contaminate the scene. "One of the men who phoned in the murders said Matt's clothes were missing. He appears to be right," she said before easing the drawer shut.

If this room had been searched by an intruder, nothing had been tossed about, probably because there was barely anything to toss. A bed and a dresser took up most of the space. Liam's eyes rose to the window. A breeze had the metal blind gently tapping against the frame.

"Odd to have a window half open with the furnace on." He moved closer and examined the sill. "I'm going to check outside."

"I'll keep searching in here," Thorburn said without looking up.

He used his phone as a flashlight to examine the ground under the window. A narrow swath of grass abutted a brick pathway running parallel to the house. The grass looked trampled, but he couldn't make out any footprints. He straightened and squinted toward the back of the property. Devina and Stu had a sizeable, fenced vegetable garden to his left next to a shed. A large clump of towering pines stretched beyond the fence while a small barn framed the right side of the yard. He walked toward it and pushed open the heavy door. He could smell the chickens before his flashlight beam revealed them roosting in cages lining the wall in two tiers. Somebody would have to look after them now that the Petries no longer could. He left the barn after a quick walkabout and crossed the yard to the garden shed. Inside, everything was in order, rakes and shovels hanging from the far wall. A wheelbarrow, snow blower, and ride-on lawn mower took up most of the floor space.

Thorburn joined him a couple of minutes later where he stood behind the shed, staring out at the fields and the woodland on either side, dark and foreboding in the moonlight. "It took me a few moments to find you. Is everything all right?" She shut off the flashlight on her phone. They stood silently listening to the night sounds: an animal rustling through the underbrush, the hoot of an owl in a nearby tree, the wind wrapping itself around the branches of the pines and swaying them to and fro. "I didn't find anything of interest in his room." She spoke softly, as if not wanting to disturb the peaceful scene.

"We'll need to search the field and woods at first

light," he said at last. "The boy, Matt Clark, could be out there, hurt or…"

"Don't say it." Thorburn cut him off. She gave a small laugh. "Sorry, I just want to believe he got away until the truth comes out. Someone might have taken him."

"Perhaps. We'll have to search for him anyway. The open window in his bedroom suggests he could have exited the house that way. Whoever killed Stu and Devina might have heard him and given chase." Liam shrugged. "It's one theory among many."

"It's odd, isn't it, that Lanny Dooley and Calvin Frisk had no idea about his relationship to the Petries?"

"I'll ask Forensics to keep an eye out for correspondence when they go through the paperwork, phones, and computers." He took one last look into the darkness and turned toward the house. "Let's have a quick check of the upstairs bedrooms before I call in a report to HQ. Forensics is already going through the deceased couple's bedroom but doesn't hurt for us to get the entire lay of the land. We can get a team together to visit the neighbours as soon as the sun's up in five hours, but until then carry out a Google search on the Petries and Matt Clark while I get the ground search organized. There'll be no sleep for us tonight, I'm afraid." He looked skyward over the pines. "Bad weather is moving in, unfortunately."

"I'm too wired for sleep anyway." They'd reached the back steps into the house. She stopped and looked back at him. "Thanks for … letting me get my bearings. Not everyone would be as patient with an inexperienced partner."

He nodded but didn't say anything, not convinced she

wanted a response. He watched her climb the stairs, putting away his unease at her connection with Auger, his mind already sorting what needed to be done before dawn. The clock was ticking, and the first forty-eight hours were critical if they were to have any chance of finding Matt Clark and the killer — if someone else was involved. He just prayed it wasn't Matt they'd end up hunting down for murdering the two people who'd opened their home to him for the summer. A troubled eleven-year-old capable of such evil hurt his brain to contemplate.

CHAPTER 5

W eak morning light guided the search team and a flurry of reporters with cameras and microphones to the Petrie farm. Through the living-room window, Liam spotted Ella Tate and her protégé, Sherry Carpenter, from *The Capital* standing on the driveway behind the police tape. HQ had issued an AMBER Alert shortly after 3:00 a.m., followed five hours later by a press release. They had not located a picture of Matt Clark, but Lanny Dooley had given a good description when Thorburn called him the night before. They hadn't been able to determine any next of kin, however, and the alert was thin on details. If there'd been time, Liam would have gone over to speak with Ella, but he was wanted in the backyard.

As soon as the search teams with two sniffer dogs were brought up to speed, they set out to comb the fields and woods behind the Petrie house. The air was cool and crisp, with a dense layer of clouds blocking the sun. A dampness in the air spoke of the rain to come. Liam joined one of the teams with two fellow detectives from Homicide, fondly nicknamed Boots and Jingles, ignoring the fatigue that had settled as a dull ache behind his eyes. Thorburn stayed inside to continue her online research into the Petries. The team of police walking slowly through the cornfield toward the woods stretched in two jagged lines with handlers and their dogs, straining at the leads, a few steps ahead. Liam used a pole to poke at debris, relieved not to hear a shout from anyone that they'd found the boy's body.

Twenty minutes in, the skies opened and a half-hour downpour muddied the ground and puddled in the hollows. The dogs appeared less determined in pulling their handlers forward, the rain watering down scents and making them snuffle more thoroughly through the vegetation. Liam had put on a raincoat and boots before setting out, as had the others, and they continued to press forward through the driving rain, slowly and methodically checking every square inch of land. The smell of wet loam and rotting corn husks filled his senses, his boots squelching in the muck with every step. He worked hard to concentrate as the rain pelted his face and blurred his vision.

They reached the edge of the forest, and the dogs sniffed up and down the perimeter, seeming less certain than before. The searchers gathered under a cluster of pine trees as thunder rumbled a short distance away. The officer in charge raised his voice above the sound of the rain rustling through the leaves and striking the ground.

"This swath of woodland covers a couple of acres with a stream running through it. The next property over is a dairy farm owned by Calvin Frisk. We'll keep our formation and go up the east side and return by the west half if we don't find anything."

Boots came up behind Liam. The hood of a black poncho protected his bald head. "Not enjoying this weather. Any ideas on why the couple was murdered?"

"Nothing yet. Forensics is going through their paperwork and devices, in addition to the autopsies. Hopefully, they'll find something."

"This is a helluva disturbing situation." Boots saluted before trudging back to Jingles. The two of them chatted for a moment and then moved farther down the line.

Liam turned toward the woods. This would prove to be rougher going, but at least the trees gave some protection from the relentless rain, which had succeeded in washing away footprints and scents. He thought, however, that the farther they got from the house without finding Matt's body, the more likely he was still alive. The question was whether he'd been taken or somehow made a clean escape — and if he'd gotten away, why hadn't he shown himself to the police?

————

"THIS PLACE GIVES me the creeps, knowing what happened." Sherry slumped back in the passenger seat and squinted toward the Petrie farmhouse through the windshield, streaked with droplets. Sporadic gusts of wind splattered sharp slices of rain onto the roof and pummelled the side of the car. "What the hell kind of person kills a couple of harmless, middle-aged people living the life on Sunnybrook Farm?"

Ella looked up from her cell phone. "But we don't

know they were harmless, do we? They could have been into something illegal. Maybe they were hitmen hiding out in this secluded location after a life of contract killings."

Sherry scowled. "You've watched one too many action movies, Tate. This boy who's gone missing, what if he's the killer? The public could be naively on the lookout for him while he's armed and dangerous, prepared to shoot anybody who gets in his way. Have the police thought about that?"

"He's only eleven years old, still in grade school." Ella studied the front door of the house as someone stepped outside. She had to admit that although the idea of this boy shooting his caregivers seemed irrational, it wasn't impossible. Children had done vicious, horrible things before, even if these were the exceptions rather than the norm. "You're right, though. All scenarios should be considered, and I'm sure the police are doing just that."

"Have you found anything more about the Petries or Matt Clark online?"

"Not too much. Devina Petrie's Facebook page is private. However there's a webpage for Petrie Farm where they take orders for produce." She held up her phone screen for Sherry to see before scrolling through vibrant photos of vegetables and a flourishing garden. Devina and Stu smiled in several as they showed off baskets of beans, peppers, tomatoes, and potatoes. In one pic Stu stood in a cornfield, holding up a cob with the husk partially stripped away. In another, Devina posed with homemade soaps and candles at the kitchen table.

"They looked like a nice couple." She clicked on the

comments page. There were twenty or so endorsements, along with questions about hours of operation and what was in season. Devina had answered or thanked every entry. A few were obviously from friends who mentioned events in Ashton that Devina or her clients might be interested in attending. The last comment was from three days before they were murdered, inviting Matt Clark and his friends to work at the local fall fair, since they were looking for young people to help out. Jean Bowser gave the dates and inserted a poster. This was the only comment without a response underneath. Likely, Devina or Stu hadn't checked the site the last couple of days before they died. This was harvest time, and they had a huge garden to empty and what looked like an acre of corn to bring in.

"I can't find any social media sites for Matt Clark," Sherry said. "Odd for a kid that age not to have an online presence. Not even a TikTok account."

"There must be a zillion Matt Clarks."

"There are several in Canada, but I've weaned out the ones who don't fall into his age group. Of course, he could have come from the U.S. or overseas. So far, the kid's a mystery. We'll have to talk to neighbours to get a lead."

"The Petries kept a low profile too." Ella looked toward the house as the front door opened. She recognized the two officers who stood talking in the entranceway. There'd been no sign of Hunter since she arrived, and her hope rose and fell every time someone came or went from the house. She wanted to send him a text yet didn't dare leave an electronic trail. They'd collaborated unofficially on a few cases, but his position on the force demanded more secrecy about their alliance than hers, even though he only fed her enough information to point her in the right direction on cases.

"You still seeing that cop, what's his name, Stefan?" Sherry's voice drew Ella out of her reverie.

"We've been on a few dates." Ella shrugged, not wanting to discuss her personal life with a colleague. It was bad enough that Tony nagged at her for being too solitary and dolled her up like a perspective bride. There was one way to shut Sherry up, though — turn the tables. "What about you? Got some hot guy ... or girl ... hiding in the wings?"

Sherry laughed. "I can assure you I'm into men, and as it so happens, I've been dating a chef. He owns a little bistro in the ByWard Market called Gleason's. Have you eaten there?"

"Nope." Tony might have, though. She'd have to remember to ask him.

"Well, we will have to rectify that soon. Bernard makes the most divine escargot and coq au vin."

"I have a feeling we could be busy the next while." Ella tried to keep the disappointment from showing on her face as two more cops left the house without any sign of Hunter. "As soon as this rain lets up, I'll film you with the house as a backdrop, and we'll get the footage to Canard, sparse as our story will be. Then I suggest we drive into Ashton and talk to some locals at the pub. Surely somebody knows something about this family."

"And I wouldn't say no to beer and a sandwich." Sherry pulled out her notebook and began jotting points for the interview. "Give us an hour, and Ashton Brew Pub here we come."

CHAPTER 6

Lanny Dooley's call arrived as Rosie was walking toward her car to phone Acting Staff Sergeant Quade. Hunter was still out with the search party, and she needed instructions from central command before joining the door-to-door. She stopped partway down the driveway in the misty drizzle and answered.

"Detective Thorburn? Sorry to call, but my son Jimmy tells me he was fishing with Matt on Saturday, and they parted close to dusk on the highway."

Rosie's heart quickened. "Is Jimmy home now? I'd like to come over and speak with him, if you're available."

"I'll put on some coffee. Come around to the back door."

She confirmed the farm's location on the other side of Ashton in Beckwith County before signing off. A quick call to Quade with an update about her impending visit to speak with Matt's friend, and she was on her way.

———

JIMMY WATCHED the black sedan pull into the driveway from the window on the second floor landing and let the curtain fall back into place. His parents had kept him and Theo home from school while "things got sorted," as his mom put it. "A week off this early in the term won't hurt," she'd added. "We need space to grieve." His dad had told him to stay upstairs until called to speak with the detective, and he'd been pacing up and down the hallway, feeling like a caged animal. At last, the cop knocked on the door, and his dad thumped down the hall to let her in. Jimmy tiptoed to the head of the stairs, staying out of sight while he listened to his dad greet the detective and invite her into the kitchen. He watched the tops of their heads bob past. The detective had long, reddish-brown hair tied in a ponytail and looked young.

He slid silently on his bum down the steps and crept closer to the kitchen. They were talking in hushed voices, so he couldn't make out what they were saying. A chair scraped on the floor, and Jimmy leapt back toward the stairs. His dad appeared in the doorway to the kitchen, and Jimmy pretended he'd only just come down from his bedroom.

"Jimmy, time to meet Detective Thorburn. She wants to talk to you about Matt."

The woman was sitting at the table, but she stood when he entered and smiled as if she was glad to see him. "Hello, Jimmy, please have a seat. I'm Detective Rosie Thorburn — you can call me Rosie — and I have a few questions about your friend, Matt. He's missing, and I'm hoping you can help us figure out where he's gone and why."

She hadn't mentioned that Devina and Stu were dead. Jimmy thought that might be a big fat clue. He held back, and his father gave him a gentle shove toward the table.

"Don't be shy. The lady won't bite."

"Your dad tells me that you like to fish. Is that right, Jimmy?" Her hazel eyes were friendly.

He nodded. "Me and Matt have a place we usually go."

"Were you fishing there on Saturday?"

"I met him on my bike at the end of his driveway. We rode toward Ashton and found a spot on the Jock River further along. We caught six perch and we both took three. Matt caught a couple of rock bass and gave me one. It was a good day."

"What time did you get home?"

"It was almost dark. Matt said bye and biked toward Ashton while I went the other direction to get home. The sun was going down, so we had to hurry. My mom and Devina don't want us riding along the side of the highway in the dark, even though we both have lights on our bikes. That's the last time I saw him."

"The sunset was around seven forty-five," Lanny added. "Your mother wasn't too happy that you came home so late."

"She said to be home before dark, and I was. I texted her a couple of times."

"Dark being a judgement call. Well, you know how she worries."

The detective waited for them to finish their exchange and focus on her. She gave Jimmy an encouraging nod. "Did Matt tell you where his real home is and why he came to stay with Devina and Stu?"

"He lives with his mom, but he never said where. He told me she had to work, and Devina offered to take him for the summer. He didn't know if he'd be starting school here next week. He said it was up in the air. He was happy to have the first week of class off anyway."

"So his mom and Devina were friends?"

"I guess." Jimmy shrugged. "Matt never said anything about his family."

"Do you have a photo of him?"

"Nope. He doesn't have a phone, and said he hates having his picture taken."

She seemed to be thinking about what he'd said, and during the silence, Jimmy tried to stop himself from imagining the awful things that had happened to Devina and Stu. *Shot. Both of them.* Sunday night, his dad had come home and poured a big drink of rye before telling his mom what happened. Jimmy was halfway up the stairs on his way to bed after staying up late to watch a movie and had crept back to the hallway to listen. His mom had begun crying and asked a bunch of questions before she pushed past him to run upstairs to her room, not even stopping to find out what he'd overheard or to order him to bed. His dad had found him there and told him that his mother was in shock. She and Devina had been friends a long time. And the police were right now searching the fields and woods for Matt's body, Jimmy's dad had told his mom before she left with Theo for her dance class that morning.

"Where is your wife, Mr. Dooley?"

"Hope took our daughter to ballet. Theodora is

seven and thankfully has no idea what's going on. We're trying to keep her life on an even keel. She has Down's."

And she takes all of Mom's attention. Jimmy thought the words but didn't say them out loud. He'd have included his dad, except the farm took up most of his time and Theo came a distant second. It didn't matter, though, not since Matt arrived at the start of the summer. His first real friend and now... Jimmy looked out the window and tried not to cry. The detective seemed to notice, and her voice softened.

"What kind of person is Matt? Can you tell me anything about him that would let us know him a bit better?"

Jimmy scrunched up his face as he thought over her questions. "He turns twelve tomorrow. We were supposed to have a party." *And I don't turn eleven until the end of December.* "We both like being outdoors and stuff."

"He was a good friend to you."

Jimmy nodded, his vision watery with unshed tears. He was starting to realize how little he had left to look forward to with Matt gone.

"I won't keep you much longer, Jimmy, but can you tell me if Matt was scared or angry on Saturday?"

"He never said anything. He was happy about his birthday coming on Tuesday. Devina was going to bake a chocolate cake and promised him a surprise. He thought it might be a dog."

The detective looked over his head at his dad. "I guess that's all for now, but we'll want to ask more questions in a bit and speak with your wife."

Lanny nodded. "This will take a while to sink in." He ruffled Jimmy's hair. "Why don't you go outside and play in the yard, son, while we finish talking? Don't go anywhere on your bike for now."

Jimmy jumped out of his seat and said goodbye while turned away from them so they wouldn't see him crying. He left by the back door and jogged to the barn where he could hide out until the detective was gone.

CHAPTER 7

B_oston_
Sam Green leaned against the counter and poured a second round of coffee, smiling and laughing at the men's banter, ignoring their suggestive hints at something more. She drew away from them and picked up a couple of menus on her way to a new table by the window, aware the men's eyes were focused on her as she walked across the chequered linoleum floor. *Even in a diner,* she thought. *Men are so boringly predictable.*

The suppertime rush was over, and Sam took advantage of the lull by slipping into the back hallway to check her messages. Disappointed not to receive any, she clicked on a news app and scrolled through. All quiet except for the usual inflation warnings, wars overseas, and political muck. She tucked the phone into her apron pocket as one of the men from the counter approached. He wore a tailored blue suit, and his hair was cut short. A fashionably trimmed beard kept him from looking too corporate, although the Rolex spoke to his status.

"What time you off, pretty lady?"

"Let's not do this, shall we?"

"Do what?" He feigned pouting for a moment before grinning. "Listen, life is too short to beat around the bush. I find you attractive and would like a chance to get to know you better without the apron on."

"Your wife might not appreciate that sentiment." She glanced pointedly as his wedding band. His direct-ness might have flattered some women, but she wasn't one of them.

"The wife and I have an agreement."

"Oh, yeah? Tell me about that."

"I have girlfriends, and she has credit cards. We both get what we want without any drama."

"Lovely. Well, I'm not interested in being part of your arrangement. Please step aside so I can get back to my job."

He blocked her path a few moments longer before something in her expression seemed to get through to his astounding ego. On her way past, his hand landed on her hip, but she kept walking and didn't look back. She stayed busy clearing tables until he rejoined his friend and they exited the diner together. He'd left a twenty-dollar tip and his cell number as a parting gift. She pocketed the money and tossed his number in the trash.

"You're throwing away a gift horse. He's CEO of one of those high-tech start-ups."

Sam turned and saw Belinda standing at the cash watching her. "Do you want his number? He seems to collect girlfriends who don't mind that he has a wife."

"No, thanks. Not my jam, as they say."

"Nor mine. I prefer peanut butter."

Belinda laughed. "Say, you can clock off if you want. I'll finish cleaning up."

"Thanks. I have an appointment, so I will take you up on that and skedaddle a few minutes early."

"I saw you checking your watch and phone. Figured you had a doctor's appointment." Belinda glanced pointedly at Sam's stomach before turning away.

I never should have shared, Sam thought.

She said goodbye to Franco and Amir in the kitchen and exited by the back door. She'd arrived by city bus before the lunch shift but welcomed the walk to her apartment in the gathering dusk. She stayed on the well-lit streets, watchful but not overly concerned by the lack of pedestrians. She'd made up an appointment because of an uneasy feeling that had plagued her all day. She wanted to be safely locked in her home before complete darkness set in.

At the corner of Elm and Willow, she paused and scanned the street in front of her building. All looked quiet. A car turned onto Elm and slid into a parking spot, but she recognized the woman who stepped out of the passenger seat. She leaned in to say goodbye to the driver before entering Sam's complex. The car pulled away from the curb, and Sam took a step forward. She spotted the red glow of a cigarette in the doorway across from her building at the last second and moved back into the shadows. Was this a real threat, or was she simply being paranoid?

There was only the one sighting of the glowing cigarette, but she waited anyway. Five minutes later, a man stepped forward from the same entranceway and looked in both directions before slipping back out of sight.

The uneasy feeling growing inside her all day suddenly seemed less absurd. She should have received a phone call by now and knew this was at the bottom of her angst. A man waiting in the doorway across from her apartment could be a coincidence, but was she willing to ignore her instincts? She'd come up with a hundred reasons why the call had been delayed, but none that made any sense as the day wore on. This, combined with the man loitering across from her building, meant she could not return home tonight. She took one last look toward the place where the man stood waiting in the dark and turned to walk back the way she'd come. If she hurried, she could get her knapsack out of the locker at the YWCA before it closed for the night. She'd find a hotel nearby and book a room while she figured out her next move. Taking care of her immediate needs would keep her from panicking over those things she could not control.

CHAPTER 8

The utter darkness that only comes in the country had settled around Liam where he stood at the edge of the Petries' garden, looking up at the night sky. A few hours earlier, a fitful breeze had sprung up, helping to hasten the rain clouds on their way, and the stars glittered like fistfuls of sequins strewn across a black canvas. The scent of grass and a ripe harvest reminded him of his youth and the last days of summer before freedom ended and another school year began. He'd been an earnest student, believing that good marks would make his aunt not regret taking in him and his sister Hannah after their parents were killed in a car crash in Belfast. That need to please had never left him, even after he understood it came from childhood insecurity. His parents had abandoned him and Hannah through no fault of their own, but their deaths had marked the both of them just the same. They still clung to the bond they'd forged through that tragedy and the frightening move to Canada, not out of necessity now, but because they'd become each other's trusted confidant — the person whose love would remain a constant, no matter what the world threw at them.

There were footsteps on the hard-packed earth, and Thorburn appeared next to him. She stood silently breathing in the crisp air, and he sensed her fatigue. He half-turned and looked at her profile. "We've done all we can for today," he said. "Let's go home and get some sleep."

"I wish we'd been able to locate Matt Clark. I don't like to think of him with a killer, although on the plus side, he's likely still alive."

"He might not be with the killer." *If there even is another killer. Matt's innocence hasn't been proven yet*, he thought but kept this to himself.

Thorburn shivered and wrapped her arms around herself. "Are the searchers done combing the fields and woods?"

"They plan a second pass through tomorrow and will widen the perimeter to be on the cautious side."

"What will we focus on in the morning?"

"Quade plans to speak with media and ask for anyone who saw something to come forward. A call line will be set up, and we'll continue visiting the nearby farms. Good work speaking with Jimmy, by the way."

"He didn't tell me much."

"Which is interesting in and of itself. Matt was more private than seems normal for a kid that age, not even posing for any photos. Hard to believe in the social media generation. We still haven't found a picture of him to include with the AMBER Alert."

Thorburn turned her head to look at him. "You think he was hiding out here?"

"The idea has crossed my mind. He might have been sent to live in the country because he was hanging with the wrong crowd. Perhaps his parents wanted him to get his head straight. We also need to find out more about Devina and Stu Petrie. Hopefully more information about their lives will lead to the motive and who shot them." Liam took one last look at the night sky. "I'll walk you to your car. Let's meet in HQ at 7:00 a.m."

"Exactly six hours from now." She yawned before turning her face away.

"Often we get no shut-eye the first forty-eight hours after a murder. This is a gift horse." He needed to sleep. The weekend baseball tournament and the day's search had worn down the last of his energy. If he was to be any use tomorrow, he had to lose consciousness for a couple of hours. Quade had already told him and Thorburn to go home, and he hadn't put up much resistance. He just hoped he could make the twenty minute drive into the city without nodding off at the wheel.

———

ELLA WOKE after her usual four hours and lay a bit longer, staring at the curtain swirling into the bedroom. She'd begged off joining Stefan for a late-night drink after returning from Ashton with Sherry and thought it time she cut the cord completely. He was too intense for her liking, and she wasn't as attracted to him as she should have been if this relationship was to develop. He was a good man, though, and deserved to be with someone who would give him the same level of commitment. She took a deep breath and let it out slowly, trying to centre herself for the day ahead. Stefan wasn't going to even make the six months she usually gave her partners.

She took a quick shower in tepid water and put on black leggings and an oversized green sweater that Tony said belonged in the donation bin before padding barefoot into the kitchen and plugging in the kettle to make instant coffee. Tony had bought her a coffee machine that took up a great deal of space on the counter, but she still hadn't gotten around to using it.

Sunlight filtered through the tree outside the living-room window, and she took a moment to survey the space with a critical eye. The room was cramped and had little style to speak of. The couch was old and second- (or maybe third) hand, and her oak desk was ancient and cumbersome, shoved against the wall next to the window. Her computer and sound equipment for her podcasts took up nearly all of its surface. Tony had convinced her to buy a new leather chair and reading lamp, which she'd wedged in on the other side of the window, but she preferred sitting in her desk chair. He was now trying to talk her into a new couch, but she'd resisted so far. She didn't care about owning stuff and didn't want to start acquiring items she'd be sorry to give up down the road. Maybe it wasn't in her to become attached to things ... or to people. She accepted the first part of the supposition but discarded the second. There were people in her life she'd be bereft without — *was* bereft without. Her eyes landed on her brother Danny's urn sitting on the wide window ledge in the sunshine. She still couldn't part with him, even as the anniversary of his murder loomed.

She crossed to her desk and booted up the computer, sipping on a cup of coffee and checking phone messages while she waited. Hunter had set up an account on WhatsApp under the pseudonym "Braveheart," and she went there first. He hadn't sent any new leads on the Ashton murders, so she was on her own for this story. The Ashton Brew Pub had been quiet last evening, and nobody had given any background about the Petries. She'd be covering much the same ground today as the police, trying to piece together the facts: background on the victims and what had led to the killings. This would begin with a thorough web search, followed by another drive out to Ashton to speak with the neighbours. Hopefully, she'd have better luck today getting people to talk. Her editor at *The Capital*, Canard, had given her an end-of-day deadline for a deeper dive into the Petries and Matt Clark, and she had a lot of digging to do before setting out on the road.

CHAPTER 9

The policewoman came again, this time with her partner, late Tuesday afternoon. Jimmy watched them get out of their car from his bedroom window, and the pain in his stomach worsened. He didn't like talking about Matt or Devina and Stu and knew instinctively that was why the police had come. It scared him to think about somebody entering a house and shooting everyone. Even Mom had told Dad last night to lock the doors when they were in bed. His dad had grumbled but did as she requested. She'd warned him not to go outside unless they knew exactly where to find him. Their farm was a six-minute drive by car from the Petries' property on the other side of Ashton in Beckwith Township. He and Matt rode the distance easily on their bicycles, although they always got a lift home when it was dark with their bikes in the back of the truck or van.

Jimmy walked as quietly as he could down the stairs and stopped at the bottom. He could hear the two officers speaking with his dad in the living room. The woman detective said they'd found Mattie's bike leaning against the side of the house, so they knew he had made it home on Saturday, probably interrupting whoever was inside shooting the Petries. The question was why the person hadn't shot Matt too. Or maybe they had and moved his body? The police weren't sure. There was another option they also had to consider. Her voice dropped, and Jimmy crossed the hall to stand in the entrance to the living room. All three of them turned to look at him.

"Ah, there you are, son. Come stand over here." His dad motioned to the spot next to him, a few feet away from the man, who told him that his name was Detective Hunter. He didn't look like a policeman. His black hair was long and curly, and he was wearing blue jeans and a black leather jacket. His eyes were bright blue, reminding Jimmy of bachelor buttons — his mom's favourite flower. He was standing beside the woman cop who'd been by the house the day before. She'd said to call her Rosie.

"Was Matt a good friend to you?" Detective Hunter asked, smiling.

"He was the best." Jimmy brightened for a moment before the ache in his tummy came back. He dropped his head and scuffed at the floor with the toe of his shoe.

"Did he like living with the Petries?"

A short nod.

"Was he angry with them on Saturday?"

Jimmy looked up, trying to read Detective Hunter's expression. He shook his head harder this time. "Devina was going to bake him a birthday cake."

"How old are you, Jimmy?"

"Ten." He waited. The detective paused for a

second but didn't comment on how much older he looked. Most people thought he was thirteen or fourteen.

My, aren't you big for your age!

"And Matt turns twelve today, is that right?"

"Yup. I turn eleven in December." It felt important they know he would be a year older soon too.

The two detectives looked at each other and then at his dad before Detective Hunter smiled back at him. "Did Matt ever practise shooting guns at cans with Stu or Devina?"

"Sometimes. Stu said it was a necessary skill to have living in the country, and Matt was getting to be a good shot."

"Did Matt own a gun?"

"I think he used Stu's rifle."

"Did they practise a lot?"

"I guess." Jimmy didn't add that Stu let him shoot at cans too. His mom would go ballistic. She hated guns.

Detective Hunter thought for a bit. "Did Matt talk about his family or say where he lived?"

"He has a mom. He said his dad didn't live with them anymore."

"Do you know their names?"

"No. He called her Mom."

"Does he have other friends around here?"

"I don't think so. We ... that is Matt just hung out with me." His voice swelled with pride, even to his own ears. Matt had picked him over all the other kids. The wonder of it never got old.

"Okay, Jimmy. You've been a big help." The detective ducked his head like he was about to leave, then raised his eyes to stare at him. "Has Matt contacted you since Saturday?"

Jimmy shook his head. "He doesn't have a phone. He said he doesn't like anybody knowing where he is."

"Were those his exact words?"

"I don't know." Jimmy blinked back tears. He hated being a baby.

Big fat goof. Why're you crying, baby? Baaa … b … b … beee.

The tall man crouched down until their eyes were at the same level. "We're going to find Matt, and I'll come tell you when we know where he is. He's lucky to have such a good friend who cares about him like you do. Here's a card with my phone number. You and your mom or dad can call me anytime if you remember something about Matt or want to talk about what happened."

Jimmy tried to smile, but his mouth wasn't acting properly. The man put a hand on his shoulder before he straightened.

"You can go play in your room, son." His dad tousled his hair as he passed by.

"I know Jimmy's big for his age, and you expect him to be more mature than he is, but he's only going into grade five," Jimmy could hear his dad explaining to the detectives as he slowly walked toward the stairs, scuffing his shoes on the carpet. "He's not behind intellectually or anything, but his size marks him as a target at school. Thanks for giving him your card and making him feel seen. We will call if he remembers something that might be important."

Jimmy didn't wait to hear the detective's reply. He climbed the steps to his bedroom at the end of the hallway but stopped on the landing to look out the window. He could see the door to the barn on his right and the long driveway directly in front of him. As he watched, his mother's blue van appeared at the end of the laneway. He squinted. Theo was in the front seat, and he remembered she'd been at a birthday party in Richmond. She was popular in her class and had lots of friends. Their mom liked to chauffeur her around because it gave her a chance to socialize with the other mothers. Theo and their mom had a bond that he'd envied before Matt came along, before he had someone to talk to and go fishing with. He was going to have to get used to doing stuff alone again, keeping out of sight so his mother wouldn't keep telling him that all he had to do was try harder to make friends. As if it was that easy.

His mom parked at the edge of the grass, and Jimmy watched her help Theo out of the passenger seat with two red balloons on strings and a loot bag. Theo had a big smile plastered on her face, like she usually did, and a few seconds later they disappeared from view. His mom's hair was pinned up in a messy bun, and she was wearing a clingy red sweater he'd never seen before. Her tight blue jeans and ankle boots made her look young, like someone in high school. The boys in his class stared and said rude things to each other as soon as she was out of earshot. Whenever she stood close to them and asked how they were doing, they'd clam up or give one-word answers. After she'd gone, leaving a trail of her musky perfume behind, they'd punch him and act as if she hadn't just made them turn into tongue-tied idiots. Jimmy wished sometimes that she wasn't so pretty and friendly with everyone she met. He wanted a mother like

Evan Rose's — one who didn't attract attention or have the boys talking behind her back.

He heard her and Theo enter the house by the back door. A minute later, he listened to his mother walk to the front of the house and stop in the hall to talk to the detectives. Theo was clumping up the stairs and would soon be in his room to tell him all about the party. She'd want to share whatever was in the loot bag. He was about to turn away from the window when he saw the back door of the van swing open. He pressed himself flat against the wall and watched with his mouth gaping as Matt Clark jumped onto the driveway and, crouching low, ran toward the barn. He was carrying a knapsack over his jacket. He pried the door open wide enough to slip inside the barn moments before the two detectives stepped outside the front door of the house.

"What are you lookin' at, Jimmy?"

He turned. Theo was standing behind him, her puzzled eyes staring, the beaming smile on her face drooping into a frown. She was short and round, dressed in her favourite pink dress with the scratchy crinoline. Her poker-straight brown hair was tied back with a lopsided black velvet bow, and someone had painted blue hearts on both of her pudgy cheeks. A smear of chocolate icing covered the edge of her mouth and streaked down her chin. The two red balloons bobbed on strings above her head.

"Nothing, Theo. I was waiting for you to tell me about the party."

Her smile returned, and she grabbed his hand and pulled him across the hall into his bedroom. Once inside, she wrapped her arms as far as she could around his waist and tilted her face to look up at him. "I was the prettiest one there," she said without a trace of modesty. "I'm going to wear this dress on my birthday too." She stepped back. "I brought you a balloon to make you feel better." She held out a string, and he took it from her. He thought of Matt hiding in the barn.

"A red balloon, my favourite colour," he said. "I'll find *The Little Mermaid* for you to watch while I feed the chickens by myself tonight. My way of saying thank-you." He knew she liked feeding the chickens but could never resist watching the movie. It was like a drug — she'd be in a trance once it started. It was the same when she was allowed time on her iPad. A bomb could have gone off in the next room, and she wouldn't have noticed.

Her smile got even wider. "And I'll wait for you to come back so we can share my candy."

CHAPTER 10

"**I** feel for that kid," Thorburn said, surveying the even rows of corn before getting in the passenger side. "He's the size of a teenager, and it's easy to think he's slow when he's likely a normal ten-year-old. His dad said Matt was his only friend." She swung her gaze in Liam's direction. "Hope Dooley is attractive and young-looking. Hard to believe she's forty and the mother of those two kids."

Liam put on his sunglasses and got in next to her. He turned the key in the ignition while thinking about the Dooleys. Thorburn's comments didn't seem to require a response, so he didn't provide one. He'd only be agreeing anyway. Hope hadn't appeared to be a typical farmer's wife, although he supposed the stereotype of a ruddy-cheeked woman in an apron baking bread in the kitchen didn't hold any longer. Even so, he thought it must be hard for her to live way out here in the middle of nowhere. Difficult for Jimmy, too, who appeared to be a social misfit in school with a sister who had special needs seemingly taking the majority of his parents' attention. He wondered what kind of friendship twelve-year-old Matt Clark had with Jimmy, who was about fifteen months younger, a wide gap when it came to maturity. Was the relationship lopsided? Had Matt used Jimmy's situation to his advantage? They needed to return and find out more about Matt when Jimmy wasn't so upset by his disappearance and the murders. He wondered if Ella Tate would take on the task. She was good at encouraging people to tell their secrets.

The day was getting on, and he glanced over at Thorburn. "I thought we could drop by the Ashton Brew Pub for a pint and a chat with the bartender. They tend to know the local gossip."

"And could tell us about the Petries," Thorburn nodded. "Good idea."

"I've been known to have the odd one or two." He grinned at her. "Do you need to call your boyfriend to let him know you'll be late?"

She shook her head. "Brad's doing a double shift. The paramedics are working long hours with the staff shortages."

"Tough job."

"He's good at it, although he's been exhausted lately." She bit her bottom lip as if to cut off commenting further.

"I can imagine." He wondered if Brad's job was impacting on their relationship but decided it was none of his business.

They reached the village of Ashton, basically a corner store and a pub where they also brewed craft beer. The Jock River flowed under a bridge next to the bar, a picturesque country setting. The highway wound up a hill and around the bend toward Beckwith Township, really another village with houses and farms strung along the route.

"Ever thought of moving out of the city?" Thorburn asked.

"Not especially. You?"

Liam glanced over at her. She'd turned her head to stare out the side window. "Brad keeps asking me to move back to our hometown or somewhere in the vicinity of Collingwood."

"You both have high-pressure jobs. I guess it's natural to want to return to a simpler time now and then, but it's not the answer for everyone."

"That's a very diplomatic response. Sometimes I think giving in would be the easiest thing, and if not for this job, I'd probably already have capitulated and moved back there with Brad."

"But that's not what you want to do."

"No."

Liam inwardly squirmed. This was more personal than he liked to get with colleagues. He knew bits of Quade's life from when they'd been partners, but it was mainly superficial stuff. He steered away from anything deeper, probably because staying detached was the only way he could do this job effectively. Everyone moved on, and he didn't need to open himself to more loss. With relief, he realized by her silence that Thorburn had ended the conversation.

He pulled into the pub's entrance off the highway and drove the length of the one-storey structure into the parking lot. "Ever been here before?" he asked.

"No. The building has that Bavarian look about it."

"The part closest to us is the brew pub, and the bar is near the front of the building."

"Too bad we can't drink on the job. A cold brew would go good right about now."

"I'd say our work day is over. A pint is definitely in order."

The interior resembled its British relative, dimly lit, a ramp leading into the small main room where tightly grouped tables were arranged to encourage socializing, although today the seats were mainly empty. The walls were crowded with flags and paraphernalia, cheering up the dark wood panelling. The bartender stood behind the counter to their left, and just past her was the entrance to another room that had a bank of windows overlooking the Jock River. The server led them into this room, and Hunter's eyes landed on Ella Tate and Sherry Carpenter sitting at a table with a view. He motioned to the table next to them, and Thorburn nodded before taking a seat. Hunter glanced at two couples sitting farther down in the long room. Ella followed the direction of his eyes as he settled into the chair across from Thorburn.

"They don't know the Petries well," Ella said to Hunter. "We already checked them out. The server lives in Carleton Place, and the bartender only knew them on sight because she works days. Apparently, Stu came in Sunday nights to play darts and drink beer, but none of that crowd is here today."

Sherry reached across the space between the two tables, extending her hand to Thorburn. "We haven't met officially. I'm Sherry Carpenter. I work the crime beat for *The Capital*. I'm glad to see you've recovered from your ordeal a few months back."

"Thanks. Good to meet you. I'm Rosie Thorburn,

Hunter's temporary partner, as you appear to already know."

"Most women would try to make that partnership permanent," Sherry said, deadpan. She wriggled her shoulders as if she was about to eat something delicious.

Ella rolled her eyes. It took Liam a moment to clue in. He ducked his head to hide the red blush heating up his cheeks. The server returned with menus, letting him off the hook. He and Thorburn ordered burgers and beer as the server brought over the machine for Ella and Sherry to pay.

"We were about to head out," Ella said. "Unless you have anything you'd like to share with us about the investigation?"

"Not at this point." Liam widened his gaze to include Sherry, not wanting to acknowledge his connection with Ella. "We haven't found Matt Clark yet, but you could ask people to be on the lookout."

"Any photo of him to share, Detective?" Sherry asked.

"We're still trying to locate one."

Thorburn added, "It is odd, though. Most kids post selfies and chronicle their daily life online."

Ella tilted her head from side to side as if weighing her thoughts. "He was only eleven. Maybe his parents kept him away from all that. They did send him here. Not exactly the hub of social activity. Does he own a cell phone?"

"Not that we've found." Liam thought, impressed that Ella was thinking along the same lines as he'd been. Was Matt's aversion to social media and his summer in this isolated village prompted by his mother's lifestyle choice for him, or was there another reason?

Ella met his gaze one last time before she stood. "Well, it's been a long day. We'll leave you to enjoy your meal."

The server arrived with their food and drinks, and Thorburn and Liam dug in without talking much. Fatigue had hit them both at the same time. Liam chanced a glance at Thorburn's bowed head and wondered how far he could trust her. Auger had recently derided her policing ability, but Liam wasn't convinced of his motive. He'd brought Thorburn into the unit and appeared to control her, until Quade assigned her to work with Liam. Was she secretly reporting back to Auger? The two of them were barking up the wrong tree if they thought he'd help them oust Quade from the staff sergeant position. Perhaps she'd shared a personal problem earlier to get him to open up. Liam swallowed a mouthful of beer and picked up his fork. The sad thing was that he believed Thorburn would make a good detective, given time. He hoped whatever was going on between her and Auger wouldn't end up ruining her chances.

CHAPTER 11

Jimmy didn't make it to the barn until after supper. His mom had chores for him to do inside the house and said the chickens could wait a few more hours. She'd fed them that morning, and they weren't starving by any means. He kept quiet rather than argue and make her suspicious. It wasn't as if he'd ever been in a rush to feed them before.

He snuck two granola bars and a juice box into the pockets of his jacket before stepping out the back door into the thinning sunshine. His stomach had been so upset all through dinner that he had trouble eating his mom's stew. She hadn't noticed, though, because she was so happy telling his dad all about Theo's dancing and her day hanging out with the other mothers. His father had grunted at the appropriate times as he ate. Jimmy half-listened to her rattle on while worrying about Matt. Why was he hiding in the barn, and would he still be there when Jimmy's mom finally allowed him to leave the table?

He sped up his pace crossing the yard and entered

the chicken coop, taking a moment for his eyes to adjust to the greyish light. The chickens flapped around him as he threw handfuls of grain on the ground, not too much, as his dad had instructed. Dust motes swirled in the weak shafts of sunlight that filtered through the small windows, high up on the walls. He worked quickly and slipped back outside five minutes later, checking that nobody's face was watching him from a window in the house. The coast clear, he scooted across the yard to the main barn and pushed the door wide enough open to slip inside. He held his breath, standing in place while his eyes focused on the tractor and farm equipment. They used to keep horses in this barn but hadn't for a few years. His dad didn't want to exert energy on looking after animals, especially ones that weren't all that useful. "They're an expense we can't afford," he'd said to stop Jimmy's tears when the man came to take Flicka. Corn, asparagus, beans, squash, and peppers kept his dad busy spring to fall. In the winter, he drove the snowplough for the provincial government, keeping the country roads passable and working long hours, often through the night.

"Matt!" Jimmy called as he started moving deeper into the space. "I know you're in here. I'm alone, and nobody else saw you get out of the back of Mom's van." He stopped and listened. He took a few more steps as his eyes adjusted to the thicker gloom. "Matt, it's okay. I'm here to help you."

"I don't need any help." Matt's voice came from the far end of the barn where the empty horse stalls were. "Turn around and pretend you never saw me. I'm leaving in a few hours when it gets dark."

"I brought some food." Jimmy kept walking,

searching for Matt as he moved closer. He was almost at Flicka's stall. He hadn't been back here since they took her away. Matt was in the last stall, sitting on the dirt floor, tucked into himself like he was trying to become as small as possible. His face and hands were dirty, and a twig stuck out of his hair. Jimmy slowly lowered himself against the far wall and set the granola bars and juice box in front of Matt. "What's going on? Everybody's out looking for you."

Matt's eyes were wild-looking when he held Jimmy's gaze, like Flicka got when a noise scared her. "Stu and Devina…" His voice cracked, and he stopped talking. He dropped his chin to his chest, and his shoulders shook as he sobbed.

Jimmy waited. "My dad and his friend Calvin found the Petries. The police have been here twice. They asked me if you were mad at them."

Matt jumped up from his crouch. "I would never, ever have hurt them. The cops are fucking crazy if they believe—" his voice dropped, "if they think I did … did … *that*."

Jimmy stood too but didn't move any nearer. "I know you didn't. I'm not telling them anything." *Because I don't know anything.*

Matt panted and took in gulps of air. It took a moment for him to gain control of himself. "I got no idea who killed them. A man … I'm sure it was a man … came into the house when I was in my bedroom. I climbed out the window and ran into the woods in the dark. I could hear the guy searching for me. He had a flashlight, I think it was a phone app, but he never got close. I kept moving deeper into the trees. It sounds nuts, but I'm not making it up."

"You must have been scared shitless."

Matt closed his eyes and swayed. Jimmy edged closer in case he fell. "Let's sit down, Matty. Somebody might come looking for me. Mom's really freaked after what happened."

"Nobody can know I'm here." Matt dropped heavily onto the ground and rested his back against the cinder block wall.

Jimmy crouched down next to him. "Have you talked to your mom?"

"I don't have a phone. Devina always made the calls. I don't even know Mom's number."

"What about your dad?"

"My parents are separated. I have no idea where he is."

"That sucks."

"Yeah. It happened in the spring. That's partly why I'm here, I think."

"They didn't tell you?"

"Mom said to enjoy my summer, and we'd be back together in the fall." Matt rubbed his forehead. The smear of dirt spread across his temple. "But I know Dad was in some kind of trouble at work. I'm scared the Petries' murders have something to do with me."

"How could they? Nobody knows you're here, do they?"

Matt was silent for a moment. "I overheard my parents talking about how bad things were at his office. My dad even cried. Then they split up, and I got sent here and told to stay off social media and keep my head down. If his work mess was the reason … I don't want anyone else to die. You have to act like you never saw me. I'll get some sleep and be gone before sunrise."

Jimmy couldn't let his only friend leave this easily. "Mom and Theo are going to Ottawa in the morning for a doctor's appointment, and Dad will be bringing in crops. You can come inside and take a shower, and I'll make some breakfast. We'll have all day to figure out what to do."

"I don't know—"

"You need a plan, and I can help." He waited until Matt nodded.

"As long as you don't tell anybody, I'll sleep here for tonight." Matt reached over and shoved him on the shoulder. "You're a real friend, you know that?"

Jimmy beamed inside, the happiness overshadowing his worry, but not for long. "Are you going to be warm enough? It's getting cold at night. I can leave a blanket outside the back door when everyone's watching TV. They always watch two sitcoms between seven and eight."

"I'll check then. What time is it? I don't have a watch."

"Six thirty. I'll put the blanket on the back steps in half an hour."

"Okay." Matt was calmer now. He picked up one of the granola bars, opened the wrapper, and took a bite. "It'll be good to sleep anyway."

Jimmy started walking away but stopped and turned. "Say, happy birthday, Matt. Guess this isn't a great way to spend it."

"You got that right, but thanks."

"We can celebrate when this is all over."

"Sure." Matt met his eyes for a moment, and he smiled before moving deeper into the shadows and out of sight.

As he entered the house, Jimmy thought about where he could get a blanket without his mother missing it. He settled on taking one out of the hall closet from the back of the pile. The family was watching *Young Sheldon* when he crept downstairs with the thickest blanket he could find. He eased the back door open and set it on the steps, putting two apples on top before going inside.

CHAPTER 12

B *oston*
It took a moment for Sam to realize where she was. The hotel room was small and smelled of air freshener, but the bed was comfortable enough. She'd fallen asleep as soon as she crawled under the covers. The clerk had put her on the fifth floor next to the exit, as she'd asked. She'd made up a story about having a fire phobia and being unable to get out of the building in an emergency. Lying was becoming as easy as breathing.

She lay still, listening to noises in the hall. A door banged open, startling her, and a man's voice called out that it was room service. It took a moment before she realized that he was speaking with someone in the room across from hers. She took a deep breath and swung her feet onto the floor, all the while chiding herself for being so jumpy. If she didn't get a grip on her fear, it was going to be a very long day. First a shower, and then she'd have some decisions to make. Luckily, this was her day off from the diner, and she had time to notify the manager if she wouldn't be in tomorrow.

She put on the same clothes she'd worn the day before, except for a change of underwear and socks. She scrubbed yesterday's panties and bra and spread them on the back of a chair to dry. Her phone still hadn't rung or signalled a message. She tossed it on the desk and phoned room service on the landline. *I'll only spoil myself this once*, she told herself. *Just till I get my bearings.*

She scrolled through the *Boston Globe* while she waited. A knock at the door made her jump, and she called for room service to leave her meal outside. She listened to their footsteps recede down the hall before sliding the tray inside. The decaf coffee smelled heavenly, triggering hunger pangs that reminded her she'd skipped dinner. She poured a cup and then settled at the desk with the plate of eggs, ham, home fries, and toast. Her cell beeped as she was pouring a second cup from the carafe. She took her coffee and phone and went to stand in front of the window while she read the message. Rain streamed silently down the triple-pane glass, falling from a leaden, overcast sky.

Check the Ottawa news. Then call me. K.

She set down her coffee cup and opened the Ottawa news app. *Double Murder Near Ashton.* The headline sent a surge of panic through her entire body. She frantically scrolled down the rest of the story. The bodies were discovered two days ago. No names given. Family was still being located and notified.

Katherine picked up on the first ring. "Did you read it?"

"The article doesn't say who was killed. Do you know something more?"

"The couple had a boy who's gone missing."

She fought down a surge of nausea. "How old?"

"The article doesn't confirm his age, but says he's around ten. More details expected soon."

"Matt turns twelve today." She bit her bottom lip while she thought. "I expected a call from him yesterday, but none came through. It wasn't like Devina to forget." She focused on the rain streaking down the window. "I think somebody was outside my building last night."

"Are you kidding me? Did you go inside your apartment?"

"No, I'm in a hotel downtown. It might have been my overactive imagination, but better to be safe."

"What are you going to do?"

"Keep moving, I guess." She remembered the phone call that hadn't come. "I have to head up there."

"It's not safe, especially in your condition."

"Being pregnant isn't a sickness, Katherine. I'm capable of renting a car and crossing the border."

Silence.

"I have to make sure Matty's okay."

"This is all so horrible. You never needed to agree to any of this. Wyatt should have—"

"Wyatt should have done a lot of things, but he didn't, and here we are."

Silence.

"Katherine, don't bail on me now. You're the only one I can trust." Sam hated the pleading note in her voice, but she was beyond desperate.

"So that's why I'm going to drive to Ottawa and check on Matt for you," Katherine said. "It's only a couple of hours from here. I'll speak with whoever's in charge of the murder case, but I won't share any information about you or Matt's situation. Stay put, and I'll call as soon as I know anything. Me going makes the most sense, since I live in Montreal. The only border I need to cross is provincial, so I can't be traced, not that anybody knows we're connected."

Sam ran scenarios through her head and realized this one was the best option. Still, she didn't like having another friend jump into danger on her behalf. What if it really was Stu and Devina behind the news headline? How could she live with herself? "Promise me you'll be careful, Kate. This isn't a game."

Katherine's voice reassured her, "I'm always careful, and you can trust me not to give anything away. You're likely worrying for nothing, and if I can give you peace of mind, it's the least I can do. You'd do the same for me."

"In a heartbeat. I don't know how to thank you."

"Your friendship is thanks enough. Say, are you still using that alias?"

"Yeah, but not for much longer." The thought was a good one. Sam Green would soon be in the rear view and she could return to being herself.

CHAPTER 13

Ella thought she'd sleep soundly but found herself wide awake at 3:00 a.m. after conking out on the couch for a few hours. She wondered if it might be time to see a doctor about her insomnia — if she had a doctor, that is. Family physicians were as hard to find as hen's teeth. She'd have to make time to visit a clinic.

She put on an extra sweater, since the apartment had cooled, and padded over to sit at the computer. The Ashton murders file she'd started Monday was open on the screen, and she scrolled through its contents. The facts were few and far between, even for this early in an investigation. She leaned back in the chair with her fingers intertwined behind her head and spoke to Bart Simpson, the poster taped to the wall directly above the desk. "This is most peculiar, my friend. Who exactly were Stu and Devina Petrie? What have they done and to whom that led to their deaths?" Ella closed her eyes. "I need to find out more about them. The key to the mystery has to start there."

Before beginning an Internet search, she opened the messages on her phone. Sherry had texted soon after Ella dropped her off at her apartment the evening before, but Ella hadn't noticed the alert. *Two fresh shootings in Vanier, so I'm working those tomorrow. Canard says for you to stay on the Petrie murders. Ciao Bella!* Ella skimmed through the other messages but found nothing of import. Stefan hadn't sent his usual end-of-day note, giving her pause. Was he backing off and giving her space, or had he decided she was too much work? Either way, she felt guilty at the surge of relief. She hadn't looked forward to the awkward conversation when she promised that she was the one with the problem, not him. She'd made the same speech so often, her mind wandered when she said the words.

She stared up at the poster of Bart Simpson. "Not sure what to do about Canard treating me like I'm his employee, buddy. I barely have time to work on my podcasts." She sighed and rubbed her eyes. She couldn't deny the money from the paper came in handy, but she was becoming less convinced that the paycheques were worth the lack of autonomy. She stood and stepped in front of the window. Her brother Danny's urn sat on the ledge, and she rubbed her fingertips across its ceramic surface while she thought. This restless, unsettled feeling wasn't new, but it had deepened since Danny died. She kept trying to find solid ground, but her feet couldn't gain purchase in the quagmire of memories. The harvest moon was hidden behind a bank of clouds. Wispy strands of fog softened the light from the street-lamp to a yellowish glow, making it impossible to see into the shadows.

Ella returned to her desk and opened a Google

search. Work would take her mind off her troubles, as it always did. At 4:30 a.m., she lifted her fingers from the keyboard and stretched. She hadn't found a lot but had enough leads to make another trip to Ashton in the morning, now only a few hours away. Her eyes felt gritty, and fatigue left her light-headed. She made a quick visit to the bathroom and was mercifully asleep moments after she dropped onto her bed and crawled under the covers.

―――――

A RUMBLE of thunder woke her early, and she set out for Ashton at 9:00 a.m. after a cool shower and a cup of coffee, taking a second one with her in a travel mug. The three and a half hours of solid sleep had revived her somewhat, enough for her to look forward to another day of interviews. The windshield wipers kept a steady, thumping beat the entire way with the rain pattering on the roof of her car. She passed by the driveway to the Petries' house, knowing she'd find nothing useful there, forcing herself not to check if Hunter was on site. She entered the village centre a minute later and slowed as she reached the Ashton Pub. She turned off the highway, driving the length of the building to the parking lot at the rear of the long, one-storey structure, then pulled up the hood of her coat and walked back to the road, dashing across the intersection to the corner store. The bell tinkled as she stepped inside, shaking water from her clothes. She looked toward the cash register and smiled. Her sleuthing of the night before was about to bear fruit, if the age of this woman was anything to go by as she looked up from the newspaper spread out on the counter.

"Yes, can I help you?" A red and black checked shirt fitted snugly over a bulging belly, and her white hair was tied back in a ponytail. Tiny lines deepened around her eyes and mouth when she smiled.

"I hope so." Ella moved to stand in front of her. "Are you Nelly Depper?"

"I am." The smile dimmed, and her eyes turned wary. "I don't believe we've met."

"No, we haven't. I'm Ella Tate and am here in my capacity as a reporter for *The Capital*. Let me first say I'm deeply sorry for the loss of your friends. This must be a very difficult time for you and the community."

"How did you know—"

"I read your comments on their farm website and kept digging. You and Devina Petrie were friends in high school."

"Yes, we go back a long way. I must tell you, though, we weren't particularly close these last few years."

"Any reason?"

"None I want to talk about with a reporter."

"Fair enough."

The bell tinkled, and Ella took a walk around the store while Nelly served two customers. She didn't seem happy when Ella set a pint of milk on the counter after both women left the store. Ella fished around in her bag for her wallet. "The police have no idea why the Petries were killed. I was hoping you could tell me about them."

Nelly punched in the sale and didn't speak until she dropped the receipt next to the milk. Her expression was more resigned than friendly. "I'll be spelled off for a break at ten thirty if you want to meet me in the pub across the street."

"I'll get a table in the back room, near the windows."

"Don't worry, I'll find you, but I honestly don't know anything that will help discover who killed them."

"My sole objective is to learn more about them. We'll leave solving their murders to the police." Ella hoped a lightning bolt wouldn't strike her dead for the lie as she opened the front door and walked outside into the pouring rain.

CHAPTER 14

Ella ordered an Ashton Pale Ale, even though it was midmorning, and looked through the raindrops streaking down the window at the Jock River meandering past. The water level was dangerously low for this time of year, so she didn't begrudge the last few days of steady precipitation. The weather had become so odd. The forecast called for wet, cooler-than-normal weather for the rest of the month to complement the hotter and drier-than-normal summer. Winter promised to be a roller coaster. She checked her watch a few times, fearing Nelly had bailed when she still hadn't arrived by ten forty-five. The older couple in the corner were paying their bill when Nelly finally rushed in, her face flushed and hair damp from the rain.

"Sorry, my replacement was late." She pulled out a chair and shrugged out of her yellow slicker as she sat down.

"I'm just glad you made it. Let me buy you a drink or coffee, or whatever you'd like. Is it too early to order lunch?"

"That's okay. Reba — the server — knows my order. Same thing every morning."

Reba waited until the couple left through the side door to arrive at their table. She was sixtyish, with a runner's toned body and beaming smile. "Coming right up," she said, nodding at Nelly. She looked at Ella. "Can I get you another?" "Something to eat, maybe?"

"A coffee would be great, thanks."

Two coffees arrived in short order, followed by a heaping plate of poutine that Reba set in front of Nelly. She picked up the fork and grinned. "My daily guilty pleasure."

Reba hovered. "Everett joining you as usual?"

Nelly shook her head, her eyes darting over to Ella. She dismissed Reba with a wave of her hand and said, "So what do you want to ask me?"

Ella took a sip of coffee before saying, "I'd like to know what kind of people Stu and Devina were. The good, bad, and ugly. I assure you, though, that I won't print anything unkind. It would serve no purpose."

"So why even utter something derogatory aloud?" Nelly took a big forkful of French fries, gravy, and cheese curds and stuffed the lot into her mouth. Ella waited while she chewed and swallowed. Nelly set down the fork and leaned forward. "Devina was a free spirit. She missed out on the hippy generation by ten years, but she could have been a flower child. Soon as she turned eighteen, she left Ashton, her family farm, and all her friends, and didn't arrive back here until five years ago with Stu in tow."

"Did you stay in touch when she moved away at eighteen?"

"For a while. She travelled around a lot, said she

planned to live in all fifty states. In the end, she spent most of her time in California, interspersed with living in cities in the southern states. Monterey, Phoenix, and Vegas were her main locales, I think she said. She settled in Florida as well for a time."

"How did she support herself?"

"Waitressed and dealt cards in casinos. Picked fruit when all else failed. You have to envy her willingness to do whatever it took."

"And Stu?"

"She said they met in a Vegas casino. He was playing blackjack at her table. He asked her out for a drink, and they hit it off. Got married a few months later in one of those Elvis chapels. Guess he must have known a good thing when he saw it. I believe that was toward the end of her foot-loose life, about three years before they moved here."

"What was your opinion of him?"

"Stu? He was friendly and integrated himself into the Ashton community more than Devina when it comes right down to it. He joined the dart league and worked on some charity fundraisers. Devina threw herself into farming and making crafts. She was the driving force behind their business."

"That conflicts with your depiction of her as a flower child."

"Right? She was a woman of contradictions, although to be fair, farming and candle- and soap-making are back-to-the-land. I understand she was ready to settle down when her parents passed, and Stu figured why not move to Canada? He worked construction and had no real ties."

"Had he married before?"

"I don't think so but don't know for sure."

"And they never had children, either together or with other partners?"

"None they spoke about."

Ella watched Nelly pick up the fork and continue eating. "Could they have come here to escape from something or someone?"

Nelly appeared to consider the idea as she chewed. "If they did, they kept whatever it was to themselves."

"You knew they were looking after Matt Clark for the summer?"

"Of course. I'd see him and Jimmy Dooley fishing on the river almost daily. Sometimes Matt helped out with Stu's causes. Seemed like a good kid. Polite whenever we spoke."

"I saw your name on their farm Facebook page a few times."

"Easiest way to contact Devina."

"Do you know why Matt was here for the summer or where he comes from?"

"Nope. Maybe Stu told one of his dart league friends, but Devina never shared any information with me. This is a small community, and we're all in each other's pocket, so that kind of news would have gotten around. Frankly, I was surprised Matt hung out with Jimmy, who might look big for his age, but still … Jimmy started grade five after Labour Day, and Matt will be entering grade seven from what I understand, which is a chasm in kid years. Stu said they'd be registering Matt by next week if he didn't leave before then. Guess that's a no-go now. Matt's good-looking and appears athletic, while Jimmy has that gangly awkwardness of a kid not comfortable in his own skin. He's isolated on the Dooley farm and introverted as all get out. Matt didn't join any summer sports leagues or seek out a more popular crowd. Kind of unusual, really. It felt like he was putting in time, waiting to go back home."

Ella paused for a few beats. "You said that you weren't close to Devina when she moved back here. Had something specific happened that kept you apart?"

"You don't miss much, do you?" Nelly set down the fork. She'd eaten all the poutine and drank the last of her coffee before answering. "We had nothing in common anymore." She shrugged. "Life happens. We grow up and take different paths. Didn't mean I wanted anything bad to happen to her. Christ, it's devastating to think about." She turned her face to look at the trees and water deep in the ravine. "Could have been someone from their past catching up to them, but who knows? Ashton is a quiet, peaceful place, and nothing like this has ever happened before. Makes me think it had to be someone from away." She turned her eyes on Ella and gave a half-smile. "Well, if that's all your questions, I need to get back to the shop."

"Thanks for your time. I'll cover your bill."

"That's all right then." Nelly struggled into her jacket and stood. "Stu and Devina didn't deserve their lives to end this way. I hope the police bring them some justice."

"I hope so too. Say, is there anyone I should speak with? Was Devina close to anybody else?"

Nelly hesitated. "Nobody I can think of offhand."

Liar. Ella's instincts kicked in unbidden. She'd interviewed enough people to know when somebody was holding back or trying to make her think black was white. "Thank you for sharing your break with me," she said, hoping to keep the line of communication open in case she needed to speak with Nelly again. By then, Ella hoped to have learned more about the Petries and their relationships so that she'd be the one with the upper hand and in a position to cut through the bullshit and unearth the truth.

Reba arrived at her table a few minutes after Nelly left, holding the debit machine in one hand and the coffee pot in the other. "Not trying to rush you," she said. "Stay for another cup if you like."

"I'll pay up now and will take the refill." Ella grinned. "Say, who's Everett?"

"Everett?"

"Yeah, the man Nelly usually meets on her break."

"Why, Everett is Nelly's brother. He'd have coffee with her, and then Devina Petrie often joined him when Nelly went back to the store. I can hardly believe Devina and Stu are gone. It's just plain surreal."

"Did you know them?"

"Not like we socialized or anything, but you get to recognize people on sight, and everyone's friendly. Their murders have rocked this village, believe you me."

"How can I find this Everett?"

"He has a house nearby on the Flewellyn Road, this side of Dwyer Hill. There's a mailbox with a moose on top near the highway at the bottom of his driveway. Nice guy. He used to date Devina, from all accounts, before she went off to find her fortune. The love of his life, if you believe the gossip. He has to be devastated. I haven't seen him since … well, since her death."

"Last name?"

"Johannson."

"So Nelly must be married, since her last name is Depper."

"Married and divorced. Made her kind of bitter, if you ask me. Eating a mound of poutine every morning isn't helping her to post attractive photos on Tinder." Reba's tinkling laugh made the comment less cruel than it sounded. "She had a thing with Calvin Frisk some years back right after her divorce. I believe she still holds the torch for him, but I'd be gobsmacked if he ever looked her way again."

Ella's reporter senses tingled. Everett was a person who potentially knew more about Devina than anyone else. Nelly had gone out of her way not to mention he was her brother, which seemed mighty curious. Was he in need of protecting? Interesting that he and Devina met for coffee most mornings. Perhaps Stu hadn't known about their ongoing relationship. Had jealousy simmered like a pot on low boil? People kept secrets for all kinds of reasons; in this case, one of them might have erupted into murder. A bit more digging, and she intended to find out where Everett and his sister Nelly fit into this tragedy.

CHAPTER 15

Jimmy's mom and Theo were running late. Theo had spilled a bowl of cereal and milk all over herself and had to change her dress. She'd cried and screamed, not calming down until Jimmy had gone upstairs with her to help pick out another one. She'd insisted the dress had to be blue and pink, even though the only one with these colours was in the laundry. He finally convinced her to wear a blue skirt with her pink top. It had been difficult staying patient, but he knew she'd escalate if he didn't. Theo could throw one hell of a tantrum when she got going. He wished he could join in sometimes, but his parents wouldn't have been amused.

Finally, his mom was ready to leave. She'd let her hair hang loose and was wearing another new sweater, this time bright orange with sparkly flecks sewn into the wool. Jimmy could usually sense her mood, but the last few days she'd been closed off, probably because she was mad at his dad. The evening before, when they thought he was in bed, he'd heard them arguing about how little

time she spent working around the house. She'd
suggested hiring a cleaner, and he said that would be a
waste of money when she was perfectly capable. Jimmy
hated when they fought about stupid stuff.

"Jimmy," she said, louder than normal, to snap him
out of his daydream, "I've left sandwich meat and
cheese slices in the fridge and some soup you can heat
up for your father when he comes in for lunch. Get that
going around eleven thirty."

"Sure, Mom." He'd help out if it meant she stopped
being so unhappy and if it made his dad quit expecting
her to keep the house tidy when she'd rather be doing
anything but that. She'd had a career in fashion, taking
courses at college and modelling part-time before she
got married. Jimmy guessed that was why she liked
shopping so much and dressing up Theo.

His mom paused and studied his face before picking
up her purse from the table. "I'm so sorry about your
friend Matt, and Devina and Stu... Well, what
happened to them is really, really tragic." She crossed
the space and gave him a hug. He could feel her trembling before she released him. Her eyes were sad and
wet with tears that she blinked away. "We just have to go
on." She smiled and turned to help Theo fit into her
coat. Five minutes later, she hustled Theo across the
yard to the van and they were gone in a cloud of dust.

His dad was already working in the fields, so Jimmy
had the house to himself. He put on a waterproof jacket
and ran over to the barn to get Matt. The rain had let
up for a bit, and the air was spicy with loam, earth-
worms, and wet grass smells. If this were a regular fall
morning and school was out, he'd have gone to the
creek across the highway to play in the stones and mud.

He guessed he'd be doing a lot more of that once Matt was gone for good. The idea brought on a fresh wave of sadness.

He pushed the barn door open and let his eyes adjust to the dim light. "Matt," he called, peering toward the back of the barn. "Coast is clear."

He heard footsteps on the dirt floor, and moments later, Matt was walking toward him carrying the blanket and his knapsack. He stopped a few yards away. "Are you sure you want to do this, Jim? I can hang out here and leave when it gets dark. You don't need to get involved."

"Nah, it's okay."

"Shouldn't you be in school?"

"My parents are giving us the week off because of everything that's going on. Mom managed to slot Theo into some ballet classes with the younger kids, otherwise she'll be a big pain. She doesn't care that she's in with the three-year olds as long as she can dance."

They didn't speak as they exited into the sunlight and raced to the back door of the house. Once inside, they stopped and stared at each other. Something in Matt's eyes seemed older, but when he grinned, Jimmy saw the old Matt. "I'd kill for a shower, and that's something I never thought I'd say." Matt looked down at his dirty clothes. "I stink."

"Let's go upstairs. I'll get you a towel. We should have lots of time. Dad comes in for lunch, but he doesn't stay long. You can hide in my room while he's here."

"What about your mom and Theo?"

"Yeah, they won't be home until suppertime. Trust me, Mom likes to be away from here as much as possible. Keeping Theo busy outside the house makes them both happy."

Matt gave him a look but didn't say anything. Jimmy had the feeling, not for the first time, that his friend saw through his lame attempts at being funny. Matt could say a lot without saying anything at all.

Jimmy tossed Matt's clothes into the washing machine in the basement along with his own from yesterday. Then he waited at the head of the stairs while Matt cleaned up in the bathroom. If his dad had entered the house for some crazy reason, Jimmy'd go into the bathroom and pretend to be the one in the shower. Luckily, there was no need for plan B. Matt was quick and waited in Jimmy's bedroom after he finished, putting on Jimmy's housecoat, even though it was a few sizes too big, while Jimmy ran down to put the damp clothes into the dryer. Then he made sandwiches and poured glasses of milk. He added a slice of cake for Matt, not daring to take another for himself because his mom would be sure to notice how much was missing.

They sat on the floor to eat, their backs against the side of Jimmy's bed. "So what do you want to do next?" Jimmy asked.

"I guess get in touch with my mom. I need to tell her what's going on."

"Where is she?"

"I'm not sure."

"Why not? Isn't she at home?" Jimmy realized how little he knew about Matt and his life.

"No, she's on vacation."

"What about your dad?"

"He travels."

"Well, they've got to be somewhere. What does your dad do?"

"He's between jobs." Matt rubbed his forehead. "Look, I'm not real comfortable talking about my family."

"Why not?" Jimmy's forehead furrowed as he tried to understand why somebody wouldn't want to talk about their parents.

"They're private people."

"That's weird, I mean all kids talk about their parents."

"Not me. I think … I think my mom sent me here to get me out of the way. They separated in the spring." Matt had an odd look on his face, as if he wasn't telling the truth or was keeping stuff back. Jimmy couldn't forget the real fear Matt had shown when he first found him in the barn.

"You can stay in my room if you want. I have a big closet, and we can make a space when you need to hide. It's only Theo who comes into my room anyway. I'm responsible for keeping it clean in here, and Mom just stands in the doorway to talk to me."

Matt thought for a minute. "Maybe for a few days while I try to track down my mother, if you're sure. I don't want to get you in trouble."

"I'm not scared of my parents. Besides, they're never going to find out." He paused. "We could go to the cops."

Matt shook his head. "No way, not until I talk to Mom." He picked up the plate of cake but stopped with a forkful halfway to his mouth. "Was that the doorbell?"

Jimmy jumped to his feet. "Stay here. I'll go see who

it is. If you hear anyone coming up the stairs, get inside the closet and don't make a sound."

"Jimmy, you need to be careful. Come back here if it isn't somebody you know." Matt's voice had an urgency Jimmy'd never heard before. He hesitated.

"I'll be careful," he said at last, ignoring the anxiety shooting up from his belly. "It's not like anyone knows you're here, and nobody's out to kill me last time I checked."

He leapt down the stairs and hesitated in the hallway. A fluttering in his chest accompanied him as he tiptoed into the living room and crossed to the window. He positioned himself behind the curtain and craned his neck to peek outside. A car he didn't recognize was in the driveway, and a man in a ball cap and black jacket stood on the front steps. The man was looking around while he raised a hand and pounded on the door. Jimmy moved away from the window and slid down the wall into a crouch. The doorbell peeled a second time. Jimmy thought about Matt's warning and the Petries dead in their living room. He tucked his head, squeezed his eyes shut, and prayed the man would go away. The front door was locked thanks to his mom's paranoia, but he wasn't sure about the back one. For the first time, he thought that having Matt in the house might not be such a good idea.

CHAPTER 16

"There's a woman here to see Detective Hunter. Says she knows Matt Clark's mother."

Rosie Thorburn lifted her eyes from the computer screen and stared at the officer standing next to her desk. It took a moment for her to absorb his words. "Hunter's gone into Ashton." Her eyes darted across to Auger. He was on the phone with his back to her, and her skin crawled at the thought of approaching him for assistance. She made a decision. "I'll meet with her. Name?"

"She didn't say. Follow me and I'll point her out. She's downstairs in the lobby."

The officer waved Rosie over to the woman standing in front of the plate glass window staring out at Elgin Street. Rosie took a moment to study her profile. She appeared to be in her late forties or early fifties, cropped brown hair, slender, dressed in grey slacks and a cream-coloured wool sweater with a multicoloured silk scarf tied at her neck. High-heeled black boots and a matching leather satchel slung over one shoulder completed her ensemble. *Elegant Parisienne,* Rosie thought, looking self-consciously down at her own severe blue pantsuit and scuffed, flat-heeled shoes, already feeling at a disadvantage. She approached and cleared her throat.

"I'm Detective Rosie Thorburn, and I understand you might have information about Matt Clark?"

The woman spun around. Her face matched her clothing, beautifully made up with subtly applied colour accentuating her cheekbones and generous mouth. "Yes, if we could go somewhere more private…?"

"Of course. Could you first tell me your name?"

"Katherine Fielding."

Rosie led her to a second-floor meeting room, and they settled in across the table from each other. "I'm sorry there's nowhere more comfortable," Rosie said as she took out her notebook and pen. This woman had too much style to be sitting in this austere room, looking as out of place as a monarch butterfly in a jar full of grey moths. Rosie tried to mask her feeling of inadequacy and plunged in. "Let's begin by telling me your relationship to Matt Clark."

"I know his mother, Glynnis. We were colleagues for some years, although not recently. Glynnis lives in New York City, and I relocated to Montreal to be with my husband a few years ago. He's since passed away, but I like the city and decided to keep it as my home. I'm really here to find out if Matt Clark is in fact the missing boy being reported by media."

"Yes, that's his name."

"The Petries are the murdered couple then?"

"Yes." Questions swirled in Rosie's head, and she had to take a moment to organize her thoughts. The team wouldn't be impressed if she forgot to ask something important. Auger was already making snide comments when they were alone, intended to make her doubt herself. He'd stopped sending suggestive emails since she moved over to work with Liam Hunter, instead giving her the cold shoulder except for the disparaging words. She'd let his harassment go on too long. Nobody would believe she wasn't being vindictive if she spoke up now. They'd think she was trying to get back at him for speaking poorly about her work. There was also the issue of concrete proof, of which she had none. She focused on Katherine Fielding's eyes, staring at her curiously from behind tortoise-shell-rimmed glasses. "Sorry." She halted and regrouped. "Do you also know Devina and Stu Petrie?"

"Not personally. Glynnis met Devina working in a Vegas casino when they both were starting out. They shared an apartment at one point. I can't tell you much more about their relationship. I've never met Devina or her husband. Working in Vegas was only temporary work for Glynnis. I believe you'd call it a gap year after high school. She went to college and ended up in the publishing industry in New York."

"Then how did you meet Glynnis?"

"I owned a restaurant in South Keys Florida, and Glynnis worked for me one summer after her last year of college before she got a job offer in her field. This would have been, oh, twenty years ago now, but we remained good friends. I imagine she also stayed friends with Devina too. Glynnis is someone you can't help but like being around. She's funny and kind-hearted, perhaps too much so. People tended to take advantage."

Rosie hesitated. Katherine was answering her questions but not providing much useful information that would further the case. While she considered how best to phrase her next question, Katherine interrupted her silence. "Glynnis will be frantic when I confirm what she feared, that the missing boy is her son. What are you doing to locate him?"

"There has been a search of the surrounding fields and woods without any sign of him, which actually gives us hope that he's alive. We've put out an AMBER Alert and are following up on any leads. I'm sorry not to have better news. How can we reach Glynnis? We've attempted to locate his relatives without success. The AMBER Alert was necessary, but we've limited the information we're giving to media until we reach his family."

For the first time, Katherine appeared uncomfortable. Her gaze shifted away from Rosie's. "Glynnis is on vacation and has a new cell number I don't have. She called me from the hotel she was staying at in Boston, I believe. She won't be there any longer, though, so there's no point in naming the hotel. What can I tell her about Matt when she's in touch again?"

Rosie felt the interview slipping away from her. "Of course you can tell her to contact the Ottawa Police Service, but what about Matt's dad? What's his name, and how can we reach him?"

"They're separated. I have no idea where Wyatt is and doubt Glynnis knows either."

"What's Wyatt's profession?"

"I believe he's between jobs. He was in accounting. Management level."

"Is Matt Canadian or American?"

"American. The family lived in New York City until

recently." Katherine frowned. "Look, I really only came to find out about Matt. What else can you tell me about what happened?"

"Not much, I'm afraid. Has he ever been ... violent? Is he troubled at all?" Rosie tried not to react to Katherine's glare.

"Are you kidding me? You think Matt killed those people? Are you people nuts?"

"We're looking at all possibilities."

Katherine laughed. "Matt isn't a killer, not by any stretch. He's only just turned twelve years old, for God's sake. Don't even think about barking up that tree." She made a show of checking her watch. "Damn, I'm late for an appointment. She reached into the side pocket of her purse and pulled out a business card. "Please phone or text me with any updates. I can pick up Matt anytime, anywhere." She stood.

Anxiety gripped Rosie, and her mind went blank for a moment before she forced herself to focus. "Why was he staying with the Petries for the summer?"

Katherine paused, partially turned away from the table. "No idea. I have nothing helpful to tell you, I'm afraid. Thanks for meeting with me." She reached out her hand. "And your name again?"

"Rosie Thorburn. My partner Detective Liam Hunter will likely be in touch soon. He'll have more questions and can give an update."

"I'll anticipate his call then."

Rosie watched her leave and remained seated while she read through her notes. *What hadn't she asked?* She skimmed through her writing again and felt heat flush her cheeks. Katherine had not given the last name of either parent. How could she have missed that? The sick feeling in Rosie's stomach let her know that she'd messed up. *What else had she neglected to ask?* Her sparse writing barely elicited anything useful. She reluctantly gathered up her things and made her way down the hall to Major Crimes. The office had the quiet hum of busyness, and she looked for Hunter, hoping he had returned from Ashton, but he wasn't at his desk or anywhere she could see. She crossed the room, unable to avoid Auger's stare as he watched her settle into her chair.

"Who was that you were meeting with?" he asked.

"Katherine Fielding. She's a friend of Matt Clark's mother."

Auger's expression turned incredulous. "You interviewed her alone?"

"Why wouldn't I?"

"She's kind of a major breakthrough. I would have thought a more senior detective should take that on. I've been at my desk all morning, and you should have run this past me with Hunter out in the field." He paused and leaned back in his chair. "So, where are the kid's parents?"

"She didn't know."

"Really? She didn't know? I find that hard to believe. Tell me you at least got a photo of the kid."

Rosie shook her head, the sick feeling in her stomach growing into near panic. Heat rose upward from her chest, and her face had certainly blushed to a bright red. She took a cleansing breath and worked to still her rapidly beating heart before managing to say, "Katherine wasn't very forthcoming."

Hunter picked that moment to walk into the office, and she silently gave thanks while dreading the disapproval in his eyes when he learned about this. She'd messed up, believing she had the skill to take on the interview alone. Auger was on his feet before she could get to hers. He looked down at her and spoke in a low voice with his back to Hunter. "You've badly over-stepped, Thorburn, and will have to face the repercussions. Next time, check with me before assuming you can handle anything halfway challenging. That way you might — just might — be able to keep your job."

CHAPTER 17

Liam glanced over at Auger and Thorburn as he crossed the floor to his desk. Neither looked happy. Thorburn's slumped shoulders and ruddy complexion reminded him of a naughty child being chastised for wrongdoing. Auger stood and said something to her as Liam slid into his desk chair. A moment later, Auger strode past him on his way to Quade's office. Liam watched him rap sharply with his knuckles before disappearing inside, pushing the door shut behind him. He looked back at Thorburn. She sat without moving, gazing straight ahead.

"Come over here and talk to me, Thorburn." Liam raised his voice, concerned by her trance-like stare.

She turned toward him and seemed to come back to herself. "Give me a sec."

He waited while she fiddled with something with her back to him. She pulled a tissue out of her bag on the floor and wiped her cheeks. Finally, she stood with a notebook in her hand. She rolled the visitor chair closer so that she sat facing him on the other side of his desk.

Her eyes skimmed over his before she looked down at her lap. "I'm sorry. I know I messed this up."

"Whatever are you talking about?"

"The interview. You weren't here so I met with Katherine Fielding — she's a friend of Matt Clark's mother, and was downstairs in reception. I should have waited…"

"Why? You're perfectly capable of speaking with her. What did you find out?"

"The thing is she was evasive. I must not have asked the right questions."

"That's interesting and perhaps revealing. She likely had something to hide. Did she tell you how to reach Matt's parents?"

"They're recently separated, and she had no idea where the dad is now, but they had been living in New York City. His mom is on holiday in Boston, but that's all she knew, or at least, all she told me that she knew. Matt's American." She studied her notes before looking up at him. "She thought Matt might have been sent to live with the Petries because of the separation. Here — have a look at what I wrote." She slid the notebook across the desk.

He read quickly. Thorburn's neat cursive was clear and concise. "Glynnis and Wyatt. She didn't confirm their last name as Clark, but we can assume Matt has the same last name as his dad. Wyatt's an accountant, but she didn't name the company where he works. You're right, Rosie. I'd say she was being deliberately evasive."

"Here's Katherine's business card. I told her that you would be in touch with more questions. I believe she only came to the station on a fishing expedition about Matt."

"I agree and will follow up with her right away. Good work." If he'd come across as critical or unapproachable before, he regretted causing her to question her own abilities. Her discomfort was on him. For the first time, Thorburn smiled, her relief palpable, making him feel even more of a jerk.

"Thanks, Hunter. What would you like me to do now?"

"Check in with Forensics and Brigette Green for updates." An email message pinged on his computer. "Gotta go. Quade wants to see me. I'll call Katherine as soon as I find out what the boss wants." He stood. "Let's get your things moved over here. You can use Quade's desk while she's acting."

Thorburn's smile widened, and Liam wondered why he hadn't thought to have her change desks earlier. He'd come to realize that she never asked for anything, and it was up to him to anticipate how to make her working life easier. In some ways, she reminded him of his sister, Hannah. Neither asked for much and always seemed surprised when something good came their way.

———

AUGER NODDED at Liam as he took the seat next to him. Quade's expression was serious, and Liam braced himself for bad news.

"Auger has brought to my attention that Rosie Thorburn's inexperience could be a liability for the murder investigation. He's suggested I work with HR to get her transferred to a less critical position in another unit.

This would give her a chance to learn and progress under less stressful conditions."

Auger nodded. "I have to admit some fault on my part for bringing her into the Homicide unit. She would have been better served in a placement with more learning opportunities where errors don't create such an impact." He looked down at his hands folded in his lap. "There's also the issue of her near-death experience. I sense a trepidation in her that wasn't present before. It's as if she doesn't trust herself, and that could lead to consequences if she's ever confronted with trouble again."

Quade was watching Auger closely. Her gaze shifted over to Hunter. "What are your thoughts?"

"Thorburn's inexperienced, but she's steady and keen. Of course she was impacted by that experience. Who wouldn't be? She's had counselling and been green-lighted. I'm fine in the mentoring role while she regains her confidence."

"The question is whether the unit would be better served with a more seasoned investigator. We have a difficult case facing us and can't afford to keep her as your partner if she's not up for the job. It's setting her and the investigation up to fail. I'd like your objective opinion." Quade continued to study him, her face devoid of emotion. "I can speak with Thorburn and then get HR involved. I'll frame the change as being in her best interests over the long term. If we can avert setting her up to fail, I'm in agreement with Auger."

Liam was having trouble understanding where Auger's sudden concern for Thorburn's career was coming from. Something felt off. He remembered Thorburn's eyes when she apologized for taking the initiative by interviewing Katherine Fielding on her own. He leaned back and crossed his legs. He normally avoided confrontation but would make an exception. "I'm going to respectfully disagree with you both. Thorburn has been nothing but professional and willing to work at whatever task needs attention. She's smart and insight-ful. I'm happy to continue mentoring her in this posi-tion. She's earned a chance to prove herself, and I for one believe in her."

The room was silent when he finished speaking. He could sense Auger's displeasure as Quade sat thinking. She tilted her head from side to side as if considering going one way or the other. She sighed and grimaced. "Okay, Hunter. Let's leave things as they are for the time being. We can keep the transfer option open if it becomes necessary."

"I'm only after what's best for the unit," Auger said before pushing himself out of the chair. "But I bow to your judgement and hope this decision doesn't come back to bite us." He laughed as if making a joke. "I guess you won't be able to say that I didn't warn you when Thorburn makes her next misstep and you have to explain it to the Police Board."

CHAPTER 18

J immy gathered his courage and scooted across the living room floor, down the hall, and into the kitchen. He crouched low so that he couldn't be seen through the window and crawled on hands and knees to the back door, reaching a hand up to turn the lock. Already he could hear footsteps on the stairs leading onto to the small deck that his dad had built two summers before. He huddled against the door and prayed the man wouldn't look directly down through the window, because he'd be seen for sure.

The doorknob turned and rattled. Then … silence. Was the man deciding whether or not to break in? Jimmy knew it wouldn't be difficult. The lock was cheap. They'd never been concerned about intruders before. In fact, he couldn't remember the last time they'd locked up the house entirely during the daytime. "We've got nothing worth stealing," his mom had proclaimed more than once. Sometimes she said it while giving his dad a sorrowful look and punctuated the statement with a deep sigh. Like a smart fish, his dad never took the bait.

Jimmy held his breath and listened. He'd push his entire weight against the door if the man broke the lock to keep him from entering. He hoped the man didn't have a gun. The house seemed to be holding its breath along with him, the creaks and humming appliances silent for once. Jimmy spotted an ant making its way up the wall near the boot rack and focused on the black dot's progress. He began counting to take his mind off the person standing on the other side of the door, trying to still the panic.

The doorknob turned and rattled one last time before the heavy footsteps descended the steps and onto the lawn. Jimmy ran hunched over like Quasimodo through the kitchen and into the hallway, where he stood motionless, watching the front door. Time crept past, feeling like forever while in reality it was only seconds, but at last he heard a car door slam. He propelled himself into the living room after he heard the car engine start. He made it to the window in time to see red taillights turning onto the main road from the end of the driveway. Not trusting his eyes, he waited a full minute before dropping the curtain back into place and racing upstairs, calling out to Matt when he reached the landing. "Coast is clear. You can come out now."

He reached the bedroom in time to see Matt crawl out of the closet. His face was flushed, and the wild look in his eyes had returned. He stood and gulped in fresh air after being shut in the stuffy closet. He looked at Jimmy. "Who was that?"

"Some strange guy. Probably looking for my dad."

"I don't think it's a good idea for me to stay here. Whoever that was could be coming back."

"Nah, they drove off. It's okay." Jimmy didn't want

Matt to leave. He wouldn't mention the man turning the door handle and trying to get inside. He hoped Matt couldn't see any traces of the panic he'd felt moments before. "I'll take the dishes downstairs. Your clothes should be dry by now. You can play video games if you want."

Matt took a second before nodding. "Thanks, but I'm going to lie down on your bed if that's okay. Decide what to do next."

"We can figure it out together when I come back upstairs."

Jimmy hurried out of the room and down the steps. Maybe it would be safer for Matt to leave. It might be a big mistake letting him stay in the house if somebody was trying to track him down. Whoever killed the Petries could be after him. A crazy idea, but somebody murdering the Petries was even crazier. Jimmy ran through his mind how little he knew about his friend, how many secrets he was keeping. He could tell his parents Matt was hiding in his bedroom and let them decide what to do. Jimmy entered the kitchen and first unlocked the back door in case his father came up to the house and tried to get inside. He'd be suspicious to find the door locked.

Detective Hunter had seemed okay. He could tell him and keep his parents out of it. That way, he wouldn't get into trouble and could avoid getting punished. He set the dishes on the counter before opening the dishwasher, then straightened and stared out the window. The thing was that if he turned in Matt, he'd be breaking a promise, which would be worse than getting caught lying to his parents. They'd have to forgive him eventually, but Matt would leave and never look back. He'd lose the only friend he had.

———

ELLA CRANED her neck as she slowed to find the moose mailbox, the air clearer now that the rain had stopped. She'd stayed at the pub for most of the afternoon, writing an article that she'd sent along to Canard a half hour earlier. He'd liked the update and promised to give it front-page status in the morning paper and on the paper's website. Even though she was eager to get back to the city, Everett's relationship with Devina nagged at her. There was more to their friendship than anybody was saying. Ella had already made one pass along this stretch of road and turned in somebody's driveway fifteen minutes up the highway to try again. Surely, a moose shouldn't be that hard to spot. At last, she saw what passed for the animal, although it had the face of a rabbit, in her opinion. She pulled over to the shoulder to let three cars whiz past before crossing the highway and easing up the driveway.

The white clapboard farmhouse sat on a grassy piece of property with a large red barn at the bottom of a gentle slope off to the left. A fence encircled a large pasture, containing a number of cows standing and lying close together. Ella counted forty and thought they might be a dairy herd. The scene was bucolic, with the brilliant blue sky and the sun slanting through the maples in the front yard. The yearning for a life like this caught her by surprise.

There were no vehicles in the driveway, but she parked anyway and walked to the front door. A woman answered her knock, wiping her hands on a dishtowel as she smiled at Ella and asked if she could help her.

"I hope so. I'm looking for Everett and wonder if he's home." Ella studied the woman. She was fit, late forties or early fifties, grey hair pulled into a messy bun. Jeans, a red plaid shirt, and running shoes made her appear at home in this country setting. The woman was studying her as well. Ella was aware that she had no style, her blonde hair shaggy and her clothes old and functional. She'd dressed in a black sweatshirt and ripped jeans over desert boots and thrown on a sweater for warmth under her blue raincoat on her way out the door this morning. She reminded herself to do some laundry when she got home or she'd have to recycle the outfit tomorrow, uninspired as it was.

"I'm Everett's wife, Miriam. He's gone to town for groceries but should be back soon. And you would be…?

"Ella Tate. I'm a true crime podcaster and freelancer for *The Capital*."

Miriam's hands stilled, and her smile vanished. "You're here about poor Devina and Stu. We're all completely devastated."

"I know this has been a difficult time."

"If you add horrifying, I'd say you're about right."

"I'm collecting background about them to make the public realize these were real people with hopes and dreams. It's too easy to feature the sensational so that readers become desensitized."

Miriam nodded. "You got that right." She opened the door wider. "Why don't you come in for a cup of coffee while we wait for Everett? He should be along soon."

"Thank you. That's very kind."

The kitchen, a large, bright room, didn't disappoint. The rustic pine cupboards reached the ceiling with a table made from the same wood set up against one wall. The oak chairs were mismatched and comfortable with bright yellow or red pillows tied onto the seats. Water-colour paintings of flowers filled one wall. Ella smelled rich coffee and freshly baked bread as she sat and waited for Miriam to pour them each a cup from a pot on the stove. She set the coffee mugs on the table along with a blue-and-white striped jug of milk and invited Ella to help herself.

"What led you to Everett?" Miriam asked as she scooped sugar into her coffee. "Did you run into his sister Nelly by chance?"

"As it so happens, I did. She said that she and Everett meet for coffee most mornings at the Ashton Pub. This morning she invited me to join her for her break after we spoke in the store."

"That poutine will be the death of her." Miriam's face reddened. "I didn't mean ... that's more insensitive than I meant it to be, given all that's gone on. It's just all that fat and grease every morning isn't good for the heart. We worry about her."

"I hear you. It's a sad fact foods that taste the best are the worst for us."

"Everett put those morning visits with his sister into his daily routine. It was their chance to catch up and stay connected."

Ella hesitated while she thought how best to phrase the next question. "The server told me that Devina sometimes came by as well and had coffee with Everett. Were you aware of their meetings?"

"Of course." Miriam's eyes widened for the briefest of seconds before she smiled and waved a hand in front of her face. "They've known each other a very long time. The bond goes deep when you've grown up together."

"I understand they dated in high school?"

"In small communities, everyone dates everyone in high school. Those relationships are not long-lasting or life-defining."

"How did you get along with Devina and Stu?"

"Well, Devina wasn't as social as I remembered from before she left town to find her fortune, but Stu took part in community events. He could be counted on to pitch in with volunteer duties or to give a helping hand whenever somebody needed it. He didn't have any farming experience before they moved here about five years ago, but he was willing to learn. They were raising chickens and had that big vegetable garden." She let out a sigh and looked at her hands. "I've been going over the past few mornings to feed the chickens. I'm not sure what will become of them now."

"I see by the farm's website that she made and sold craft items."

"That's right. She was working hard to get her business off the ground, and I rarely saw her. We were friendly whenever our paths crossed. It's actually good that she found the time to take a break from work to have coffee with Everett. I was hoping she'd branch out eventually and socialize more."

"You didn't join them at the pub for coffee?"

"No, most mornings I take a yoga class or get groceries." Miriam paused and turned her face toward the back door as if listening for something. "I believe that's Everett pulling into the driveway. She pointed at Ella's mug. "Refill?"

"Thanks." Ella thought Miriam sounded relieved to have a distraction from their conversation. She listened to the clump of footsteps climbing the back steps, and a few moments later the door opened and Everett filled the entrance to the kitchen. First impression was that he was a grizzly bear of a man, broad shoulders under a red plaid shirt, bald head, and grey beard to his chest. His dark, piercing eyes surveyed the room, skimmed over her, and landed on his wife. He bent and unlaced his boots before stepping onto the tile floor.

"Reporter?" he asked, nodding toward the table.

"Ella Tate with *The Capital,* getting background on Devina and Stu."

Everett grunted and poured a cup of coffee. Miriam looked small next to him, although she had to be five-six or seven and solidly built. Everett said something in passing to her that Ella couldn't hear before taking a seat in Miriam's vacated chair. He watched Ella while he took a sip and lowered the mug. "There's not much we can tell you. They were good people, and now they're dead."

"You knew them well."

"As well as anyone knows anybody."

Ella sensed Miriam watching from behind her. "Are you aware of any reason somebody would harm them?" she asked, resisting the urge to turn around.

"None whatsoever. I spoke with both recently, and neither was worried or upset about anything." He looked over her head. "Did you notice anything, Miriam?"

"Not a thing." Her voice was coming from deeper in the kitchen.

Ella angled sideways and saw Miriam with her back turned, putting dishes into the sink. Ella swung around to look at Everett. "Did they say why Matt Clark was staying with them?"

"Devina knew his mom from her time working in the States and was doing her a favour. Apparently the woman had recently separated from her husband and was having a hard time."

"The mom's name?"

"Not sure I ever knew it. Devina and Stu didn't talk about Matt much, or his situation."

"Did you find that odd?"

"No. He's a good kid and seemed useful. He made friends with Jimmy Dooley and was usually off somewhere with him, from what Devina said. They liked to fish and could be found at the river most days until dusk. Have the police got any leads on Matt's whereabouts?"

"Not that I've heard."

Everett nodded. "He's got a chance of still being alive then. I was worried when we heard they were searching the fields."

Ella wanted to ask him if his feelings for Devina were of the romantic sort, but she couldn't find the right moment with Miriam behind her listening. She doubted he'd tell her the truth anyway. But why meet Devina every morning for coffee after Nelly returned to the store? It might have been a perfectly innocent friendship, but the two of them meeting alone on such a regular basis triggered a warning bell. "Would you happen to have a photo of him?"

"No, you, Miriam?"

"I had no opportunity to take his picture, not that it was a priority." Miriam walked closer to the table until she was in Ella's direct line of vision. She and Everett exchanged a look. "I'm sorry, but I'm going to have to end the chat. We've got some work to do in the barn before it gets dark."

"And I should be going. Thank you so much for your hospitality and for sharing your memories of the Petries." Ella clumsily gathered up her bag and notebook and stood. Neither Miriam nor Everett made any move to stop her or to invite her to drop by again. They seemed eager to have her gone.

Miriam opened the back door for Ella and stepped back to let her pass. The sun had begun its descent, and a shaft of light caught them in its sparkling glow. "The murders had to have been done by someone outside the community," Miriam said, squinting into the glare. "Nothing else makes sense."

Ella stood on the doorstep, looking out at the fields bathed in pale, slanted light, darkness not far off. Nelly Depper had made much the same observation. "Nobody can be ruled out yet," she said, glancing behind her at Miriam, who'd stepped deeper into the cool shadows of the hallway. "As much as we want to believe our friends and neighbours aren't involved, the truth will come out eventually. It always does."

She tilted her head and nodded in Miriam's direction before starting down the stairs toward her car, not sure if she'd imagined the apprehensive expression on Miriam's face before she turned and firmly closed the door.

CHAPTER 19

Tony's apartment door stood propped open, and Cher was belting out "If I Could Turn Back Time" from the stereo system in his living room. Ella hesitated on the second-floor landing, tired from her day in Ashton but fully aware that Tony would not forgive her if she crept past him to the third floor without stopping to say hello.

"*Merde*," she said under her breath before crossing the hall and poking her head inside. "Tony, you up for some company?" she called at the same moment that Cher ended her lament for better days. Tony and Luvy appeared in the doorway to the living room. Tony set the miniature dachshund on the floor, and she scampered over to Ella for her usual ear rub.

"There you are, girl," Tony said and waved her into the kitchen with the apron tied around his waist. "I've put a chicken casserole in the oven and was about to make a pitcher of Bloody Caesars. You got dinner plans?"

"I'm beginning to think I do. I'll go freshen up and will be right back. Can I bring anything?"

"Lordy, no. I've got you covered."

She changed her clothes — jeans into sweats — and took a moment to wash her face. She could hear Tony speaking with a woman as she started back down the stairs. Piper, Lena's nanny, turned to look at her as she reached the second-floor landing. She'd begun minding Lena the month before, taking a year off before starting university the following autumn.

"Hi, Ella. I was asking Tony if he could look after Lena until Finn gets home. I have plans for the evening, and he's got a client who showed up unexpectedly."

Tony held a squirming Lena in his arms, a bag with diapers sticking out the top at his feet. Lena reached her arms toward Ella. "Mama," she said. "Mama."

Ella took her from Finn and two chubby hands squeezed around her neck. "You have to stop calling me that," Ella whispered into Lena's ear. Piper and Tony grinned at each other, and she frowned at them both. "Seriously, when Adele comes home, this baby had better not be getting us confused."

"It's just—" Tony broke off with a laugh. It took a moment for him to suck in enough air to finish the sentence. "You are the least likely woman to be voluntarily called 'mama' by any child."

"Are you saying I'm not mother material?"

Tony ignored the question and said goodbye to Piper before herding, Ella, Lena, the dog, and the diaper bag inside his apartment and closing the door. "I'll see about those Caesars, shall I?" He clattered down the hallway before she could respond.

She settled with Lena on her lap in one of the

peacock blue chairs after grabbing a few storybooks from Tony's bookshelf. He kept a stack along with toys next to a playpen for those evenings and weekends when he looked after Lena. Adele had only been gone a few months, but Lena was now firmly ensconced in each of their lives. Ella read three stories before the baby's head snuggled against her chest and her eyes closed. She laid the sleeping child gently inside the playpen and covered her with a blanket, standing for a moment to watch her breathe softly in and out. Adele was missing out on so much.

Tony walked into the room and handed Ella a drink. They stood in silence, staring at Lena, until Ella made her way to the couch. Tony joined her a few seconds later. "How are the murder cases unfolding?" he asked. "Any new information come to light?"

"The police appear to be looking for a stranger or someone from the Petries' past."

"And you?"

"I'm keeping an open mind, but yeah, someone outside the community seems probable."

"Are you conferring with the good detective?"

"No. Hunter's been distant lately."

"Since you started going out with his colleague, perchance?"

Tony had asked the question lightly, but she knew what he was getting at. "Hunter has no interest in dating me, Tony. We've got a loose collaborative relationship when mutually beneficial. That's it."

"If you say so." He didn't look convinced, and she scowled at him. "No word on the missing boy?" he asked, ignoring her glare.

"Not that I've heard. My guess is that he was taken

by whoever shot the Petries. I have no evidence, however." She had tried unsuccessfully to temper the worry she felt for the boy. By all accounts, he was a good kid. Had he witnessed the killings? Was that why he was abducted, if in fact that was what had happened? She knew the only way to help him was to figure out the who and the why — to control what she could and let go of the rest. Hopefully, Major Crimes was way ahead of her. Hunter was being uncharacteristically quiet about the case — no messages or offers to meet — and she promised to put herself back on his radar in the morning.

———

LIAM LEFT a third message on Katherine Fielding's phone before driving home through another bout of driving rain, slick like oil on the pavement whenever he passed a streetlight. The low cloud cover made the darkness even gloomier, and his spirits only lifted when he turned into his driveway and saw the porch light on. Stepping inside the house, he could hear Hannah, Jack, and Hugh laughing in the kitchen The boys ran to wrap themselves around him when they heard him shut the front door. Hannah leaned on the doorjamb at the end of the hallway and smiled at him. "If the mountain won't come for supper, supper must come to the mountain."

"And the mountain is delighted."

"Mommy made lamb stew and homemade buns," Hugh said. "If we clean our plates, we can have a double helping of trifle."

"It has strawberries and whipped cream." Jack

jumped up and down on stockinged feet before racing toward the kitchen. He stopped at the entrance. "And I get to serve the stew. I'm going to get lucky."

"I beg your pardon?" Hannah asked.

"He means Lucky the cat." Hugh grinned, and Hannah swatted his head as he passed.

"Tell me he's too young to know about getting lucky." She shook her head as both boys disappeared from view. "I'm milking the idea that chores are a reward as long as I can, Liam."

"A bit brilliant, really."

"Their cups are still half full."

After the boys had eaten and cleared the plates, they went into the living room to watch a movie. Hannah poured Liam and herself a second glass of wine from a bottle in the fridge. She sat across from him. "The Ashton murders appear brutal."

"Is that what media are calling the deaths — the Ashton murders?"

"It is. Any progress solving them or finding that young boy?"

"No word on him, and it's early days in the case. We're still sorting through the evidence." Liam set down his wine glass, not eager to talk about work. "How's the new man in your life progressing?"

Hannah didn't question the change of subject, and he silently saluted her tact. She'd grown used to him steering away from whatever case had consumed him during the day. "I let him know that I intend to date other men, so he's free to do the same, although he'll likely stick with women. I've discovered that I'm not ready to settle down ... or settle for that matter. And you?"

"Married to the job." He grinned and raised his glass to clink hers. "Long live the foot-loose Hunters."

"Amen to that."

She studied him over the rim of her glass. "There's a new temp hired at work who appears to be single. She's about your age and quite lovely."

"Ahh, thanks but no thanks. I haven't time to invest in a relationship." He could see the wheels in Hannah's head turning. "Really, sis, now is not a good time."

"Uh-huh." She couldn't have sounded any less convincing.

"I mean it."

"Of course you do."

After Hannah took the boys home, Liam lay on the couch with Lucky purring on his chest. Without his sister and nephews to ground him now and then, his life would be an empty expanse broken only by work, sleep, and the odd game of baseball, which sadly had ended for the season on the weekend. The idea of a trip to get out of his rut was beginning to take hold. He'd have to start investigating destinations. Figure out a place that would suit him. It would give him something else to think about on his time off other than the cases. "Might even be time to get lucky," he said, scratching the cat under her chin. "And by getting lucky, I do not mean you."

CHAPTER 20

Boston

Glynnis checked both ways before pulling out of the car rental parking lot. No longer using the alias Sam Green, she felt a sense of relief. She was tired of being in hiding and wanted her real life back. All the subterfuge and planning hadn't kept Matt safe, and it was time to reassess and start over. Wyatt wouldn't be pleased, but he was in no position to criticize her decisions. She'd done everything he asked of her, and now she'd damn well forge her own path.

She navigated out of Boston and followed the GPS instructions to get on the 89 heading north to the Canadian border. The sun was peeking over the tree line off to the east, and the skies were clear. It should be a good travel day. She'd have to use her passport and would hope that it didn't trigger any alarms. The idea of being tracked still seemed surreal. She half-convinced herself that it wasn't possible for these people to find her so easily.

She'd reached Katherine by phone early evening the

day before. Katherine's confirmation that the Petries were dead and Matty was missing panicked her for a few minutes, but she forced herself to stay centred. Matt wasn't dead. If he had been abducted, he'd be used as the bargaining chip, and that gave her time to find him. She'd wanted to reach out to Wyatt but wasn't sure how. Even if she could speak with him, there was no certainty of safety for him or her. The worst outcome would be for him to back out of the plan. She couldn't let that happen. No, all things weighed, she'd need to handle this problem by herself.

Traffic was light except for the transport trucks moving produce and goods. She didn't trust these long-haul drivers to be fully alert, knowing many motored on minimal sleep or with the help of uppers and coffee. She held her breath and accelerated in the outside lane as she zipped past one carrying paper products. There was always another string of transports around the next curve to navigate.

She pulled off the highway at a rest stop twenty miles from the border, checking in her rear view to see who drove into the parking lot with her. Two cars had followed hers, and she slid into a spot where she could watch the passengers exit. A young couple and a baby got out of the green SUV as soon as it stopped, but she had to wait five minutes before a middle-aged man left the black Volvo with a Jack Russell terrier on a leash. Neither driver looked threatening or appeared to pay her any attention, so Glynnis stepped out of her rental and stretched. It was time for a quick trip to the restroom before buying an herbal tea and sandwich. She returned to her car with her purchases and ate and sipped while surveying the comings and goings.

Not for the first time, she kicked herself for agreeing to a separation from Matt in order to keep him as safe as possible before the grand jury took place. Wyatt had said he wouldn't give evidence if she or Matt were in danger, so he convinced her to hide out before contacting the FBI. At first, he'd vetoed her taking the job in the Boston diner, but she argued for some normalcy. With a new haircut and colour, nobody would recognize her, and the work gave her a reasonable cover. It wasn't until she'd arrived in the new city that she realized she was pregnant, but she stuck with the plan, deciding that telling Wyatt about the baby growing in her belly would serve no useful purpose. The idea of sending Matt to an isolated Canadian farm for the summer had also been logical on paper. She hadn't realized how difficult it would be not to have him with her. She should have fought harder to keep him. It wouldn't take much for her to break down and cry over his disappearance, but what good would that do anybody? He was a capable kid. Resilient. She wouldn't let herself believe the worst. Not yet.

One final bite of sandwich and she put the lid back on the tea. If the border wasn't too busy, she should make Montreal by nightfall. She hadn't called ahead and would sleep in her car if Katherine was still in Ottawa. There'd be no checking into a hotel where they'd request her name and credit card information. Perhaps she was being overly paranoid, but going off the grid was her only advantage. She had to remain vigilant and hope she wasn't too late to turn things around.

CHAPTER 21

Rosie woke later than she'd meant to, realizing as she stretched and looked toward the bedside table that she'd forgotten to set her alarm. There'd be no time to meditate or check the news while she leisurely drank a cup of tea. She turned her head on the pillow and looked at Brad's side of the bed before remembering that he was on nights. They'd be two ships passing, her leaving for work as he was returning. They wouldn't have a chance to resume the argument of a few days earlier, a delay she welcomed. He'd been pushing her to make decisions, but committing to his plan for their future made her want to run the other way. At least she could set all that aside for today. She flung back the covers and hurried into the shower. Twenty minutes later, she was in her car on the way to HQ.

Kurt Auger pulled into the parking garage ahead of her, and she purposefully drove to the opposite end of the lot, backed in next to a post, and waited in her car until she was certain he'd entered the building. She was a coward when it came to the man, but she was incapable of standing up to him. Her father had been a misogynistic bully too, one who constantly belittled her and her sister Sheila while slapping their brother Dean on the back and telling him he was the family's only hope. Even now, her father continued to put her down whenever she called to speak to her mom. "Not sure how you made the police service. Must be that misguided gender equality nonsense." They'd come to the hospital when she was hurt in July, and even then, he'd said he wasn't surprised she'd gotten into trouble. "Ask to be put on traffic duty," he'd said. "Your skill set would be better suited."

Hunter was already at his desk and motioned for her to take the seat across from him when he raised his eyes from his computer screen and spotted her. "As promised, your new location," he said. "I hope that's okay."

"It's fine, thanks." She felt Auger's stare burning into her as she pulled out her chair. She dared not look his way. "So what's our plan for today?"

"Brigette Green has scheduled the Petrie autopsies for ten. You and I will be sitting in. I doubt the pathologist will be through both by lunchtime, so make sure you've had something to sustain you until they take a break and we can grab a bite. They've been known to work straight through."

"Not sure I'll be up for a meal after that."

"Ah, another first for you, I'm guessing?" She nodded, attempting to tamp down her anxiety and failing. He added, "We'll play it by ear then, but you might not find the process as difficult as all that. Did you study biology in school?"

"Cutting up a human body might not be the same as a frog, but yeah, I've sliced into a few of those."

"You'll be fine then."

His confidence was reassuring, but still she worried. What if her body betrayed her and she reacted badly? Hunter was being patient, but for how much longer? With Auger angling to get rid of her, she couldn't afford to be less than perfect. She'd dealt with her father long enough to know that any opening would be used to further the campaign against her. It was as if he'd handed off the "keeping Rosie in her place" baton to Auger. She could hear her dad in her head. "She's stubborn but not all that bright. Don't shy away from making her see common sense." Her own fear of failure had grown to such a degree over the years that she'd become her own worst enemy, too scared to stand up for herself, believing she deserved the criticism while still fighting her internal demons to become a detective. The stubbornness her father complained about was the stone in her stomach that kept her going and made her rail against his dismissiveness.

She'd never shared with Brad about her father's treatment, and while he suspected some of it, he had no idea the depths. Her father reined in his behaviour whenever Brad was around, welcoming him like a second son. Their "good old boy" connection angered her even as she pretended having the two of them get along was a good thing. Brad couldn't understand why she didn't call her parents more often or want to live close to them. At times, she hated him for not seeing the truth, for pushing her to live the life he wanted. Somehow, she had to find the strength to break free and cut a new path … to find a way to change whatever it was about herself that men like Auger seemed to recognize and use to their advantage.

———

THE DAY WENT BETTER than Rosie could have imagined. Once she got past the smells and the blood, she settled into the rhythm of the autopsies. Coroner Brigette Green was present, but a forensic pathologist named Riley Seiman performed the post-mortem, dictating his findings into a recorder as he sliced, sawed, weighed, and analyzed. Hunter's steadying presence next to Rosie helped her to stay focused. Each autopsy took three hours, with a coffee break in between. By the final cut, exhaustion had replaced any initial queasiness. The relief that she'd been able to overcome her anxiety was tinged with elation. Her body hadn't let her down.

"I'll have a preliminary report to you within two days," Seiman said as he peeled off his latex gloves. "I can confirm, though, that both died by gunshot wounds, as you already surmised. Stu Petrie took one in the chest that stopped his heart immediately. Devina Petrie has bruises on her arms consistent with a struggle. They've become quite noticeable in death. The shot went through her chest as well at closer range, with no chance of survival, even if help had been at hand. The residue on her hands confirms that she was a shooter."

"Could she have struggled with somebody, the gun went off, and killed her?"

"A plausible scenario."

"Anything else you can share off the top?"

"Both were in good health. There's nothing more that stands out. Have you got the ballistics report?"

"Not yet," Hunter said.

"The tox screens won't be completed for a few weeks. However, I don't see habitual drug use for either. Nothing intravenous, certainly."

"We'll wait for the written report with the initial findings, then, but thank you for sharing your preliminary conclusions."

Hunter held the door for Rosie and they stepped into the hall. "You did great," he commented as she walked past.

"Piece of cake." She grinned. "I found it fascinating, to be honest, once I got over my initial trepidation."

"The first time is a test of fortitude. You passed with flying colours. Feel like getting a bite to eat while we discuss next steps? I find a beer helps to clear out the smell."

Brad would be at work, and she could use a bit of time to decompress. She studied Hunter's face, trying to see if he had ulterior motives. She was leery of dinner alone with colleagues after Auger. She'd never gotten any unsettling vibes from Hunter, but that meant nothing. Her track record was reason enough to be careful. "You don't have somewhere else to be?" she asked at last.

"My cat can entertain herself for another hour, but if Brad is home waiting for you with supper made, we can go over things tomorrow morning in the office. Feel no pressure, since our work day is over, for all intents and purposes."

He'd given her an out, and she considered what this could mean. Would he have been so nonchalant and mentioned Brad if he planned to try something when they were alone? Was she being paranoid? The idea that she might be became the deciding factor. "I'll get my jacket. Do you want to walk somewhere or take our cars?"

"Let's stretch our legs and get some air. How do you feel about pizza? We can try Colonnade, if you don't mind going that far."

"Colonnade works."

It was still light, but the sun angled lower on the horizon, the rays slanting through the high rises and directly into the eyes of drivers heading west. The air had cooled since Rosie left the house in the morning, and she was sorry to feel the first tickle of autumn in the air. She'd be longing for summer by November. Hunter seemed content to stride along beside her without talking once they left the station, and she enjoyed the silence, which was more companionable than uncomfortable.

The warm smell of garlic and tomatoes greeted them as they entered the crowded, noisy restaurant. A hostess led them past a table of ten into the back room and sat them at a table for two in the far corner, leaving menus and promising a server would be right over. Rosie looked around. "I've never been here before."

Hunter looked up from the menu. "That's right, you lived in Toronto until a few months ago. Are you glad you made the move?"

"Brad had a job offer from this city — he's a paramedic — so when Auger asked if I'd like to work in Ottawa Homicide, all the stars appeared to align, even though Brad had planned to turn down the position." She frowned before opening her menu and studying the pizza selections. In Toronto, they'd been closer to his family in Collingwood, and he hadn't been so insistent about moving back home. In hindsight, she could have gotten out from under Auger if she'd turned down his offer to move here.

"Did you consider Auger a mentor?"

More like a predator. Hunter's question felt odd, as if it hid a deeper meaning. "He hired me." She didn't dare say more and give him a reason to question her loyalty to the team. "Any recommendations?" she asked to change the subject.

"We could share a vegetarian if you like."

She nodded and they ordered a couple of beers to go with the pizza when the server arrived. The couple at the table next to them left, and they were out of earshot of the other customers. Even so, Hunter spoke quietly, and she lowered her voice to match.

"I've tried to reach Katherine Fielding, but she hasn't returned my calls," he said. "Rather odd for someone who was so eager to find out about Matt Clark."

"She appeared to want information but not to give it. I'm sorry I wasn't better at questioning her."

"You did as well as any of us would have. She was being deliberately cagey."

Rosie kept her eyes lowered. "Auger said that I should have asked him to take the lead."

Hunter hesitated and she prepared herself for his response. His voice was mild, almost amused when he commented, "Auger had his own caseload to keep him busy and has no jurisdiction over ours."

She smiled and relaxed into the seat. Their food and drinks arrived, and Hunter said they should take a break from the case while they ate. She felt exhaustion settling in by the time she'd wolfed down two slices of pizza and finished the glass of beer. Hunter was watching her when she set her fork on the empty plate and looked up. "Well, that was delicious. I'm amazed at how hungry two autopsies can make a person," she said.

"Do you want to share the last slice?"

"No, I'm full up. You have it."

He reached for the piece and asked, "How's your recovery coming along?"

"Physically, no issues. I've had three sessions with the psychologist, and he says I'm fine to carry on. No lasting side effects from the incident in July." She averted her eyes so he wouldn't read the truth.

"I feel bad about that. I was responsible for you being in that situation." She could read real anguish in his expression.

"You do?" She couldn't hide her surprise. "I was the one who didn't take the proper precautions."

"I'd argue that you couldn't have known. I sent you into the field alone when I should have had your back."

The server returned to their table with the cheque, and they had her split it down the middle while Hunter polished off the last few bites. *He's being careful not to treat this as a date*, Rosie thought. *He's nothing like Auger.*

"Good," Hunter said, pulling a credit card out of his wallet. "That should do it for today. I suggest we push for the ballistics report first thing tomorrow and then make another drive to Ashton to speak with the neighbours."

"Go over the same ground?"

"Yup, and hopefully someone new comes forward. Patience and persistence."

"Patience and persistence. Sounds like something you'd crochet onto a pillow or a wall hanging."

Hunter laughed. "I plan to have the words tattooed on my arm in capital, neon letters before much longer, because lately, I have difficulty remembering to follow my own advice. Not the persistence part; it's the patience bit that's getting tougher to maintain over the long haul."

CHAPTER 22

Jimmy woke and rolled onto his side. Matt was still sound asleep, tucked in next to him in a makeshift bed on the floor. Jimmy had found a musty-smelling sleeping bag in the basement and given Matt one of his pillows. Nobody could see him from the hallway, although Jimmy had shut the door anyway. The plan seemed to be working because Matt hadn't been detected since he'd brought him upstairs two days ago. It was going on seven thirty, and he could hear his dad moving around in the kitchen. He'd likely been up since six and already out in the barn.

"Matt." Jimmy leaned off the side of the bed and gave the sleeping bag a shake. "Matt, time to get up."

Matt's eyes opened. He looked startled for a few seconds, as if not sure where he was. Then he took a deep breath and relaxed. "What time—?"

"Seven thirty. Theo will be up soon, if she isn't already. You should get in the closet. I'll bring up something to eat once everyone's out of the house."

"I need to use the can."

"Can you wait a few hours?"

"Don't think so."

"We'll go together, then, and hope Theo and my mom stay in bed for a while."

"Sorry, Jimmy."

"Nah, it's okay."

They crept across the hall to the bathroom, and Jimmy turned his back while Matt had a pee and washed his hands and face. Jimmy listened for sounds of someone moving around and jumped when a door slammed down the hall. It came from the direction of Theo's room. A moment later, he could hear her outside the bathroom, singing a favourite song in her off-key voice.

"What now?" Matt whispered.

Jimmy tried to think. Theo wasn't going anywhere, and he had to keep her from finding out about Matt. She wasn't good at keeping secrets, even when she bought in. She'd gotten him into trouble more than once by blurting something out. "I'll get her to go back to her bedroom for something. You sneak across the hall and into the closet once she's out of sight."

"Gotcha."

If Theo was suspicious, she didn't show it when Jimmy asked her to find a pen in her room for him to borrow. She talked the entire time, and he walked her back to the bathroom none the wiser. His mom passed him in the hall as he was about to enter his room. She was dressed in jeans and a sweater but hadn't put on make-up, as she always did when she was going out. "Eggs and bacon sound good?" she asked.

"Sure, Mom. Does Theo have a dance class this morning?"

"It's at one today. Guess I'll have no reason to avoid housework after breakfast." She smiled, but he knew she hated doing chores. "Tell Theo if she hurries, she can feed the chickens. Get dressed and come on down. It won't take me long to scramble some eggs."

He dressed quickly in jeans and a sweatshirt while telling Matt what was going on through the open closet door. "Might be a while before I make it back here, but hang tight. I'll get some food to you."

His dad was still in the kitchen when Jimmy took a seat at the table. He had a full cup of coffee and was leaning against the counter. His mom worked next to him at the stove with her back to the room. The sky through the window above the sink was grey and gloomy, and Jimmy's spirits slipped. He hated rainy weather.

"You and Theo spending the day at home for a change of pace?" his dad asked. His voice was jokey, but his mom didn't seem to find him funny.

"You make it sound like I'm neglecting my duties. Driving Theo around and making sure she has a full life isn't nothing." She lifted the frying pan and began scooping eggs onto three plates. "I might not be milking cows, but that's your life choice."

"I'm working for us, Hope. For you and Jimmy and Theo. All I ask is that you meet me halfway."

His mom was silent for a moment, and Jimmy sat very still. He hated rainy days, but he hated when his parents argued even more.

Her shoulders relaxed. There was a pleading note in her voice that hadn't been there before. "We could sell this place and move into the city. I could get a job, and the kids would have so many more opportunities. We could spend time together without you being exhausted and stressed." She walked over to the table and set down two plates of food.

His dad put his coffee mug on the counter and zipped up his jacket. "Maybe you're right. This isn't the life you wanted, and I know you've tried. We could spend the second half of our married life doing what you want."

"Oh, Lanny, I…"

She turned to face him, and Jimmy saw them exchange a long look that he couldn't decipher. Would his dad really give up this farm that his father and grandfather had owned and passed down to him? Jimmy'd always thought he'd be next in line, and then he'd get Flicka back — not the real Flicka, because she'd be too old, but one just like her. He even dreamed about his dad having a good year and buying her back, knowing in his heart this wasn't likely to happen.

Theo bounced into the kitchen, breaking the moment and drawing everyone's attention to her, as per usual. His mom fussed with Theo's breakfast, and his dad kissed her on the forehead before going outside and back to work. It was as if the tension of a minute ago had never happened.

"Your dad would like you to give him a hand in the barn when you're done eating," his mom said. "Theo and I will work inside cleaning up the joint."

"It's a work morning," Theo said. "Yippee."

Jimmy had no choice. He slipped a few strips of bacon into his pocket for Matt when he went upstairs on the pretence of getting a warmer hoodie. Matt would need to wait until the afternoon for some real food. Jimmy hoped Matt wouldn't decide to make a run for it before his chores were done and the others were out of the house.

————

ELLA TEXTED Hunter before setting out on her bike to Daisy's café for breakfast. The first raindrops began falling as she was pedalling up Bronson, but she kept going. Luckily, she'd packed a rain jacket that she could pull out of her knapsack for the ride home.

Hunter was not in their regular booth, waiting for her, and her heart dropped a notch. He'd been decidedly cooler since she started dating Stefan, likely because he didn't want their odd partnership to become common knowledge. Over the past year, Hunter had fed her bits of information to put her on track for a story in return for her intel. So far, they'd managed to help each other on a few cases, and from what Hunter had said, Quade was looking the other way. Still, they had to be careful not to flaunt the collaboration. Maybe Hunter had decided the risk wasn't worth the reward. It was surprising how bereft this made her feel.

Daisy grinned at the sight of her as she settled into the booth and arrived seconds later with the coffee pot and a copy of *The Capital*. "Where's your fella?" she asked, filling Ella's mug without asking. "Off rounding up bad guys?"

"In all likelihood. There are enough of them out there lately." Ella looked through the plate glass window and frowned. "He's busy these days anyway. We've … fallen out of touch." She drew her gaze back and picked up the cup. "I'll have the usual, Daisy. Thanks." She'd tried unsuccessfully to correct Daisy before about

Hunter not being her boyfriend. Let her think they'd broken up.

Daisy patted her shoulder. "Sure thing, sugar. I'll get the kitchen right on it."

Ella read the front page, pleased to see her article mentioned in the header. She turned to page three and skimmed the story, printed as she'd written it, without edits. Satisfied, she leaned back, drank her coffee, looked out the window, and mentally organized the day ahead. A flash of lightning lit up the gloom followed by a torrent of raindrops drumming against the glass. She thought about the bike ride home and decided this might be a good day to stay inside and work on a podcast. She'd begun posting once a week, expanding her repertoire to include twenty minutes with an expert in a crime-fighting related field. Her followers had grown from seventy to 120,000, expanding her influence and upping her profile. A new sponsor was bringing in a modest cash flow. She'd snagged a great interview with an art fraud investigator late last week and needed to edit the footage. An update on the Ashton murders would be the lede in Saturday's podcast, but for this, she'd wait until later today for the most accurate news.

Daisy set a plate of bacon, eggs, and hash browns in front of her with a side of toast, breaking Ella's reverie. "Looks like you've got company."

Ella looked toward the entrance as Hunter started across the floor toward her. He glanced behind him, and Ella's eyes were drawn to the door opening a second time as Rosie Thorburn stepped inside, shaking out her umbrella. Hunter reached Ella's table a few seconds ahead of his partner.

He spoke in a low voice. "Sorry, got your message as

Thorburn and I were heading out. I suggested we stop for breakfast first."

"No problem," she said, even though it was one. They wouldn't be able to speak freely.

Hunter turned as Thorburn stopped alongside him. "Look who I found. Feel like company, Ella, or do you want to dine in peace?"

"Sure, have a seat if you don't mind watching me eat ahead of you."

Daisy waited for Rosie, then Hunter to slide onto the seat across from her before pouring coffee. She took their order without giving any indication that she knew Hunter. Ella silently applauded her discretion, although Daisy appeared to give Thorburn the once-over.

"This your usual spot?" Thorburn asked Ella.

"On occasion." She avoided meeting Hunter's eyes. "It's close to my apartment. So, how are things with you two?"

"Busy. Hunter's showing me the ropes on a murder case. My first."

"Well, you've got a good mentor. Have you come up with any insights you can impart?" Ella widened her gaze to include him.

Thorburn jumped in. "Sorry, we can't share evidence unless we have clearance."

Hunter shifted slightly away from her and gave Ella an apologetic shrug. "How about you, Ella? Uncovered anything helpful?"

"I've been speaking with neighbours and people who knew the Petries. Nobody says anything bad about them."

Daisy arrived with two more plates, and the conversation veered away from the case. "I'd like to join a gym," Thorburn said. "I'm starting to feel out of shape."

"I was planning to go this afternoon, if you'd like to try out my friend Finn's place on Catherine Street. It's not all that far from the station."

"Would you mind? I can make it around five if all goes well today."

"I'll give you the address and we can meet there."

Thorburn nodded. "I've been needing to change things up a bit, so this might be the push that gets me out of my comfort zone."

"Yeah, I hear you." Ella speared the last strip of bacon. "It's too easy settling for the usual routine instead of going for something that involves work." She grinned at Hunter before popping the bacon into her mouth. This meeting was a bust, but at least he'd showed up. They'd need to connect later when he was alone. She signalled Daisy for her bill and left them still eating as she went outside to unlock her bike, the rain soaking her jeans before she'd made it to the corner.

CHAPTER 23

Thorburn parked in the Petrie driveway, and they made a dash through the rain to the front door. Forensics had not released the scene to the family, but they'd gathered most of what they needed, and Liam wanted another look now that they could move around more freely. The house had a forlorn, deserted look shrouded in wispy tendrils of fog, made more depressing by the leaden sky and cold rain. They covered their wet footwear in white booties even though it was unnecessary and stood for a moment in the front hallway in the dampness and chill. "We could turn on the furnace while we're here? Forensics must have turned it off for some reason." Thorburn waited for him to nod before she went to locate the thermostat.

Liam entered the living room first, needing to get a renewed sense of where Stu and Devina had stood and fallen when each was shot. Chalk outlines of their bodies marked the floor. He paced the distance. A sticker above the couch indicated where a bullet had lodged into the wall. He heard Thorburn in the doorway and turned. "I'm trying to figure out the sequence of what happened."

Her eyes darted between the chalk bodies and landed on him. "What are you seeing?"

"Stu was likely sitting on the couch or standing near it when Devina entered the dining room with the rifle. She'd have gone to get it from the back hallway for some reason, I'm guessing because a third person was in the room threatening them, but this is only a theory for now."

"Could it have been a murder-suicide?"

"Devina has bruises and scratches on her arms and hands, indicating a struggle. Stu was on the other side of the room and has no obvious defensive wounds. A third person is the more likely scenario."

"The unnamed visitor." He could picture Devina and the visitor standing near where Thorburn was now, just inside the entrance to the living room, closer to the dining room than Stu.

Thorburn stepped up beside him. "It could have been Matt back from his day of fishing with Jimmy Dooley. Something might have set him off, and he frightened Devina. That would have put the confrontation close to sunset."

Liam pulled another strand of thought. "Matt might have been the one to bring the gun into the room, going into the house through the back door, and then coming up behind Devina in the dining room."

Thorburn looked in that direction. "Stu sees him and stands. Matt fires and shoots him, then struggles with Devina for the gun. It goes off and kills her."

They were both silent for a moment, picturing the scene. Liam said, "Or this might have happened before Matt made it home. A visitor was in the living room who scared Devina enough that she left them and got the gun from the back entrance, where Stu kept it and the ammo in easy reach to scare off groundhogs."

"Or the visitor might have gotten the gun from the back door on their way in. The Petries never locked that entry, so the person could have surprised them. Maybe Devina was on her way to the kitchen to make supper, and Stu was on the couch." Rosie's eyes scanned the room.

"We're sure it was the same rifle kept by the back door that killed them both?" Liam asked.

Thorburn nodded. "The ballistics report arrived overnight. The Petries' rifle was used in both deaths."

"I don't believe Matt was involved in the shootings," Liam said. He couldn't put the boy in this room with the Petries as they were being gunned down. "I believe he was in his bedroom and escaped through the open window. He might have been in the house while events unfolded or arrived soon after and the killer was still here."

"Then Matt could be in hiding?" Thorburn asked.

"If the killer didn't catch him. The question is where did he go that would feel safe? The nights are getting colder, and remaining outdoors overnight without food or water doesn't appear a viable option for long."

"His bike is still here, so he'd be on foot."

"Matt has one friend: Jimmy Dooley. The Dooleys live quite far from here. It would be difficult for Matt to get to their farm without being seen by somebody."

"We've already spoken with Jimmy twice. He seemed as out to sea as the rest of us. Matt didn't confide in him much about his life, even though they hung out."

"No." Liam rubbed his temple, where a throbbing had started to spread. "Matt knows other neighbours, though. He helped out at various fundraisers and worked with Devina to sell crafts and produce. We'll need to visit nearby homes and check the outbuildings. For damn sure, Matt'll have taken shelter today if he's out there." Liam paused and listened to the rain striking the roof and gusts of wind rattling the window panes. The autumn weather was starting out with a wallop. "Let's get a detailed map of the area and go about the door-to-door search systematically. We can borrow a few officers to check out the sheds and garages while we speak with the owners. If we return to HQ now, we can start after lunch."

"Let's hope the rain lets up by then."

"If I had to guess, this is going to be an all-day downpour. It's as if the heavens are in sympathy with the Petries and their fate, making our lives miserable too so we don't forget." He took one last look at Devina's chalk outline before turning away and stepping into the hall.

———

ROSIE TEXTED Ella that she wouldn't be able to make the gym today but hoped they could try tomorrow. She looked at the Johannson house from under the hood of her raincoat and started up the driveway with an officer recruited to scout around outside while she carried on the interview. The door was opened by a woman named Miriam, pretty, fiftyish with a trim, muscular body. Rosie hoped she would age that well. Even standing in the doorway, she could smell fresh baking and coffee.

"Please come in out of the rain," Miriam said after they'd made introductions.

"Officer Pine would like to search the outbuildings for Matt Clark, if this is okay. We're still trying to locate him."

"Of course. Nothing is locked." Miriam nodded in the direction of the barn. "You'll find my husband Everett working inside."

Rosie nodded at the officer before he turned and began sloshing through the puddles on his search of the property. She followed Miriam into the large kitchen and gratefully accepted a cup of coffee. "I understand you've been feeding the Petries' chickens and collecting the eggs."

Miriam sat across from her, hands wrapped around a mug. "Yes, who…"

"The officer who's been monitoring their house. We've located Devina's uncle in Vancouver, and he'll be coming in a few days to make arrangements. His name's Terrence Garnett."

"I've never met Terrence, but I'll be on the watch for him."

"How well did you know Devina and Stu?"

"We were friendly, but Devina kept to herself for the most part. Stu was out in the community more than she was."

"Did your husband and Stu spend time together?"

"Not really." Miriam lifted the coffee cup and sipped, taking her time before answering. "A reporter was by and knew somehow that Everett and Devina dated in high school. She thought it might be important, but I can assure you, it's not. They were still friendly, and some might misconstrue that. Says more about the people spreading stories than about us."

Rosie blinked. Where had this come from? Had Ella Tate been by, following up on some bit of local gossip about Everett and Devina? Rosie studied Miriam's face to determine if she was attempting to divert trouble by making this confession out of the blue, wondering if there was more to the story than Miriam was sharing. "How friendly were they?" she asked at last. Her question sounded rude to her own ears, but she didn't know how better to ask.

Miriam's expression went from annoyed to amused. "Casual friends. Nothing more secretive, no matter what titillating hearsay is going around."

"When is the last time you saw Devina or Stu?"

"Goodness, I ran into Stu a week before they died. Everett and I were at the Ashton Brew Pub when he came in and sat by himself in the back room. Everett went over and chatted with him. He didn't stay long and told me afterward that Stu was distracted and in a funny mood. Everett invited Stu to join us, but we weren't surprised when he stayed put."

"Could Stu have thought that Everett and Devina—"

"Of course not." Miriam's face scrunched into a scowl. "I can't see how this is important to solving their murders."

"It's always helpful to learn as much as possible

about relationships connected to the victims." Hunter's words echoed in her head. *Find out as much as you can. Watch their body language. Figure out what they aren't telling you and try to separate the lies from the truth.* He was proving a patient teacher, and she thanked heaven for allowing her to be his partner, if only for a short time. She had no illusions about her inexperience and the fragile position she was in. Auger had brought her with him from Toronto because he wanted the power over her. He hadn't expected Quade to shift her to Hunter's team and out from under him. She dreaded his next move.

She refocused on her questions, but Miriam had little more to impart about the Petries. Rosie was relieved when Pine tapped on the front door to let her know he'd finished searching for Matt and would wait in the car for her. They had two more properties to check out before nightfall, and she'd run out of things to ask. She wrapped up the interview and followed him outside into the driving rain.

Her phone pinged a message as she was buckling her seatbelt. She glanced down. Carlos had sent a text to her personal number asking if she wanted to meet for a drink when she was done work. He was available any time after six. She raised her eyes to look out the side window and the rain running in rivulets down the glass. Her heart beat faster at the thought of seeing him. Brad was working a night shift, and he'd never know. Was this what she wanted? Could she live with herself if this drink turned into something more? She thought about her growing discontent in the relationship with Brad. She didn't want to spend the rest of her life in a passion-less marriage because, even though they hadn't taken vows, they lived like a married couple in the same house with a joint bank account. Yet seeing Carlos behind Brad's back wasn't something she would have contemplated a few months ago. Was this who she was becoming? She looked back down at her phone screen and took a cleansing breath before beginning to type.

CHAPTER 24

The phone rang as Theo and Jimmy finished eating lunch. Their mom had made egg salad sandwiches and heated up tomato soup but didn't join them at the table, saying she wasn't hungry. Their dad had said that he was too busy in the barn to come in and eat yet, so Jimmy was tasked with bringing him sandwiches and a thermos after they finished their meal. He planned on saving a sandwich for Matt and eagerly awaited his mom and Theo's departure for her dance class. He listened with growing dismay to his mother's side of the conversation.

"Sure, no problem. We'll plan on coming to the next one." She ended the call. "Stand down, Theo," she said over her shoulder. "The teacher is sick, and dance is cancelled for today."

"Mom," Theo wailed. "You promised."

"Sometimes unexpected things happen and we have to adjust, Theo. It's called life." She checked her watch. "Why don't you invite a friend over?"

Theo's face lit up. "I can ask Amelia and Becka."

"That's two friends, but fine. Do you have their pictures and numbers on your phone?"

"Yup."

"Then see if they're free. I can talk to their moms if necessary." She looked across the table at Jimmy. "You can stay in the barn and help your dad. There's not much else to do outdoors in this rain."

"I thought I'd read in my room."

"Since when have you spent an afternoon reading? Take your dad his lunch and stay out there and be useful."

Her voice brooked no argument, and he didn't dare draw attention to himself by protesting. It was true that he wasn't a reader. He'd rather be outdoors fishing or playing in the woods than lying around with a book. Hopefully, Theo and her friends would keep out of his room and Matt would stay hidden. He felt the situation spiralling out of his control and wondered how much trouble he'd be in if his parents discovered what he'd done. His dad hated lying more than anything else. He said that if he taught Jimmy and Theo one thing, it was to always tell the truth when they'd misbehaved and face up to the consequences. Jimmy imagined the punishment for hiding Matt would reach a new level, although since they'd sold Flicka, there wasn't much they could do to him anymore that would hurt worse.

JIMMY'S DAD finally released him after he'd help muck out the stalls, replacing dirty bedding with clean. It was going on five o'clock, and the cows were due for their second milking of the day, but his dad had a machine and didn't need his help with that. Jimmy was happy to leave him to it. The rain had lessened to a drizzle when he stepped outside the barn, mist obscuring his view of the front door, the house perched like some ghostly white ship in a sea of fog. He waded through puddles, jumping and sloshing in the mud on his way. If it weren't for Matt waiting in his bedroom, he'd have stopped to play.

He could hear Theo and her friends giggling and talking loudly in her bedroom as he started up the stairs, his legs and arms tired from lifting and cleaning. He stank like manure and would take a shower before dinner; his mom wouldn't let him in the kitchen otherwise. He stopped on the landing, and his heart flipped at the sight of his wide-open bedroom door. Had Theo gone inside?

He hurried across the space and into his bedroom, closing the door to the hall behind him. Matt was nowhere in sight, and his stomach clenched. He crossed to the closet. He opened the door while quietly calling Matt's name. At first, he couldn't see Matt, but as his eyes adjusted, he found him sitting with his back against the wall, hidden by clothes and boxes.

"You stink like a cow, buddy," Matt said as he stood and moved past him into the room. He stretched his arms over his head and arched his back. "Am I ever stiff. I'm guessing you were helping your dad?"

"Yeah. Was Theo in my room?"

"I stayed in the closet when she and her friends came upstairs and fell asleep for a while. I heard her in here, because she dropped something, and it woke me up." He rubbed his stomach. "Say, have you got anything to eat?"

"Not yet. I'll bring something to you after I shower."

"I'm starving. Also could use the can."

"We need to wait for Theo and her friends to leave." Worry was beginning to gnaw at Jimmy about his impending punishment because hiding Matt was becoming harder and harder. He'd stopped talking about contacting his mother, almost like he was waiting for her to show, which Jimmy thought was no plan at all.

"Let's hope it's not much longer, or I'll have to take a piss out the window."

Theo, Amelia and Becka chose that moment to leave her bedroom and go downstairs, their voices loud and boisterous as they passed by Jimmy's door. Matt crouched behind the bed in case Theo decided to enter and only straightened after they were halfway down the stairs. He and Jimmy scooted over to the bathroom, and Jimmy stood guard inside the door. He peeked into the hall and listened as Matt finished up at the sink. "We should hurry. I can't hear them anymore."

"Almost done."

They tiptoed across the carpet to Jimmy's room, and Matt entered first, stopping in his tracks so that Jimmy bumped into him. "What's the prob—" Jimmy started to say and snapped his mouth shut as he looked past Matt toward the bed.

"Hi, Matty," Theo said from where she sat bouncing up and down on the mattress, her face rosy with a beaming smile crinkling up her eyes. "What're you doing here? Everybody's looking for you." She stood and jumped over to wrap herself around his waist.

Matt put his arms around her shoulders, returning the hug while he looked over her head at Jimmy and mouthed, "What the fuck now?"

CHAPTER 25

Shortly after five o'clock, Ella posted her latest podcast about the murders and turned off her computer. She packed a knapsack with gym clothes and hurried downstairs, happy at the thought of some exercise after sitting all day. It was still raining, so she drove rather than cycled to Finn's gym. He was in his office working at the computer when she arrived. She shook the rain off her jacket before going in to say hello.

"Well, if it isn't true crime podcaster Ella Tate," he said, jumping up from his desk to hug her. "Decided to whip the old body back into shape?"

"Yeah, between long hours at my desk and Tony's cooking, I need to do something." She patted her belly. "Losing my svelteness."

"Your what?"

"Let's just say I'm a few inches thicker in the middle than before I met Tony."

"It's never too late to get back on track. We could have a bout in the ring if you're up for it."

"We should save that for my next visit, since I'm not

much competition at the moment. Hear from Maisie lately?"

"Yeah, she's flourishing at McGill in the medical stream. She plans to work here in the summer, but I can't imagine she'll return after that. We're likely to find her in a community in Africa helping at a hospital on future holidays."

Ella never stood in Finn's office without remembering Finn's former employee Maisie tied to the chair and bleeding out. It had taken her a while to come back to the gym, wanting to forget that horrible day, now almost a full year ago. In some ways, it could have been yesterday.

"Lena's with Piper?"

"Yeah, I'll be heading home when I close up, so sorry we can't go for a drink tonight."

"Next time." She wanted to ask if he'd heard from Adele but knew speaking about her caused him pain. Two months with his wife gone, and they were all learning to adjust, even Lena. That was the saddest part of her absence.

She left Finn and was on her way to the change room when the front door opened and someone called her name. She turned. Rosie Thorburn was striding toward her, carrying a gym bag. Her face was flushed, as if she'd been running. "Are you coming or going?" she asked. "I hope I'm not too late."

"I've only just arrived. You couldn't have timed it any better."

"Lovely. Do I need to sign in or pay?"

"We can let Finn know you're here, and then I'll show you around. You're my guest today, so no charge."

They changed, and Finn chatted with Rosie while

Ella began her workout. She'd finished on the stationary bike and was starting on weights when Rosie joined her. Rosie had spent her time on the elliptical, and her hair was damp with sweat. "I can spot you," she said. "I need a break."

"Sure." Ella lay on her back and pushed up the first set of dumbbells while Rosie got into position.

"So, I've spoken with Finn and told him I'd be signing up. He gave me tonight as a free trial."

Ella grunted and pushed the weights up a second time. She lowered her arms. "Do you live close by?"

"No, Brad and I rent a small townhouse off Pinecrest, but this gym is close to HQ. I plan to stop in on my way home when work allows."

"I should come more regularly too. Man, this is hard work." She pushed up the weights and groaned as she lowered them. "You want a go? I'm out of shape and don't want to damage myself."

"That's okay. I was thinking we could go for a drink if you have time when you're done. No shop talk, I promise."

"But I like shop talk, the juicier the better." Ella smiled. "I'm going to take a round out of the punching bag and should be ready after that."

"I'll skip for a bit, and that'll do it for me too."

They decided to walk to the pub around the corner from the gym, even though the rain hadn't stopped completely. Ella lifted her face to the sky, enjoying the wet coolness on her skin after the workout. It was a quiet evening in the bar, and they had their choice of seats. Ella selected a table next to the window where they could watch the people walking past. She couldn't remember the last time she'd been out with someone other than for work.

Even breakfasts with Hunter were about a case or an investigation. She was curious why Rosie seemed to want to befriend her. They had little in common. Rosie struck her as a buttoned-up, careful kind of woman. Young and pretty, but with little spark or spontaneity. Ella took a sip of beer and sat back, waiting for Rosie to lead the conversation.

"Feels great to get in some exercise. Thanks for letting me know about Finn's gym." Rosie raised her glass and toasted Ella.

"Glad I could be of help. So, what does your partner — Brad, I believe you said — think about living in Ottawa, and how long have you been together?" Rosie's face tightened, and Ella wondered if she'd struck a nerve. Did her relationship with Brad have something to do with her choosing a gym near work and going for drinks? Was Rosie avoiding going home?

"Brad and I started dating in high school. We grew up in Collingwood, so a small town kind of upbringing. We split up a few times but always got back together. He agreed to leave Toronto, where we'd been living, mainly so I could take this job in Ottawa with Auger—"

Rosie's voice trailed off, and Ella took a moment to figure out what she wasn't saying. Her eyes and the way she gripped her beer glass were tells that all was not rosy in Rosie-land. Was she upset about Brad, or the job, or both? Ella didn't usually insert herself into someone's private life, but there was something about Rosie she liked, and her unhappiness was difficult to ignore. "Was moving here a good choice?"

"I think … no … things have been stressful."

"Is it work?"

"The move. Work. Brad. Take your pick." Rosie

stared out the window and took a long drink of beer. She looked back at Ella and gave an apologetic smile. "I didn't ask you here to listen to my troubles."

"Sometimes having an objective ear is needed, and I honestly don't mind." She took a stab in the dark. "Is it Auger? Is he upset that they've moved you over to work with Hunter?"

"Auger." Spoken in a flat monotone. "He's the reason I got the job in Major Crimes. I thought it was a great opportunity."

"Thought?"

Rosie was silent for so long that Ella had time to finish her beer and order a second. Rosie declined the offer of another drink. "Can I tell you something as a … a friend and not a reporter?"

"Of course."

"It was after I arrived in Ottawa that I started getting texts with disturbing photos from an anonymous account. At first once every few weeks, and then more frequently. Sometimes daily."

"Were they threatening?"

"No, there was nothing in the texts that threatened to hurt or kill me. It was what went with them that felt threatening. Auger began touching me when nobody was around and saying things — suggestive comments, like in the texts. At first, I thought it was something I'd been doing or wearing. Some silent signal I was giving off—"

"You know that's bullshit, right, Rosie? You in no way instigated this sick behaviour. Auger is your boss, for Christ's sake. He's stepped over so many boundaries and should be fired, for starters." The rage was growing, and she forced herself to calm down. "So there's no doubt the messages came from Auger?"

"I thought so... I believe so, but whoever sent them was careful. There's nothing that can be used to identify him unless you know him intimately." She gave a short laugh. "And the sender has to be a man because, well, have a look." She slid her phone over to Ella.

Ella could feel the warmth rising up her neck as she flipped through the photos of a man's genitals taken from inventive angles. She read the messages, crude and intimidating, no matter that Rosie had rated them non-threatening. "Good God," she said, rubbing her forehead. "This is like a campaign waged against you. If Auger is behind these, he's one twisted, dangerous man. When did you receive the last one?"

"They stopped when Quade moved me over to Hunter's team. Auger now takes our moments alone to tell me what a terrible job I'm doing and to belittle me. I know for a fact he's complained about my lack of judgement to Quade. I expect a call from HR at any point to let me know I'm being transferred out of Major Crimes."

"We can't let that happen. Does Hunter know about any of this?"

"No, and I'd like to keep it that way. I don't want him to treat me differently. I need to prove to him and Quade that I'm a good detective and worthy of their trust. Hunter has already given me more chances and responsibility than I ever got from Auger."

Ella tried to control her frustration at the idea that Auger was going to get away with the harassment. The reporter in her struggled with the promise she'd made to listen as a friend. "These photos and the things he's said — you can take them to Quade."

"No, it'll be my word against his, and he's been careful, as I already told you. He only says things and touches me when we're alone. It's also possible he didn't send the texts."

"Possible, but not bloody likely."

Rosie took a drink and set the glass down. "The texts and photos have stopped, and he's avoiding me now in the office, aside from the odd snide putdown. I just have to figure out how to keep him from moving me out of the unit."

"Are you comfortable telling me where he was touching you?"

"Nowhere too intimate. He'd run his hand up and down my arm or stand behind me when I was sitting at my desk and massage my shoulders. Creepy but clear of any erogenous zones. Again, he's been careful." She gave Ella a wry smile. "Thank you for listening. Believe it or not, saying all this out loud to a sympathetic ear makes it easier. I haven't even told Brad. I've not made many friends since we moved here."

"Rosie, if I can help in any way, I'm on it. You only have to ask."

"That means a lot." Rosie ducked her head and drained the last of her beer. "We should get going before I start talking about Brad. One sob story is enough for tonight." She gave a small smile and started putting on her rain jacket, averting her face.

Ella had to bite back the urge to jump in with solutions that involved Rosie standing up for herself and exposing Auger. She'd interviewed enough sexual abuse victims to know that they had to come to that decision in their own time. "We'll do this again soon," she said instead and grinned. "And maybe on our next gym outing we can even talk a little shop, although I say that in jest. We have to keep work out of our friendship so Auger has nothing to fault you for when we nail him for harassment."

"From your lips."

CHAPTER 26

Montreal
Katherine set a steaming tureen of pea soup on the table next to a plate of crusty bread from the bakery on the corner. Glynnis watched her old friend scoop out heaping amounts with a ladle and inhaled the fragrant aroma of peas and ham as Katherine set a bowl in front of her. "This smells divine. You never cease to amaze."

"Simple to whip together. The bread is fabulous, too, although I would have made my own if there'd been time."

They toasted each other with glasses of sparkling water before Katherine sat down across from her. While eating, they chatted about their lives since they'd last seen each other ten years ago. Katherine had already filled Glynnis in on her trip to Ottawa and convinced her to spend the night rather than race across the provincial border so late in the day with no plan. Glynnis fought every impulse in her body to keep moving and find Matt, but she was exhausted and knew

Katherine was right. The baby growing in her belly had sapped her energy.

Main course done, Katherine brewed a pot of tea and brought out a plate of lemon squares that they took into the living room, a few steps away in the open-concept ground floor. The property had limited frontage, and the rooms were narrow and long, the kitchen and laundry room at the back end of the house. A staircase with a wrought-iron railing curved upward to two bedrooms and a bathroom on the second floor. Katherine lived alone now, and her touch was every-where, from the lilac walls to the white shag rugs, floral paintings, and plush sofa and chairs. Her husband of six years had died from an aneurism twelve months earlier. Framed photographs of Frederick and Katherine sat atop her dresser and filled the wall in the stairwell. Glynnis regretted not being there for her after his death. They'd spoken often by phone, but there had been no memorial service, and she wouldn't have been able to leave New York, even if there had been. Wyatt had been going through his own hell and needed her nearby.

"So," Katherine began. "What now?"

The familiar worry flooded through her, the panic she'd so far kept under control. It was as if the fear she'd been living with the entire summer had mutated into the worst possible horror show. Losing Matty... She couldn't let herself go there. He had to be safe and waiting for her. "I'm going to drive to Ashton tomorrow at first light and check out Devina's farm."

"Is that wise?"

"I have to see for myself where he was staying. How it all went down."

"A detective named Liam Hunter has been leaving messages. It might be time to fill him in."

"This goes against everything Wyatt set up ... but you're right. It's time to break my silence if it helps bring Matty home. Surely, the Ottawa police aren't a threat to Wyatt. The corporation's people in the NYPD can't have influence this far north." She paused. "I can't believe those assholes found Matt in the middle of nowhere. It makes no sense. Devina and I hadn't been in contact for years until I reached out. Those bastards would never have left him alone all summer if they'd known where he was."

"Could Wyatt or Matt have let it slip somehow? Social media, perhaps?"

"I suppose anything is possible, but Matt promised to stay off all the platforms. When I spoke with him on the phone, he said his friend Jimmy didn't have any accounts, or that's what he told Matty anyway. As for Wyatt, there's no way he'd put us in jeopardy."

"When does the grand jury begin?"

"Three days from now. It's expected to last a month, maybe two. Then I can make plans."

"Something to hang on to. I can come with you tomorrow."

"No, I don't want you more involved in case things take a bad turn. I'll be in touch, though, when I can."

"My door is always open." Katherine smiled at her with sad, concerned eyes before looking away.

———

ALONE IN THE guest bedroom in the front of the house, Glynnis sat by the window, looking out at the street.

Cars lined both sides with no spaces in between, parking being a rare commodity in the city. Permits were a necessity in this neighbourhood. A woman moved back and forth in the living room window directly across from her, dancing by herself and not caring who saw. Glynnis thought if she could hear whatever music guided her moves, the woman would look somewhat less deranged.

She'd always been good at blocking out troubling thoughts and ignoring the worst situations as they were happening, but Matt's disappearance had shaken her so deeply that mental trickery wasn't working. He was the one person in her life who'd never let her down, the one she loved beyond all reason. If anything happened to him — well, that would simply be the end of her. Truly. Forever and ever.

Her parents had been dead set against Wyatt Clark from the get-go. She'd brought him home Easter weekend her last year of university. He'd been polite and had kept his hands off her in front of them, quite a feat in those early, heady days of their relationship. Her parents had pretended to like him, and it was only when she returned during summer vacation to say they planned to marry that their true feelings bubbled out. She was too young. He was too smooth. Too handsome. She'd gotten angry, told them they were trying to ruin her life. She and Wyatt eloped without their negative presence to mar the day. The wedge had been driven; her parents kept their distance.

Wyatt landed an accounting job in Manhattan with a start-up generic drug company, and she began work as an editor at a publishing firm. They were happy, and their joy compounded when she became pregnant with Matty. Eighteen months after they said "I do," he was born and she quit her job to stay home with him. That was hands-down the best time in their marriage.

Downhill started on Matt's fifth birthday when Wyatt left for work in the morning and didn't come home until the next day. He said he'd gotten involved in a file, lost track of time, and slept at the office. She might have believed him if he'd met her eyes when he said it. This began a five-year stretch of her waiting at home while he got sucked deeper and deeper into the firm, working long hours and becoming more and more distant when he was with her and Matt. He took on more responsibility, got perks, travelled. She hadn't known then that he was being pressured to perform with an unspoken threat hanging over his head. He knew too much about the company and its finances for them ever to let him leave. He confided to her only at the end after his colleague and the colleague's girlfriend were murdered that he'd been openly warned. The company's enforcer pointedly asked about her and Matt, said it would be a shame for him to lose his family in a terrible accident. They'd been in bed, her lying on top of him, whispering in each other's ears, afraid the company had somehow bugged their room. "A couple of cops in NYPD are in on it," he'd said. "I can't see any way out." She'd been shaken by the corruption and the menace that infiltrated their lives like an invisible virus. It was she who'd come up with the idea of contacting the FBI. She still had no idea how complicit Wyatt was in the illegal ventures or what he'd done to stay in the firm's good graces. She knew their relationship would take a long time to recover, if she even wanted to give him another chance.

A flash of light across the street caught her eye, and

she turned her face to peer into the shadows. Surely, nobody had followed her here? She had spent the night before in her car in a parking lot in a suburb outside of Montreal. She'd paid to leave the vehicle in a garage several blocks away. This rush of adrenaline was left over from the panic to get here undetected. Still, she moved to the side of the window and drew the blind, lifting the fabric from the side and checking that nobody was loitering on the sidewalk. She waited a full minute before looking again. All appeared quiet, people strolling past without stopping or lurking nearby. She made a quick trip to the bathroom down the hall before changing into a nightgown. The sheets were cool, and she sank into the mattress with a sigh. So much better than last night's uncomfortable, cold car seat, made even more uncomfortable by her growing belly. She wondered what Wyatt would think when he found out they were having another child. The baby's conception had been their last act of intimacy before he'd moved out.

She snuggled in and let the room's dark silence envelop her, but sleep was slow in coming. She'd kept Mattie's disappearance and the Petrie murders from Wyatt, but that didn't stop her from second-guessing her decision. She knew that if Wyatt testified, and the company had Matt, he was as good as dead, her along with him because she would do everything in her power to track them down. Yet if Wyatt didn't go through with his testimony, they were good as dead anyway. Her only chance was to find Matt and disappear again until Wyatt was free to join them in their new life — if she decided to allow him back in.

CHAPTER 27

Lucky woke Liam up by stretching out next to his head and purring like a small engine. One paw swatted at his ear, and he rolled over and gave the cat's head a rub. "Food bowl empty, or you just being annoying?" The cat meowed and jumped off the bed, tail flicking as she landed on the floor. Liam took a moment to focus on the pale lemony sunlight pouring though the slats of the half-open blind. It was going on 6:00 a.m. The Petrie murders final forensics report was promised for today, although they already knew the highlights. Thorburn and the officer were continuing the door-to-door sweep, and he'd catch up to them once the morning update with Quade was over. He'd have to try reaching out to Katherine Fielding again before setting out for Ashton. Her silence had become irksome. The day held no end of tasks to get through. Hopefully, the team would make some headway before nightfall.

He showered and dressed in black slacks, black turtleneck, and tan jacket. Lucky sat in his lap while he ate a bagel and drank a cup of coffee in the living room.

He'd been gone a lot of late, and she seemed starved for affection, even though Hannah had been bringing his nephews over late afternoons to feed and play with her. "I won't be keeping these overtime hours much longer, little friend," he said, giving her back one last rub. "Guard the castle and stay out of trouble."

Yesterday's rain had stopped, but swollen clouds lingered like a woollen blanket over the city. The streets were slick with leftover precipitation, and puddles filled low-lying sections of the road and pathways. Liam deviated from his route to visit a Tim Hortons drive-through for a large coffee and egg sandwich that he ate before getting back into traffic. The bagel earlier hadn't filled him. Even with the stop, he was first into the office and had a chance to review the night's reports while he waited for Quade. Auger was next in and stopped at his desk on the way by.

"Hear the news? Greta's decided to move back home to Regina. She's accepted a job leading their community outreach program. Means her current post will be up for grabs."

Liam waited a few beats. "You applying?"

"Sure, nothing to lose. How about you?"

"I'm happy where I am."

"Guess Quade and I will be duking it out then, that is if she wants to make her acting permanent." He lifted his hands and feigned a couple of jabs. "Being a Black woman gives her a big advantage, political correctness being what it is these days, but I have more experience." Auger gave an exaggerated shrug. "Hopefully, what's best for the team will win the day."

"I'm certain the competition will be fair." Liam watched Auger saunter over to his desk and tried not to think the worst of the man. He wore his ambition like an oversized coat that hid whatever good was going on underneath. Liam wanted to give him the benefit of the doubt, but it was getting more and more difficult to see beneath that big coat.

His cell rang as he was beginning to wonder what had happened to Quade. Her voice echoed loud in his ear. "Franny's sick, and I'm about to drive her over to the clinic. I'm guessing strep throat, so it can't wait. She spent the week at her father's and he, of course, didn't notice her high fever and cough. Can we postpone that meeting until this afternoon? If I don't make it to HQ, we can video chat."

"No problem. I'll drive out to Ashton in the meantime. Thorburn's expecting me."

"Great. I've sent Auger a message, but please check in with him. He's watching for missteps, and I don't intend to give him reason to go over my head. The man's like a buzzard hovering in a dead tree waiting for roadkill with my face on it."

Liam thought about telling her that Greta wasn't returning but decided this could wait. The office had ears. "I'll update him," he said instead. "Give my best to Franny."

"You got it."

He tossed his phone on the desk and looked across at Auger, who was deep in discussion with Boots and Jingles. Before he could stir himself to go over to speak to them, his desk phone rang. Downstairs reception line.

"There's a man here asking to talk with the lead on the Petrie case. Says he's FBI." The officer didn't attempt to hide the disbelief in his voice.

"Tell him I'll be right down."

He took the stairs to the lobby. The man who approached with an outstretched hand was of average height, wearing a well-cut navy suit and tan shoes. His black hair, combed back from his forehead, glistened with gel in the fluorescent lighting. Clear, bright eyes and a clean-shaven face made him appear boyish. Stereotypical FBI, if American television was anything to go by. "Thank you for seeing me without an appointment. I'm Agent John Rodgers with the FBI." His firm grip held a moment longer than comfortable. "The desk sergeant told me you're Detective Liam Hunter, lead on the Petrie case."

"I am that. Would you mind showing me some ID just to cross the t's?" Liam saw the desk sergeant lean forward, as if he also wanted to see the proof.

"Of course." Rodgers pulled out a badge and held it up for Liam to inspect.

Liam nodded after studying Rodgers' photo and matching it to his face. The laminated card had all the official U.S. logos. "Let's find a place where we can chat in private."

They took the elevator to the second floor and settled into a cramped room containing a table, two chairs, and little space for anything else. Liam shut the door and sat across from Rodgers. "So how can I help you?" He figured the visit concerned Matt Clark or the Petries, but he wasn't going to lead the conversation.

"We understand Matt Clark has gone missing after the couple he was living with for the summer were murdered."

"That's correct."

"Do you have any leads on the boy's whereabouts?"

"No. We've been checking all the farms, houses, and

outbuildings in the area, but no sighting. Matt could have been taken by the killer, or he's made it out of the county on his own steam. We have no idea which. I can confirm that his body was not found after we searched the land around the Petrie farm, and we believe Matt wasn't murdered in the vicinity, at any rate. Again, we're hopeful that he's still alive. Why the interest?"

"That's good then." Rodgers pushed his chair back from the table and crossed his legs. The pause felt dramatic to Liam, a tactic to control the conversation. He tried not to react when Rodgers asked, "Have you been reading about the generic drug company grand jury going on in New York City?"

Liam replayed the morning news that he'd half paid attention to on the drive to HQ. "I'm aware of it but not up on the details. Why?"

"In a nutshell, Wyatt Clark, Matt Clark's father, was the accountant for the generic drug company ZTMeds, basically an illegal bunch of drug pushers dressed up in suits. Wyatt is a key witness and set to testify before the grand jury in a few days. We have a different system in New York from Canada, as you know. The grand jury is made up of twenty-three jurors, no judge. The prosecutor argues there's enough evidence to go to trial, and they rule yea or nay without having to decide on guilt or innocence. The grand jury is held in secret with everything sealed until a trial is given the go-ahead."

"Was Wyatt Clark involved in the illegal activities?"

"Not so much a willing player, if you believe his version, but he admitted to being involved enough that the ones running the show had him on a string. You know, agree to certain perks, turn a blind eye, stay silent about money that appears out of nowhere. One of his buddies in the company developed a conscience and tried to get out of the organization. He was found strung up in his apartment with his hands and feet cut off and his girlfriend tied to a chair with her throat slit. Not long after, Wyatt approached the FBI because he figured he was next. The firm had begun monitoring his emails and phone calls, not believing that his friend was the only one wanting out. Their tentacles stretched far and wide, including into the NYPD, so Wyatt didn't trust the police to keep him or his family safe. Like I said, Wyatt had figured out a lot about what was going on in the organization, which employs over five hundred people, not all of whom are corrupt. I should add that we'd had the owners under surveillance for a few years. Wyatt's cooperation was the break we needed to move forward with a prosecution."

"You think these people took out the Petries to get his son Matt and stop his testimony?"

"A distinct possibility. These are not people who forgive, and Wyatt Clark was cooperating with authorities." Rodgers seemed to weigh his next bit of information before speaking again. "Wyatt convinced his wife Glynnis and son to go into hiding before he approached the FBI. He refused to say where they were. He's paranoid about the corrupt cops and didn't trust us to keep them safe."

"You weren't able to locate them?"

"We got a hit that Glynnis Clark crossed the border using her passport two days ago. She has to be on her way here or is in the vicinity already. She'll be looking for her son."

Rodgers hadn't answered his question, but Liam figured he wouldn't press it. From what he knew of the

FBI, they kept secrets and twisted the truth to suit the moment. "What do you need us to do?"

"We want to bring Glynnis and Matt Clark somewhere secure while the grand jury and ensuing trial play out. We'll be putting the family into witness protection eventually. If you locate them, we need to be notified."

"Of course. This information puts an entirely new lens on the murders. It's jaw-dropping, if I'm honest."

"Yeah, a lot to swallow. I'll be staying at a hotel near the airport for a few days and available on short notice. I have another colleague, Agent Carla Jones, with me. Our first concern is to make contact with Glynnis Clark and get her somewhere safe. The second is to locate Matt and have him join his mother. Our fear is that Wyatt Clark won't testify if his family is under threat, so this isn't as selfless as it sounds. We need Wyatt and will do what we have to in order for him to comply."

"Does Wyatt know…"

"That his son is missing? No, we're waiting to see if we can move his wife and son to a safe location."

"Let's hope we find Matt soon then."

Liam escorted Rodgers downstairs and shook his hand before he disappeared through the front door onto Elgin Street. They'd exchanged contact information, and Liam took a photo of Rodgers' credentials that he'd have verified. Rodgers said he understood and would have done the same. The modern world of liars and fakes. If everything checked out, Liam would let him know about the visit from Katherine Fielding, an almost certain connection to Glynnis Clark. Perhaps the FBI would have more luck than he'd had so far getting in touch with Fielding, whom he was now convinced knew Glynnis's whereabouts.

Liam took the stairs to his office on the second floor, uneasy about Rodgers and what he'd revealed about the Clark family. The murders and missing boy were diffi- cult enough on their own without this threat. He took out his cell to call Quade. She was going to have to get on top of the new twist in the case, starting with debriefing the team. The danger quotient had risen exponentially, and everyone had to be made aware of what they potentially could be walking into.

CHAPTER 28

Jimmy made it downstairs before Theo and waited for her at the kitchen table. Their mom was standing in front of the stove, spooning oatmeal into bowls as he settled into his seat. Brown sugar and fresh cream were on the table along with glasses of orange juice. There was nothing he could easily pocket and bring upstairs to Matt, so he'd have to take something out of the cupboard when he got the chance.

Theo danced into the room wearing her tutu over pink tights not even a minute later. She crossed to their mom and wrapped her arms around her waist from behind, leaning her head against their mother's back. His mom looked down and smiled at Theo's raised face. "Good morning, darling. Take this oatmeal to your brother and sit. I'll bring yours over in a sec."

"Okay, Mommy." Theo put a bowl in front of him before sliding into her chair. Jimmy nodded at her. She'd promised on her dolls' heads the evening before not to say a word about Matt being upstairs. Jimmy had his doubts she'd be able to keep her mouth shut, but so far, so good. His mom set down two bowls before taking her seat. They all looked over as the back door opened and his dad clumped inside, stepping out of his work boots.

"Rain's let up, but it's a cool morning. They're calling for sun and warm days the rest of the week beginning tomorrow. We know how reliable the weather predictions have been lately." He removed his ball cap and filled a bowl with porridge before joining them at the table. He looked across at their mom. "Calvin stopped in a few minutes ago. The police are searching properties for Matt. They were by his place yesterday afternoon. He also said a few neighbours have reported seeing a man roaming around. Calvin approached him, and the guy told him that he was a private investigator."

"Really? Who hired him?"

"Good question. Calvin thought it might be the Petries' family but wasn't sure."

"Did Calvin say what this man looked like?"

"Yeah, he wore a Yankees ball cap and had on a black raincoat. He's tall and stocky. That's all he noticed."

"Jimmy, I want you staying indoors today unless you're helping your dad. Theo and I will come directly home after dance class."

He tried not to squirm under her gaze and shot Theo a look to make sure she stayed silent. If only Matt would go to the police like he'd suggested again last night. This man sounded like the guy who'd checked out their house. Could he really be a PI? Jimmy couldn't figure out why Matt had to speak with his mother, who was travelling somewhere he didn't know, before he'd talk to another adult. Whose mother didn't tell their kid where they were going or give a way to contact them? Matt had no plan as far as Jimmy could tell. The whole thing was getting weird. "Can't I play in the yard?"

"I don't see any harm," his dad said. "I'm not far if Jimmy stays close to the house. I'll be working in the south field today."

His mom shook her head. "You won't be near enough to watch Jimmy or hear anything. There's a killer on the loose, and I won't feel safe until that person is caught. You stay inside and keep the doors locked, Jimmy. No arguing."

His dad nodded before lowering his eyes to the bowl of oatmeal. Theo blinked at him and said, "Can Amelia and Becka come over to play? They're staying home this week too until the killer's caught. We haven't finished our game from yesterday."

"We can ask their moms at dance class."

Jimmy kept his head down for the rest of the meal and offered to clean up the dishes so his mom and Theo could get ready to go. His mother gave him an odd look before leaving him to it. He was worried she knew about Matt until he realized that he had never asked to clean up before. She likely wondered what had gotten into him. He waited until his dad went outside and his mom and Theo were upstairs to gather up granola bars and pour a glass of juice. He'd make toast once they'd gone from the house.

Matt had moved from his bed on the floor into the closet when Jimmy finally made it to his bedroom. His mom and Theo were outside, getting into her van. A quick trip to the bathroom and he and Matt sat on the floor while Matt gobbled down the food and juice.

Jimmy filled him in on the police search and the PI sightings.

Matt crumpled up the granola bar wrappers. "I can't stay up here much longer. Theo is going to rat me out. I need to get moving."

"The weather is clearing up, and it's supposed to be a warm week starting tomorrow. You could hide out in the woods."

"I'm thinking I'll walk toward Ottawa along the highway and hitchhike. Maybe somebody'll pick me up. I have some money in my bag for emergencies. I can take a bus to New York and find my mom."

Jimmy's bottom lip trembled, and a wave of sadness welled up inside him. "I could come with you. I hate it here."

Matt stared at him. "That won't work, Jimmy. You're safer at home. Besides, they'll only make you come back when we get caught."

"If my parents even notice I'm gone."

Matt moved closer and lightly punched Jimmy on the arm. "When my mom and I get settled in our house, you can come visit. Maybe we can hang out next summer too at our cottage on Lake Champlain."

"Where's that?"

"Upstate New York, close to the border. Really good fishing, and we have a motorboat so I can take you to my favourite spots. If you have a phone, I can show you, or maybe on your computer."

"My computer's just set up for games. I'll go get Theo's iPad. Mom makes her leave it at home when they go to dance class. She left it in the mall once and at her friends' houses a few times, and Mom had to drive back to get it. She was pissed." He didn't say that he and his mom had decided to remove the internet on his gaming laptop after he was bullied on social media. "You don't need to be tempted to go online and see that crap," she'd said. "You can use my computer when you have homework or research to do. You're only nine years old, for God's sake. You can survive without being on those sites. We all can for that matter." He had a phone somewhere but always forgot to charge it. Nobody called him anyway.

He returned a moment later, frowning as he studied the screen. "She's got an Instagram page open." He raised his eyes to stare at Matt. "Mom told her no social media, but she has a page under the name CuteKitty-Girl. It's gotta be her friends who set it up. God, if Mom finds out…" He scrolled down and paused. "She's been posting photos all summer. Look." He handed the iPad to Matt and watched his face redden.

Matt stared at the screen and then up at Jimmy. "These are of me. She must have taken them when I wasn't paying attention to her. She's used my name and made comments." Matt checked the privacy settings. "Her account's public. Anybody could have seen them. I thought you said she couldn't read."

"She can't. One of her friends must have set this up. They would have posted when they're over playing with her."

"If somebody wanted to find me, she sent them an open invitation."

Jimmy turned his head. "I hear someone driving up our road. I'll go check if it's Mom."

He jumped to his feet and ran across the hall to look out the window. A car he didn't recognize was turning around to face down the driveway toward the road. He

strained to see inside the front seat. The man was
wearing a ball cap … like the PI his dad was talking
about at breakfast. Like the man who'd been circling the
house a few days ago. This couldn't be good. He raced
back into his bedroom. Matt was stuffing things into his
knapsack.

"I've gotta get out of here. Who's in the driveway?"

"The same guy who was around the other day. My
mom heard he was a PI."

"Like shit." Matt slung the knapsack over his shoulder. "I'll get out the back way if you can keep him busy
at the front, but don't open the door."

"Wait, wait." Jimmy jumped over to his desk and
pulled open a drawer. "Mom gives us these tracker
things hooked up to her phone. Keep one, and I'll find
you when she comes home and I can access the
program. It's some protection anyway."

Matt pocketed the small disc and took a last look
around the room before following Jimmy downstairs. He
gave Jimmy a thumbs up and scooted down the hall to
the back door. Jimmy watched him go while he waited at
the bottom of the steps. The man was now pounding on
the door with the side of his fist.

"Who's there?" Jimmy called, stepping closer.

"Are you Jimmy Dooley? I'd like to speak with you
about Matt Clark."

"Who are you?"

"A private investigator."

"I'm not allowed to open the door to strangers."
Silence.

Jimmy moved closer. "You can come back when my
dad's here." *Was he still standing outside?* Jimmy leaned his
ear against the door.

"Open up, kid. I just have a couple of questions." The man's voice was muffled, but he'd spoken loudly enough for Jimmy to hear every word.

"I'm not allowed."

"I know Matt Clark's your buddy and figure you know where he is. If you let me in now so we can talk, your parents don't need to find out. I'm guessing you don't want that to happen any more than I do."

Jimmy hesitated. If this guy was legit and somehow figured out he'd been hiding Matt … all hell would break loose. But if they talked face to face, he had a chance to convince the man that he had no idea where Matt was. Jimmy weighed which would be worse — having this guy talk to his father later or opening the door and giving Matt a chance to get away — and half-rose from his crouch. He'd answer the guy's questions without inviting him inside. Shrugging off Matt's warning to keep the door locked, he reached out a hand and turned the deadbolt, yet before he had time to grab the handle, the man had the door shoved open and had knocked him backward onto the floor. Jimmy struggled to push himself up, but the man was quick and had a knee on his chest before he could get his hands and feet under him. The man held him down, while pressing a rag that smelled sweet and strong over Jimmy's mouth and nose. He struggled and tried not to breathe, but the man was strong and the pressure increased until Jimmy felt as if he was suffocating. Pain seared through his chest. He tried to gulp in air, and the sweet, sickly smell filled his senses. His head floated strangely, and a dark tunnel twisted around him and spiralled smaller and smaller with Jimmy inside, spinning like a person free falling from a great height. The man's face blurred and faded, and Jimmy moaned in fright. The terror eased and sadness filled him, and his last thought was that Theo was going to miss him when he was gone. Then his eyes rolled back, and the blackness consumed him like a total eclipse of the sun.

CHAPTER 29

Rosie looked up the road in the direction she believed Hunter would be coming from to meet her as they'd planned. The morning was getting on, and hunger tugged at her stomach, her body needing more nourishment than the two cups of coffee she'd ingested so far since waking up late and rushing out the front door. She checked her phone messages again. If Hunter had sent one, she hadn't received it. Pine, the officer she'd been travelling with the last few days, was assigned to another team, but she hadn't protested or requested someone else because Hunter had planned to make the rounds with her today. He must have been held up at HQ, and she would soon have to make the decision to go it alone. Sitting here all day was not an option.

While she took in the cars zipping past, she thought about the evening before. Brad had been sitting in the kitchen waiting for her when she'd finally arrived home from drinking in the pub with Ella Tate. Two empty beer bottles sat on the table in front of him with a third half-full one raised to his lips. He'd studied her with angry, hurt eyes, and her brain scrambled to remember whatever it was she'd forgotten to do.

"You didn't answer my texts. I thought something had happened to you." His voice was flat, like it got when he was reining in his emotions.

She'd wanted to ask him if drinking beer was his way of helping her but grinned instead. "I went to the gym, believe it or not. I'm joining one near work."

His eyes travelled to the clock mounted on the wall above the sink. "It's eleven thirty. Does this gym stay open all night?"

"I went for a beer afterward with Ella Tate. She's the freelance reporter who rescued me a few months back, if you recall." Her indignation was tempered by the knowledge that she'd come close to going for drinks with Carlos, only stopping herself because crossing that line would mean giving up on her and Brad, not a decision she was ready to make yet.

His expression changed. He set down the beer bottle and used both hands to push himself up from the table. "I'm sorry, Rosie. It's just that I had a long day and wanted to see you when I got home. We had a twenty-year-old die in the ambulance. He'd OD'd on some street drug and we…" His voice cracked.

She'd crossed the space and wrapped her arms around him before he finished the sentence. They held each other for a long moment, and then he took a deep, shuddering breath and stepped back. "I'm going to sleep in the spare room tonight. My back is killing me, and I need to stretch out. We can talk more in the morning."

Then she'd woken up late, and they'd never had a chance to work things out. Brad was in the shower when she rushed out the door with a travel mug of coffee without even enough time to scribble him a note.

She put the car in gear and cruised up the highway, turning into the Petries' driveway. She'd take a look around and stretch her legs while she waited. There was always the hope that she'd spot something overlooked, no matter how remote the possibility. It was time to stop focusing on her own sorry life.

The clouds scudding in overhead momentarily blocked the sun, and shadow settled over the house like a shroud. The image was disconcerting, and Rosie paused mid-stride to study the perimeter of the property. There was a movement near the woodpile, and her hand reached for the gun on her hip, jolted by a groundswell of fear that made her movements clumsy. As she watched and grappled with the clasps of the holster, a squirrel darted across the expanse of gravel and scampered up a tree, its nails clawing and scraping at the bark, tail twitching. Rosie dropped her hand and laughed. "You came this close to biting it, squirrel," she said, relief coursing through her. She looked around, self-conscious that someone had seen her near panic. Luckily, only the swaying trees and empty farmhouse had borne witness to her irrational distress.

Her boots crunched across the gravel to the front door, and she used the key she'd kept from the previous visit. The hall and living room were steeped in a clammy dampness, and dust had settled onto surfaces like fine silt. The faint mustiness left a foul taste in the back of her mouth. She moved carefully forward, the light unnaturally dim as the clock neared noon. The chalk outlines and dark bloodstains still marred the floor where Devina and Stu had fallen, and she studied each spot, moving between the two locations to squat and trace their bodies in the air. These murders would have played out like a scene from a horror movie. The violence would have happened quickly. She closed her eyes and let her senses sink into the scene. She imagined the sound of gunfire, the yelling and screaming. The ringing of the phone in her pocket jarred the silence and snapped her back to the present.

"Hunter," she said, staring out the picture window. A gap in the clouds allowed sunlight to filter through the lace curtains and her spirits lifted. "Are you on your way?"

His apology caught her unawares. She listened to him explain what he'd learned during an FBI visit. It had taken him time to confirm the identity of the agent and his story, and he was about to brief Quade and Auger. He wanted her to return to HQ.

She listened and looked around the empty living room that didn't seem as safe now that she knew he wasn't coming — with the new knowledge of who might want the Petries dead. She shivered and gripped the phone tighter. "I'm in the Petrie house waiting for you, but I'll leave now. No, there's nobody else here. Okay, see you within the hour. No, … no, everything's fine."

She turned off the phone and tucked it into her pocket, eager to be out of this gloomy house. With one last glance at the chalk outline of Devina Petrie, she strode into the hallway and turned her face toward the kitchen as the creak of the back door opening and banging against the wall reverberated through the stillness. The frantic beating of her heart thumped in her ears, and she laid a hand on her chest to try to calm the alarm. The doors to the house had been locked, she was sure of it, so whoever was entering had either jimmied the lock or had a key. The sensible part of her knew that she was overreacting, but the panic from a case months before swelled inside her, freezing her feet in place, keeping her body from reacting properly, even as one hand fumbled with the gun holster. She stood like a trembling statue in the musty shadows of the hallway and waited for whoever was in the house to appear in the kitchen doorway.

CHAPTER 30

After ward, Rosie couldn't have said which of them was more frightened. Miriam Johannson had lifted her head only after she'd begun walking down the hall toward her, and her scream echoed in the small space when she saw Rosie standing motionless in front of her, gun half out of its holster. Miriam clutched at her heart, her breath coming in short gasps.

"Oh my God. Oh my God. I thought you were Devina back from the dead or the killer looking for another victim." She sagged sideways against the wall. "Why are you just standing there?"

Rosie pulled herself back from the edge of terror, moved her hand away from the gun, and took a step toward her. "I was waiting for my partner, but he's not —" She stopped herself. This woman could be harmless, but no point in telling her that Hunter wasn't coming. "He's a bit late but due any second. How did you get in? This house is still a locked crime scene."

"There's a key. Devina kept one for the back door

under a rock near the chicken coop. I've been coming by to feed them and came inside for a glass of water. I thought I'd pay my respects and say a prayer where Devina and Stu died. Remember me from your door-to-door yesterday? I'm Everett's wife. We live in a neighbouring farm."

"Of course." Rosie motioned toward the kitchen. "Get a glass of water, and we should go outside. The house hasn't been released yet."

"Sorry, I had no idea. Forget the water. I only want to get out of here. I hadn't realized how eerie this place is now."

They stood on the back deck and looked toward the garden and line of conifers beyond as a darker bank of clouds blew in front of the sun, casting the yard in shadow. "What do you call it when nature mirrors the human condition?" Miriam asked. She glanced at Rosie. "It's as if the world has been in mourning since their deaths."

"Pathetic fallacy. It's when human emotions are given to the natural world." She'd been a good English student and had considered becoming a writer at one time. "Do you recall anything more about the Petries since we spoke yesterday?"

"Not really. I was remembering how much I envied Devina when we were in high school. I was two years younger and much less sure of myself than she was. She was like this ethereal flower child, kind of dreamy and free. She wore a beaded choker and a deerskin jacket with fringes on the sleeves and midi-length cotton skirts. Her hair was long, ash-blonde and poker-straight. She had her pick of the boys. They swarmed around her like bees buzzing in and out of a hive."

"And she chose Everett back then."

Miriam wrapped her arms around herself as if she was suddenly cold. "Yeah, but she left him behind when she went traipsing across the U.S. It didn't take many years before we all grew up enough to realize looks and sex aren't everything. You need to share goals and be compatible for the long haul if a relationship is to last."

"Did you really not mind the two of them meeting for coffee in the mornings? I know I would have in your shoes."

Miriam glanced at her as if gauging her sincerity, and Rosie kept her face sympathetic. Miriam's shoulders relaxed. "It meant nothing. Everett was only being friendly."

"Still."

"Devina wasn't my favourite person, is that what you want to hear? I never wished her dead, though. My emotions about the two of them had long petered out. Everett gave me no reason to question his fidelity."

"What about Stu? Did he ever indicate what he thought about them meeting up in the mornings?"

"Not to me." Miriam was quiet for a moment, watching a crow hopping across the grass toward the garden. "Devina had changed a lot from when I knew her back in the day. She was driven to succeed with her business and almost reclusive. The dreaminess was gone. Stu was the outgoing one everyone wanted to be around. She seemed less sure of herself and infatuated with her husband. I believe she liked the security of marriage, odd after the life she'd led."

Rosie couldn't tell if Miriam was being disingenuous. Was this what longevity in a relationship did to a person? Made them not worry that their spouse was spending time with an old girlfriend? Was this about trust or not caring anymore? Rosie shivered at the thought of aging with Brad and having the passion dry up like a wizened apple. She feared it was already beginning to happen. Her questions to Miriam about the state of Devina and Stu's marriage had more to do with her own situation than the case. If what Hunter had told her over the phone was true, then the murderer was a stranger to the Petries. The killer was after Matt Clark as a way to get his father not to testify before the grand jury, and the Petries were simply collateral damage.

"Would you like some eggs?" Miriam asked. "Devina's hens are good layers, and I have more than we'll ever eat."

"I can take some, but I have to get going."

"I'll fetch the basket, and we can both be on our way."

Miriam stopped before she reached the chicken coop. "Devina's uncle Terrence contacted Everett yesterday. He plans to arrive Monday night and stay at the Petrie house. Their deaths are inconvenient, since he lives so far away. He's hired a cleaning company that's awaiting permission to enter."

"I expect that will be today. Have you met him?"

"No, although Devina mentioned Terrence and his daughter Linny in passing once. She said that she'd spent time with them in Vancouver before she and Stu moved to Ashton. It really is hard to believe she's gone." Miriam gave Rosie a quick sideways smile before pulling open the barn door and stepping into the dappled light.

———

LIAM LOOKED up from his phone. Quade stood in her office doorway, signalling for him to join her before she disappeared inside. Auger was already seated across from her desk when Liam entered. The look Auger gave him was hard to read — the words sly and triumphant came to mind. Liam nodded and took the empty seat next to him, waiting to hear whatever Auger had stirred up. Quade's grim eyes fixed on his.

"It's come to my attention that Rosie Thorburn hasn't been keeping up to date on her case files. She's neglecting the paperwork, which we know is instrumental when a case goes to court. Accurate, complete information is the bedrock of how we operate, and the paper trail is paramount although tedious, I give you that."

Liam's first impulse was to call bullshit, but he reined himself in. "We've only worked together a short while, but she's been a terrific note-taker and has input information into the system daily. I've never had cause to doubt the accuracy."

Quade's eyes shifted to Auger. "Care to elaborate?" she asked him.

"I'm reviewing a break-and-enter case back when we worked in Toronto that involved injuries from last year that is about to go to court. I've been asked to testify as the arresting officer. Thorburn was responsible for keeping the file up to date, and it's woefully thin on facts. A couple of times she confused the names of the victims with the alleged perpetrators. I'm going to have to rely on my memory and hope the defense lawyer doesn't bring up something I can't answer. I only brought this to Quade's attention because we've already identified Thorburn's inexperience as a warning sign. Frankly, I was shocked by the state of her work."

"Did you question Thorburn about the file?" Liam asked.

"When I raised the subject, she avoided answering. She certainly took no ownership for the mistakes, or perhaps she didn't understand the gaps and errors. For sure, she didn't see the importance of being thorough and accurate even in the smallest details." Auger laughed. "I believe it's a trait of this generation."

Quade shifted in her chair and sighed. "I'm going to need to speak with HR and see about getting her transferred to a less critical position where she can gain experience."

Auger nodded. "Again, I blame myself for getting Thorburn in over her head. She's bright and motivated, and I overlooked how green she was when I hired her. We'll be doing her career a disservice if she's not given the opportunity to learn without such intense pressure as comes with a murder case. It's admirable that you defend her, Hunter, and I know you think you're helping Thorburn, but in the long run, you are not."

Quade stood. "I've set up a meeting with the two FBI agents at their hotel. I'm taking Auger, and he'll help out with the file now that it's got the international element. Hunter, when Thorburn returns to HQ, go through the case notes on the Petrie murders with her and stay on site. I'll have a talk with her after I speak with HR."

Liam nodded and returned to his desk. Thorburn should be arriving any minute, and he didn't have much time to process her demotion, let alone Auger becoming his partner. It struck him that Auger would take over as lead on the murders, given the force hierarchy, but that wasn't what bothered him. Thorburn's transfer felt orchestrated, as if Auger had manipulated some facts that would be impossible to disprove. He hadn't succeeded in getting Thorburn transferred on his first attempt, so he'd come back with this new worrisome information under the guise of caring about her career trajectory. Quade had bought it … or perhaps she had no choice with Auger angling for her job. Liam wasn't convinced Rosie was a liability in Major Crimes, but Auger had overridden his vote. And there was always the remote possibility that Auger was right and wanted what was best for Thorburn's career. Either way, she needed space to develop into the cop he knew she could be; a new assignment would give her time.

He flipped through the messages on his phone. He'd expected her in the office before now. It was going to be difficult to keep quiet about what was going to happen, but this wasn't his news to reveal. Quade would make better work of letting Thorburn down easily, and he'd wait in the wings to help lift her up once that happened.

CHAPTER 31

Jimmy's eyes snapped open. He was lying on his side, squarely in the centre of the bed in his room, and his gaze focused on Theo, who was on the floor, playing with her dolls. It was as if no time had passed since blackness shut out the world. How did he get here, and where was the man who'd shoved him to the floor and covered his mouth with the sweet-smelling rag? He bolted upright, and Theo smiled at him.

"You had a gigantic sleep. Mommy said you were very tired, and I shouldn't wake you. We're going out soon."

Jimmy stared wildly around the room. The closet door was open, but nothing appeared out of place. "When did you get home?" he asked. His mouth tasted fuzzy, and his balance was off when he moved his head. He swung his feet onto the floor and held onto the mattress as he sat up. It took a moment for the room to stop spinning.

"After dance class. I learned to lift my leg really high.

Higher than anybody else. Amelia came over, and we played in my room. She left and I came in here with my dolls. Where's Matty?"

Her words flowed into each other, and Jimmy needed a moment to process her train of thought. "Matt's gone. We have to pretend he was never here." He rubbed his forehead. "You need to stop posting pictures on Instagram. If Mom or Dad finds out you have an account, they won't be happy."

Theo's brow folded together in one of her stubborn scowls. "I like Instagram. Everyone else puts pictures on it, so why can't I? Amelia and Becka said I had to be on it so we can share stuff. You have a secret, and I do too. That's fair!"

Her voice rose close to crying, and Jimmy knew a tantrum wasn't far off. He scrambled next to her on the floor and tickled her tummy until she let out a squeal. A few more tickles and she was rolling on the floor, laughing, her bad temper forgotten. They both froze when their mother's voice carried up the stairs.

"We're going to the pub in half an hour. Wash up, make sure you're wearing something decent, and get down here."

Theo pushed herself up. "Mommy was sad today. She cried in the car."

"Do you know why?"

"Uh-uh. Where did Matty go? I miss him."

"He went to be with his mother. She misses him too." Jimmy was making up a story, but Theo would never know. He needed her to keep her mouth shut. "If I don't tell Mom you've been on Instagram, you gotta keep quiet about Matt being here. Deal?"

"Deal." Her smile returned at full wattage.

He felt a bit guilty blackmailing her, but not enough to take it back. "Let's go wash up. We can see the chickens before we leave if Mom says there's time." He didn't think Theo's smile could get any wider, but it did. He wished life was as easy for him as it was for her; some days he'd give anything to have her joy instead of this rock in his belly that never seemed to go away.

He had no idea why the man had left him on his bed. Had he been looking for Matt, or was he after something else? Jimmy followed Theo out of the room, the wooziness not as bad as when he woke up. He stopped still in the hall as he remembered the tracker. He needed to get his hands on his mother's phone to pick up the signal, and he'd have to figure out how to do that without her seeing. If he hadn't promised Matt he'd stay quiet, he'd tell her everything and take whatever punishment his dad dished out. Instead, he had to keep his head down and try to help Matt without anybody knowing.

———

Rosie left Miriam Johannson in the Petrie yard and returned to her car to drive to HQ. She was about to step into the driver's seat when a car she didn't recognize turned into the Petrie driveway. The woman parked on the shoulder of the road and approached the house. She was late thirties, pretty, with a confident stride. Rosie waited and stepped away from her car, startling the woman for a moment before Rosie introduced herself. "And you would be…?" she asked.

"Glynnis Clark." The woman's eyes were hidden behind green-tinted sunglasses, her mouth set in a grim line. She took a step forward as if to walk past Rosie. Her jacket opened, and Rosie glimpsed her enlarged belly. It only took Rosie a second to place the woman's last name. Nobody had mentioned Matt's mother was pregnant, although she didn't appear to be that far along. The beginning of the second trimester maybe.

"You're Matt Clark's mother?" Her voice came out a shade below incredulous.

Glynnis Clark straightened her back as she stopped walking. "I need to see where he was staying. Devina Petrie, Stu — they didn't deserve this. Have you word about my son?" She half-turned.

"No, but we're continuing our search. Do you have any idea where he might have gone?"

"You mean if he wasn't taken." Her bottom lip trembled, the first crack in her defiant armour. "We're American, and this is his first time in Canada. He doesn't know anybody else."

"We've learned why you sent him here."

"Who … how…?"

"Two FBI agents are in Ottawa, hoping we find you so they can take you and Matt somewhere safe. My partner checked their credentials, and they are who they claim to be."

Glynnis stood still, her face deep in thought. "My husband told me to trust no one, especially not the New York police. He trusted the FBI, but someone traced Matty here and look what happened? How do I know I can believe you?"

"We have no stake in this except to find Devina and Stu's killer. I don't even know anybody from New York, truth be told."

Glynnis laughed. "You sound so earnest. It's hard to be scared of you. How long have you been a cop?"

"A full year, but I've only been a detective since July. Not enough time to become entrenched or jaded." She had no idea why she was confiding in this stranger, but her honesty appeared to be working. Glynnis had now turned around to face her, the expression on her face openly appraising.

"I'm gutted if our problems in New York led to the deaths of these two. The idea makes me ill."

"You weren't the one who pulled the trigger."

"But I somehow led those people here." She shook her head. "Matt knew the risks. I told him not to use social media and to keep his head down. How the hell did they find him?"

"From what we've uncovered, Matt kept to himself except for one friend named Jimmy Dooley. They spent most of their time fishing on the Jock River that runs through Ashton. We haven't found any photos of your son, and he's not used any social apps. Do you have a recent headshot I can share with our officers?"

"Yeah, I can send one to you." Glynnis took out her phone and removed her sunglasses. "What's your email address?"

Rosie recited her work address, and a moment later, she was looking at a photo of Matt Clark, a good-looking boy who resembled his mother, light brown hair streaked blond, wide blue eyes, and an engaging grin. She could imagine him in one of those family-rated television shows. He was going to break hearts. "How old is he in this picture?"

"I took that the day before he came here for the summer, so he's eleven." Glynnis smiled at her phone screen before tucking it away. "Does this mean you're going to turn me in?"

"You could be in real danger. I want to help."

Glynnis rubbed her forehead. "I realize my best option is to stay in hiding, but my son's safety is all I can think about right now."

"If I'm not wrong, you have another child to consider."

"Touché. You're observant." She looked down at her belly before scanning the yard and house. "I'd like to look inside, if that's okay."

"Of course. I'll text my partner that I've been delayed." Rosie gave a sideways grin. "He worries if I don't check in regularly."

Rosie guided her past the living room to Matt's bedroom. Glynnis stood in the doorway and stared at the bed where her son had slept. She slowly surveyed the space. "There's nothing here that reminds me of him. No clues." She turned to face Rosie behind her. "Your team has checked everywhere?"

"Thoroughly at least twice."

"I'll come with you, but not to the police station. If the syndicate my husband worked for made it to Ashton and this farmhouse, they'll have eyes and ears everywhere. I'll tell you and your partner what I know, but nobody else. We'll have to go somewhere safe. I'm sorry, but those are my conditions."

"What about meeting with the FBI agents in their hotel? As I said, my partner has checked them out, and they're the real deal."

"Not yet. I want to find Matt first."

"And if that doesn't happen right away?"

"We have to work through every other possibility to find my son before I commit to a plan."

Rosie studied her eyes and saw determination. This was not a woman who'd be forced into hiding until she was ready. As Rosie saw it, she had two choices: agree and play along with Glynnis or insist she go to the FBI and chance alienating her. She made her decision, knowing full well that Auger could use it against her if things went sideways. "Right, you have a car?"

"A rental. It's parked on the side of the road."

"You can follow me into the city. I know a place you can stow it until we sort things out."

"Lead on then. I'm putting myself in your care."

"I'll do my best not to let you down." Rosie tucked her hands in her pockets so Glynnis wouldn't see them trembling. Her first fear was that Glynnis would simply drive away and disappear once she got into her vehicle. The second was that she'd promised this woman something that she had no business negotiating, let alone the power to make happen.

CHAPTER 32

The Ashton Brew Pub parking lot was nearly full, and Ella cruised to the back fence where she parked in one of the remaining spots. She had Sherry to thank for the intel that brought her here. A friend of one of Sherry's contacts had mentioned that the Ashton community would be holding a celebration of life in honour of the Petries tonight, convenient since Canard had requested a piece for the next day's paper that would humanize the couple. She was tired and would be late getting home, but this gift horse was too good to pass up. She hoped nobody would object to her presence but didn't much care if they did.

The night air had cooled, but the stars glittered overhead, and the air smelled of sweetgrass and clover. She inhaled deeply as she walked past the brewery end of the low-slung building with an old town taxi cab and what looked like a black Model T displayed next to the wall on the way to the main entrance. Garden gnomes of various shapes and colours watched her progress from their positions on the ground and near the roofline.

She wondered what it would be like to waken each morning to fresh air and farmland. Would the reality of living outside the city measure up to the dream? A red metal peaked roof and red doors cheered the white washed walls and black strapping. Inside, the hum of voices greeted her as she walked up the ramp into the main room. Every seat was taken, but she managed to wedge into a spot at the bar where she could unobtrusively survey the crowd.

She ordered a Guinness and slid onto a bar stool as its previous occupant joined friends at a table. Sipping the beer while taking quick looks around, she spotted the Dooley family, including the two children, sitting at a table with Calvin Frisk. Nelly Depper was settled into an alcove with her brother Everett and Miriam Johannson. She recognized a few faces, including the server Reba from the day before, sitting at a table with a group of forty-somethings. Whoever organized the event had mounted a photo of Devina and Stu on an easel between vases of chrysanthemums and hydrangea arranged on tables and the floor next to a brick fireplace. She wished Tony were here. He always knew how to get people talking and was at ease in these situations. She had to force herself to make small talk. Fortunately, the man on the stool next to her glanced up from his beer to ask how she knew the Petries.

"I'm writing an article for *The Capital*. How well did you know them?" She tried for an expression that was a cross between respectful and interested.

"I knew Devina more than Stu. We went to school together, although our paths rarely crossed since she returned." He held out a hand. "Mitch Greenway. Nice to meet you but sorry it's under these circumstances." His grasp was firm.

Before letting go, she said, "Ella Tate. Good to meet you too. What was Devina like back then?"

"Devina? God, she was this gorgeous flower child. Dreamy, kind of floating through the teen years. I had a hopeless crush. Hopeless because I never stood a chance being two years younger and shy as a turnip. She dated Everett over there, and we all wished we were him. Don't print that!" Mitch laughed before drinking from his glass.

Ella turned sideways to get a better look at the man sitting next to her. Grey hair cropped short, clipped beard with faded red strands patched through the grey, clear blue eyes. He had the muscular arms of a man who worked hard throughout his life, although he'd grown the soccer-ball beer gut many men sported in later years. This could be her own father sitting next to her, an uncomfortable idea with a bittersweet aftertaste. Life could have been different for her family, but people made choices. "What did you think of Stu?"

"I'd see him around, and we'd pass pleasantries about the weather and farming and stuff. Seemed like an okay guy. Stu told me that he met Devina working in a casino in Vegas. They married in one of those Elvis chapels. Took me a while to figure out who he reminded me of."

"Oh yeah? And who would that be?"

"Everett Johannson."

Somebody clinked a glass and called for silence. A succession of friends and neighbours rose to speak about Stu and Devina, each small speech punctuated by toasts and cheers. Ella turned on her phone's tape recorder and caught most of it. She managed a few covert photos of the picture of the two of them on the easel surrounded by flowers that she'd use with her article.

As the people began getting to their feet to mingle, and the room's noise level rose with the number of toasts and drinks consumed, Ella pushed herself off the bar stool and started toward the back room. She'd watched the Dooley children ten minutes earlier slip away from the crowd and was curious to see what they were up to. She found them seated at a table near the row of screened-in windows, close together, their heads bowed over a cell phone screen. A light breeze chilled the air, pleasant after the stuffiness in the main room. Nobody else had retreated to this location. Ella approached the children and managed a look at the phone before Jimmy flipped it over.

"Hey," she said. "Taking a break from the noise?"

"Yeah." Jimmy's face reddened, and she wondered at his reaction. They had not been playing a video game, as expected, but she hadn't gotten a good enough look at the app to know what was holding their interest. Ella hadn't met Theodora before, and even though she knew the child had Down syndrome, she found herself momentarily disconcerted by the child's steady, guileless gaze that studied her with open curiosity. It felt as if this seven-year-old girl could see past the facade into one's soul.

"Hi Theo, I'm Ella," she said, smiling and lowering herself into the seat at the table next to them. "I've talked to Jimmy and your parents before."

"She's a reporter," Jimmy told his sister. Ella thought he poked her in the side under the table but might have imagined this. She'd followed them back here on the vaguest of hunches, and now Jimmy's guilty face had her spidey sense tingling.

"Any idea where Matt has gotten to? A lot of people are searching for him," she said. Jimmy dropped his head, and the red in his cheeks brightened to the colour of a ripe tomato while Theo visibly squirmed in her seat. "If you know where he is," Ella pressed on, "I'd like to help." She was only guessing, but things started to make sense. Matt had made one friend, from what she'd heard. Who else would he logically reach out to if he could?

"He's not at our house anymore," Theo said.

Jimmy hissed at her, "Shut up, Theo."

Theo added in all innocence, "Jimmy could get in trouble for lying, so you can't tell anyone."

"Do you know where Matt is now?"

Both children stopped moving like deer caught in the headlights, and Ella experienced the strange sensation of time standing still. The din from the other room rose and fell as they stared at her. She had the feeling they were waiting for a sign to tell her whatever was weighing on their consciences. She gave an encouraging nod and remained silent, praying nobody would come in search of them to break this spell.

"He hid in my bedroom," Jimmy said at last in a voice barely above a whisper. "But a man came, and Matt left by the back door. The man said he was a PI, but Matt didn't trust him."

"When was that, Jimmy?" She kept her voice low and soothing to match his.

"This morning."

"Who was the man?"

"I don't know. He came once before, and I didn't let

him in. This time…" Jimmy's eyes welled up. "I opened the front door so Matt had time to get away out back. The man put a rag over my mouth, and I don't remember anything. I woke up on my bed a long time later, and Theo was playing in my room."

"Good God." She couldn't help herself. "Are you feeling okay? Did you tell your parents?"

"I felt sick, but I'm okay now. I won't be okay, though, if I tell them. My dad hates lying more than anything."

"More than anything," Theo agreed.

"Can you describe the man?"

"He had a black baseball cap and he was tall and big. He had brown eyes and a green tattoo on his neck. I think it was a snake. I don't remember anything else."

"Matty is getting close to Ottawa," Theo said.

"Theo." Jimmy's voice was weary as if he knew there was no point protesting. "Stop."

"How do you know that, Theo?" Ella smiled and tilted her head.

"We have Mommy's phone. It can follow the tracker Jimmy gave to Matt."

Ella's heart began to beat faster. She kept her voice calm. "We have to find him, even if it means you tell—"

"What's going on in here?"

All three turned. Lanny Dooley loomed in the doorway, glaring at Ella. "Are you interviewing my children without an adult present?"

"No, of course not." Ella glanced over at Jimmy. He was holding the phone under the table. "I came in this room for a breather before I head back to Ottawa and asked your kids how they're doing."

"It's time to go," Lanny said to Jimmy, ignoring her explanation. "Your mom is waiting outside."

Theo stood and skipped over to her dad, grabbing his hand. Jimmy got slowly to his feet and passed the phone to Ella when his father turned to leave. "Password's 2020. She has another phone and might not miss this one until tomorrow. Please don't rat me out." He spoke low and fast, and Ella nodded as she slipped the phone into her pocket.

"I'll get it back to you tomorrow."

She followed the Dooley family out of the pub a few minutes later and got into her car. Night had settled in since she entered the bar, and the air had turned crisp and fresh. She checked the time on her car's dashboard. Going on ten thirty. Late for the Dooley kids to be out. The tracker app was open when she brought up the screen, and it took her a few moments to pinpoint Matt and figure out his location. She prayed Jimmy hadn't made up the entire story, a real possibility despite the tracker. She remembered interviewing a boy around his age a few years back who'd been adamant that a man in a white van had followed him home on two occasions. It turned out he'd fabricated the incidents to get his father's attention as his parents navigated a messy divorce.

If what Jimmy and Theo told her was true, Matt was somewhere along the Flewellyn Road, several miles away but with a good distance to go before he reached Ottawa. Ella set the phone on the console and turned on the engine. The last thing she did before pulling away was hit Hunter's number in contacts. The phone rang five times before his voicemail said to leave a message.

She asked him to call her as soon as he picked up before driving onto the Flewellyn Road.

Her headlights cut across the highway. No streetlights to illuminate the road as she drove through the countryside, stretches of field leading to homes and farmhouses at the end of long driveways, cheery porch lights punctuating the darkness. Pockets of woods and bulrushes stretched between the properties. A low cloud cover had blown in over the last few hours, blotting out the moon and stars. Raindrops landed on the windshield, and Ella grimaced at the idea of an impending storm. This was becoming the wettest September in a long while and one the meteorologists kept getting wrong in their daily predictions. Twenty percent chance of rain could jump to ninety without warning.

She drove fast and caught up to a car going below the speed limit. Letting up on the gas, she chanced a look at the tracker app. Matt appeared to be on the move but not covering much ground, so he had to be on foot. The car ahead of her slowed even more, and she pounded the steering wheel in frustration. The solid line on the road didn't allow for passing on this curvy stretch. She glanced at the phone again. The red dot had stopped moving. She was only a few kilometres away, but it felt like forever at this speed. In front of her, the brake lights went on along with a left turn signal, and the car slowed even more, coming to a full stop as another set of headlights approached from the opposite direction. At last, the car looped across the road into a driveway, and Ella pressed on the gas. Two minutes later, she caught up to the dot on the phone and eased over onto the shoulder. It took a moment to make out the taillights of a black car, the passenger back door open. She parked several metres back, turned off the engine, and got out, leaving the headlights pointed at the car while she stooped to tuck the keys and Hope Dooley's phone under the seat. A man wearing a black ball cap squinted at her as he shoved someone into the back of his car and slammed the door.

Ella ran the last few metres through drizzling rain as the man rounded the trunk to face her. "Hey, is there a problem?" she yelled, stopping a few feet away. He had a hand over his eyes, watching her through the glare from her car's headlights. He stood over six feet, with the stance of MMA fighter. Fear rippled through her, but she held her ground, attempting to look like a Good Samaritan who'd stopped to lend a hand. "Do you need my help?" she asked as pleasantly as she could. "Car trouble?" She took a couple of steps toward the passenger door, but he moved sideways to block her path. Her car's headlights snapped off, and only his tail-lights glowed red through the darkness.

"All good here," he said, stepping uncomfortably close to her. "You can go back to your car and be on your way."

That would have been the wisest course of action, but she hesitated and looked past him. Whoever he'd dragged into the back seat — and it had to be Matt Clark, if the tracker was accurate — hadn't moved, and she hated to leave him. Yet she couldn't possibly take on this man. Her only option was to retreat, call Hunter or 911, and keep following the car from a discreet distance. "Okay then," she said. "Have a good evening."

He'd watched her glance toward the back seat and must have realized she'd seen him shoving somebody inside. Before she could fully turn to walk away, he grabbed her by the arm. She pulled back, trying to release herself without success. "Let go of me." The words were a growl in her throat.

His reply was to punch her hard in the stomach with full force. She collapsed in on herself, gasping for air, seeing a shower of stars in the black. While she was doubled over, he reached both his arms around her hips and lifted her like a sack, tossing her over the side of the embankment while she struggled to break free. She flew through the air and landed with a smack on the hard-packed ground, her left shoulder taking the brunt of the impact before she rolled and tumbled into a thicket of bushes. The world went dark for a moment, but she fought to stay conscious, opening her eyes and looking up at the sky. *Breathe*, she told herself. *Don't let him win.* She tried to leverage herself into a sitting position, but pain ripped through her. She eased back and lay still until the wave of fire receded to bearable. Her head hurt, her shoulder hurt, her ribs hurt. *You're alive and need to get moving.* She'd left the kids' tracker phone in her car, but her own cell was in her jacket pocket. Gingerly, she lifted her right arm and stretched it across her stomach to reach inside. *You can do this.* The cell phone lit up and she opened contacts. The ringing echoed in her ear, once, twice, three times.

"Hey, girl. What's up?"

"Tony, thank goodness. I need you. I'm in a ditch off the highway."

"*What?* Say that again."

"This man … punched me and threw me over the side of the highway. My car's on the shoulder. You can find it."

"Where are you, Ella? What highway?"

She focused on a tree branch swaying in the wind overhead. "Coming back from Ashton on the Flewellyn Road. I think I passed Conley Road."

"Are you hurt?"

She closed her eyes. *Am I hurt?* "Tony, he has that boy. Matt Clark. I was tracking him with the phone in my car. Tony? Call Hunter." She'd said all she could. Her eyes fluttered. She needed to keep what strength she had left in reserve, to get out of this pit, and steer Hunter toward rescuing the kid. She let the pain ease away, sinking and rising out of the darkness — let the world float as the drops of rain pattered on the leaves above and dampened her hair and face. She'd be fine once Tony arrived and found her. Then the real work would begin. She'd just close her eyes and save her strength until then.

CHAPTER 33

Tony scanned both sides of the highway as he drove through the misty night. Raindrops fell in spits and spats, just enough to make the roads slick and visibility difficult, as if the dim light wasn't enough. "Where the hell are you, Ella?" he asked, squinting through the side window. He reached over and patted Luvy, sitting on the seat next to him. "We're going to find her, aren't we girl? Damnation. She sure knows how to get into trouble."

They were a few kilometres outside the city limits, and darkness filled the hollows and crevices on both sides of the road. Tony made slow progress, afraid to miss Ella's car, which should logically be on his left if she was on her way home from Ashton. Still, he wasn't taking any chances, and his head swivelled back and forth.

Her call had come as he was preparing for bed, and he'd scrambled into his jeans and sweatshirt, slipping on Doc Martens and a raincoat at the apartment door.

He'd stepped onto the landing but rushed back inside to grab a flashlight and Luvy. She wasn't much of a tracking dog, but she loved Ella and might be helpful in locating her if all else failed. He thought of knocking on Finn's door on his way past. Finn would need to get the baby up and ready for a road trip, and Tony didn't have time or patience for that. No, he'd set out on his own and call for an ambulance if necessary once he located her. He tried ringing Hunter on the way to his car, but the phone went to voicemail, and he didn't bother leaving a message. Whatever he told Hunter would sound crazy. He wasn't even convinced that he'd gotten the details correct. Ella's voice had faded in and out during her call.

He rounded a corner. The road passed over a creek with guardrails on both sides. If Ella had been thrown over the side and down an embankment, this stretch of highway fit the bill. Sure enough, he spotted her car sitting dark and forlorn on the left-hand shoulder. He pulled off the road and waited for two cars to pass by before making a 360 and sliding in behind her vehicle. He left the engine running and the headlights on. Luvy jumped into his lap, and he clicked on her leash. "I'm not losing you too in this godforsaken dark piece of wilderness."

He swung the flashlight up and down the road and over the side, but he spotted no sign of Ella. He called her name, pausing between yells to listen. Rain drizzled around him and blurred his vision. Luvy barked, and he set her on the ground. "Find Ella," he said and let her sniff the area and pull him forward. She barked and looked under the guardrail. He swung the flashlight down the embankment and called for Ella. A wavering figure looking like a drowned blonde rat staggered into its beam.

"I'm here," Ella said. "If you could come give me a hand to get to the road—" Her voice trailed off.

"Gawd, girl. Give me a sec." He raced back and set Luvy in the car before tackling the slope to reach Ella.

"Don't put that light on me," she said, and he lowered the flashlight to shine on her feet. He'd seen the odd slope to her shoulder and her hunched stance.

"Where can I grab on to you?"

"My left shoulder and ribs are screaming, so let's go with my right arm."

"Is it okay if I wrap my hand around your waist?"

"Lower down is better."

Somehow, he managed to get her up the incline and into the front passenger seat of his car. Luvy seemed to know Ella was in pain and lay quietly with her chin resting on Ella's thigh. In the overhead light, her face was pale as milk, her hair and clothes sopping wet. "The phone with the tracker app and the keys are under the driver's seat in my car," she said, leaning against the headrest. "You'll have to get the phone, because we need to use it to follow them. Did you get hold of Hunter?"

He stared at her and blinked. "Are you out of your mind? You need to go to the hospital, like, now. There's no way I'm chasing after this kid with you looking like death warmed over. I'm guessing that dried blood on the side of your face and the woozy phone call mean that you hit your head."

She ignored him. "The kid is in real danger, if what that man did to me is any indication. We have to find them before he locates the tracker. Frankly, I'm surprised he hasn't already. If this guy murdered the Petries, he might believe Matt witnessed the killings and can identify him. It would explain why Matt hasn't come forward. Poor kid must be scared out of his mind."

Tony understood fear. His voice relented. "Tell you what, I'll get the phone and keys, drop you off at the doors of the Queensway Carleton Hospital, and will carry on following Matt with the app. I'll keep trying to contact Hunter in the meantime. He's been annoyingly incognito."

"But—"

"No buts. This is my best and final offer. I'll also see about getting someone to retrieve your car later, because you are definitely not driving."

"You can't approach him alone, Tony. Promise me."

"Yeah, yeah, yeah." He waved her off and stepped out of his car on his way to retrieve her things. Technically, he wouldn't be alone with Luvy riding shotgun. Yet much as he loved a good dust up, he sincerely hoped this crazy night didn't come down to Luvy playing backup, because then his ass would be good and thoroughly cooked.

———

"I VOTE we take her directly to the feds. We can't be responsible for keeping this woman safe." Auger stared at Thorburn before his eyes moved over to Liam. They were huddled next to the stove in Thorburn's kitchen, hoping Glynnis Clark couldn't hear them discussing her immediate future. Thorburn wanted to keep Glynnis overnight to give her a chance to buy in to the idea of going into protection. Liam was tasked with the deciding vote. He'd already spoken with Quade, who had told him to use his best judgement. He weighed both options.

"I believe Auger is right on this one. I know you've developed a connection with her, Thorburn, so you can stay with her, but we need to notify the FBI agents that she's here. Waiting around for her son to show up is a remote possibility at best, and she could be in danger. I'll break it to her." He put a hand on Thorburn's forearm. "Good job gaining her trust and bringing her this far, but she wouldn't be safe staying here. You could also become a target."

"She won't trust me any longer if we turn her over."

"You shouldn't have made any promises you weren't in a position to keep," Auger said.

"She would have disappeared if I hadn't made those assurances," Thorburn responded, her expression defi- ant. "But I'll support your decision, Hunter."

He nodded. Something was going on between these two, and it wasn't what he'd thought. Thorburn had been on edge since Auger walked through the front door. The few times she'd looked at him, her eyes had been frosty as a winter evening. For his part, Auger regarded her with a cross between condescension and barely disguised hostility. They'd arrived on the team from Toronto as a unit, but whatever had drawn them together appeared to have ended badly.

His cell phone rang as he was entering the living room where Glynnis Clark paced back and forth in front of the window. He checked the screen. Tony's name again. Liam had ignored previous calls with all that was going on, but Tony wasn't normally this persistent. He swiped to accept.

"Hey, Tony, I only have a second. What's up, mate?"

"Thank goodness. Don't ask how, but I've trailed the guy who has Matt Clark and likely killed that couple. This is no joke. They're holed up in a motel I didn't know existed between Ottawa and Montreal. It's got that run-down, seventies vibe going on. I'd bet my bottom dollar on orange bedspreads and black velvet paintings. Get a pen, and I'll give you the exact location."

"Did you see him?"

"Matt? Not exactly. They were already inside the room by the time I arrived."

"Is Ella with you?"

"No. She's, uh, unavailable at the moment. She's the one who got her hands on the phone with this tracker app that led me to the kid."

Liam thought things through as Tony dictated directions. This sounded off the wall, but Tony and Ella had come up with information before when the police floundered. He had a sense this might be another one of those times, although it was going to be difficult to explain if things didn't pan out. He looked at Glynnis Clark. She was rubbing her stomach and staring at him with hopeful eyes. From what Thorburn had said, she distrusted the police and only agreed to come here because she and Rosie had made a connection. He knew that forcing Glynnis to go with the FBI now would undermine Thorburn in a way that would be difficult for her to get over. Auger was also right to want this woman in a safer location. He considered both options again and revised his initial call. She'd be fine with

Thorburn another couple of hours while he and Auger checked out this new lead. If Tony had gotten it wrong, they'd only be out a bit of time. The motel was in Quebec, so he'd have to engage the Sûreté, but he had a friend on the force who'd helped before.

"Sit tight, Tony, and do not approach. I'll make a call and will have reinforcements there within the hour. Let me know if he leaves or changes locations in the meantime."

"You got it."

Liam logged off and returned to the kitchen where Thorburn was making coffee with her back to Auger, who was speaking on his cell phone and looking out the patio door into the backyard. Liam motioned for him to end his call.

Auger spoke into the receiver before tucking the phone into his pocket. "Got something?"

"We need to get on the road for another urgent matter and will leave Glynnis here with Thorburn for now, if you're alright with that, Rosie? You can help Glynnis settle in for a short while until we get back." He didn't mention that Matt could be in a motel en route to Montreal with his abductor. Glynnis would certainly have insisted she go with them, and he wouldn't bring her into that danger. He also balked at giving false hope. "I'll check in soon, and we can revise our plan if necessary."

"Of course." Thorburn rewarded him with a quick smile before she pivoted back to the coffee machine.

Liam knew she'd be happy to keep her promise to Glynnis and not turn her over to the FBI right away. If Tony really did have Matt and his abductor in his sights, Thorburn would save face with Glynnis and would more easily forgive him for taking Auger with him to the motel, seeing as how she was his partner. He was glad now that she had no idea of her transfer or Auger becoming her replacement on the case. Her disappointment tomorrow when she learned the news would be cause enough for sorrow without adding to it now.

CHAPTER 34

The minutes crept past like hours. Tony had parked on the street across from the motel and leaned the seat as far back as it would go, then thought better of it and reversed into the upright position. A full day on his feet cutting and blow-drying hair had exhausted him, and it wouldn't take much to put him to sleep. He thought of Ella and the hot mess done to her body by the man inside the motel room. She could have died out on that lonely road, although she'd called him melodramatic when he raised the idea on the way to the hospital. *I was on my feet when you arrived. No way I couldn't make it home by myself.* The trademark stubborn lift to her chin had been meant to convince him, but she was too late turning to look out the side window, and he'd glimpsed her bottom lip trembling.

Good gawd almighty, girl. At least admit when you need help. She was one exasperating woman. Luvy pawed at his arm, her signal that she needed outside. He glanced over at the motel room door. Still shut, and no sign of movement for the last twenty minutes. The guy had pulled the curtains closed before his arrival. Tony lifted Luvy into his lap. "Sure you can't hold it a bit longer?" he asked, scratching her head. In response, she squirmed and pawed at the door until he reached for her leash on the floor. "Let's make this quick."

The rain had let up since he parked, but a fine mist moistened his hair and face and likely meant more precipitation in the offing. The foggy air provided some cover, however, so he wasn't complaining. Luvy sniffed a scraggly plant that had miraculously poked up through a crack in the pavement, and Tony checked his phone. No update from Ella. Nothing from Hunter. Was he stuck here in limbo hell waiting for help that wasn't coming? Surely, Hunter wouldn't let things lag until morning?

Luvy trotted over to an empty chip wrapper and batted at it for a while before squatting on top. "That's my girl," Tony said. "So ladylike." He debated picking up the wet wrapper and putting it in the trash when he caught a motel door opening out of the corner of his eye. He crouched down and watched as a man wearing a black baseball cap and black jacket came out of the room he'd been monitoring. The boy was not with him. The man stood and lit a cigarette while surveying the street. He was the size of a middle linebacker, and Tony shivered at the thought of being seen and yanked onto the street by one of his beefy hands. Thankfully, the man's eyes didn't linger on Tony hidden behind a car bumper, likely unable to see him through the night's hazy darkness. With a half-turn, ball-cap guy checked that the door was locked before getting into his car. A few moments later, he pulled out of the motel lot and turned in the opposite direction to Tony.

Tony watched the taillights until they disappeared

from view. The guy was heading in the direction of the truck stop at the off-ramp to the main highway. *Going for something to eat,* Tony thought. He grabbed Luvy and hurried over to his car, plunking her into the front seat and slamming the door. He speed-dialled Hunter's number as he crossed the road toward the motel.

"At last," he said when Hunter picked up. "Where's the posse?"

"Twenty minutes out. What's up?"

"The target just drove off, I believe to the diner next to the highway. I'm about to check on the status of the kid who's inside the motel room if the tracker reads correctly."

"Tony, that isn't wise. Wait for us."

"This might be our only chance to get Matt out of harm's way without a fight."

"Tony—"

"I'll be careful." He shut his phone and checked up and down the road to make sure the man wasn't return-ing. Satisfied, he hurried over to room number eleven and rapped softly on the door. Waiting thirty seconds or so, he took a silver lock pick out of his pocket that he'd retrieved from the stash of tools he kept in the car when he put Luvy inside. Ella might be surprised to learn that he'd learned the skill from his father between his annual prison stints. His dad had earned his living as a career fraudster and thief, dying in jail the last time he was arrested, thus averting a lengthy prison term. He'd been a charmer with a big laugh and wide circle of mates. Tony missed him to this day. His mother had left when he was twelve during one of his dad's brief periods out of the slammer. Luckily, a neighbour had stepped in to look after him, or lord only knows where he'd be now.

It took but a few seconds to work the cheap lock and shove the door open. The bathroom light had been left on and cast enough brightness into the room for Tony to see the shape of the boy on the double bed farthest away from the window. He took a few steps closer. Both of the boy's arms were tied to a slat in the headboard and a piece of black duct tape covered his mouth. His wide, frightened eyes followed Tony as he moved closer.

"You Matt Clark?" Tony asked.

The eyes blinked.

"My name is Tony. I'm going to get you out of here. Jimmy gave my friend his mother's cell phone, and we tracked you here. The police are on their way. I'll be right outside until they arrive."

The boy's eyes began to blink at warp speed, and a muffled noise came from behind the tape over his mouth. His body bucked on the bed.

Tony hesitated. Leaving Matt here was a risk. The man could use the boy as a hostage, and he might get caught in the crossfire. Which was the wiser course of action? Leave or take him? The sheer panic in the boy's response settled it. He lifted a hand to quiet him. "All right, Matt. I wouldn't want to be left here either. Let's get you out of this room." He thought for a moment. "I'm going to take some photos because we want to make this guy pay. Hold tight." He took out his phone and snapped pictures of Matt and the room while Matt watched with pleading eyes. He forwarded the pics to Hunter with the message: *Can't leave him here.*

It took a few minutes to untie the rope and release Matt's arms. As he worked at the knot, Tony kept an ear out for the man's return, not certain what he'd do if he heard a car pull up. He kept the tape over Matt's mouth to save time but also to keep him from screaming. That's all he'd need, some Good Samaritan rushing in and thinking he was into some sick bondage game with a pre-teen.

Once Matt's arms were freed, Tony half-pulled and half-carried the boy off the bed. Matt was slight but heavy enough, and they shuffled toward the door until Matt got his feet under him and he began dragging Tony. Matt pulled the door open, and the outdoor lights disoriented Tony for a moment. He breathed in the fresh air, trying to replace the stale stink of the motel room and get a second wind. Matt was clawing at the tape on his mouth with one hand, without success. Tony signalled for him to wait.

"Leave the tape until we cross the street. I'll get it off without hurting you. My car's just over there. Let's get you inside, and I'll move us farther along the street. The police are minutes away." Tony panted out instructions as they darted toward his car. A vehicle's headlights drew closer from the same direction as the diner, Tony guessed half a mile away. "Inside and down on the floor," he said, opening the back door. "I'll get the tape off once this person goes by. We can't be sure it's not that creep returning."

Matt didn't need a second invitation, scrambling inside at record speed. Tony slammed the door after he was safely stowed and climbed into the front seat, slumping down as the approaching car turned into the motel lot and pulled into the space in front of room number eleven. Tony started the car while the man got out of his and fumbled with the room key, juggling a bag of fast food in his other hand. Tony waited until he had the door open before shutting off the engine as a

Quebec police car and two black sedans silently filed into the motel lot.

Tony turned and looked down at Matt's upturned face. Luvy had already scrambled into the back seat to welcome him. "The police are here," he said, smiling, "and all will be well. Your friend Jimmy came through big-time." He got out of the car and helped Matt up onto the seat. It took a moment to get the tape off his mouth and wrap his arms around the boy. "You're safe, Matt," he said, patting his back while Luvy leapt up and washed the lad's face with her tongue. "And you've made a new furry friend by the looks of it."

CHAPTER 35

First thing the following morning, Ella checked herself out of the hospital and caught an Uber to her apartment. Tony had offered to skip work and come pick her up, but she'd refused. He'd already filled her in about his part in the rescue and arrest at the Quebec motel the night before, and she owed him too much ever to repay as it was.

Almost every part of her ached, from her head to her shoulder to her ribs. She'd been assured all would heal given time; even the mild concussion would leave no lasting effects. The nausea and sleepiness from the night before had receded to manageable levels, although she'd skip working on her computer for the day. Her vision blurred when she focused too long on her phone screen. Her left arm in a sling was another reminder to take things easy for the rest of the week, as her doctor had advised. She'd already called Canard to let him know.

She thanked the Uber driver and took a moment to breathe in the fresh, bracing air as she slowly started up the walkway to her apartment. Yesterday's rain had moved on along with the cloud cover, and she squinted to lessen the sun's glare. She was surprised but not surprised to see her car parked in the driveway. Tony had somehow gotten it back to the city, likely by enlisting the aid of one his many friends. He was resourceful and usually seemed to know what she needed before she did. Making a detour to the car, she took her sunglasses out of the console, relieved to put them on and cut the dizzying brightness. She retrieved her keys from under the seat where someone had replaced them.

The house was still, with the empty feel it got when everyone was out. Finn would be at the gym, and Piper would have taken Lena to playgroup for the morning. She trudged up the stairs and passed Tony's closed door. He had told her today was a packed schedule at the salon. Inside her apartment, she stripped off her muddy clothes, released her arm from the sling, and stepped into the shower. Washing her hair with one hand took effort, but since Tony had left early for the shop, there was lots of hot water that didn't run out even with the extra time. Sometimes having short hair was a blessing. After towelling off, she dressed in workout pants and a long sweater before entering the kitchen to make a cup of instant coffee. It was only then that she saw the plate of homemade carrot muffins next to a cell phone on the counter. A note stood propped against the salt and pepper shakers. She reached for the piece of paper.

Thought you might want to return the phone to the kid. I can tomorrow if you aren't up to it. See you anon. T.

She looked up. *Jimmy.* She'd been able to keep his name out of the part he played in hiding Matt but wasn't sure how long she could keep his secret. In any case, she had to get the phone back to him so he could replace it before his mom found out it was missing. He was only a kid, but he was a source, and she'd do all she could to protect his privacy, even from his own parents, because that was his request. This might skirt an ethical line, since he was a minor, but she had to go with her conscience on this one. Her word had to count for something.

She plugged in the kettle, wanting a jolt of caffeine and one of Tony's muffins before setting out for Ashton. The idea of driving exhausted her, but she remembered Jimmy's panic that his parents would find out he'd been hiding Matt, and she felt a responsibility, misplaced or not. Her phone rang as she was finishing her coffee. She checked the caller and picked up. "What's going on, Sherry?"

"Canard is sending me to give you a hand. I hear you suffered a tumble."

"You could say that. Feel like driving out to Ashton?"

"When?"

"As soon as you can pick me up."

"On my way."

Ella clicked off and sent a silent thank-you to Canard. She hadn't been looking forward to driving with one hand and had put off taking one of the painkillers to stay alert. She'd give in and take a pill now, then collect her things and wait downstairs for Sherry. By the time she arrived, the pain should be under control and she'd be able to function. Sherry could help her type an update for the paper after Jimmy had the phone back and they returned home. Hopefully, Hunter or Thorburn would respond to her message in the meantime to debrief her on the man who'd abducted Matt and likely had murdered the Petries. There was still a lot more story to uncover and report on. The thought of what lay ahead gave her a burst of energy. These were the moments she lived for: exposing those who'd done harm to others while helping to bring some kind of restitution to their victims.

———

Jimmy spent the morning watching Theo, even playing dolls with her for an hour to keep her away from their parents. He didn't trust her to stay quiet about the missing cell phone or Matt, but she'd been okay up until ten minutes ago, when she began getting restless. His parents had been in the kitchen for a while, and Theo was hungry. He'd offered to go make her a sandwich and bring it to her, but she was having none of it.

"I want to make my own sandwich. You never get it right."

"Double peanut butter and strawberry jam. It's not rocket science, Theo. I can make it like you want."

"No." She scowled, uncrossed her legs, tossed her Barbie doll onto a pile of clothes, and got up from the floor. "I'm going to see Mom."

"Theo—"

"Leave me alone. You can't make me stay here if I don't wanna."

The back door opened, and voices greeted each other in the kitchen as they reached the bottom of the stairs. Jimmy grabbed Theo's arm and drew her closer. "Let's wait to see who that is," he whispered into her ear.

He felt her body relax. She nodded and they stood silently, listening.

He recognized the voice of their neighbour, Miriam Johannson. A moment later, he heard Mr. Johannson's booming laugh. Theo nudged his arm. "I don't like Mr. Johannson. I'm going to my room to play until they leave."

"What about your sandwich?"

"I'm not *that* hungry."

He moved closer to the kitchen after he was sure Theo had climbed the stairs. The Johannsons didn't visit that often, so something must have happened, and they'd come here to tell his parents. His mother's voice rose more clearly than the others, and he tuned in to her words.

"Thank goodness he's been found safe. I hated to think—"

Muffled words from his dad. Mrs. Johannson's voice rose. "Why would this man kill Stu and Devina and abduct Matt? It makes no sense."

Jimmy jumped when his father appeared in the kitchen doorway and spotted him. His dad hesitated a moment before walking toward him. "What are you doing out here, son?"

"I was going to make Theo a sandwich, and I heard voices."

"Miriam and Everett came to tell us that Matt was found safe and sound last night. They heard a report on the radio."

"Really?" Jimmy tried to sound surprised. "Where … where was he?"

"They aren't sure, but he was with somebody the police arrested."

"Do the police think Matt killed the Petries? Because that definitely didn't happen."

"The reporter gave no other details. Come make the sandwich and stop lurking out here like a peeping Tom." His dad's voice was gruff. He put a hand on Jimmy's back and gave a gentle push in the direction of the kitchen. "It's a relief to know your friend is safe, though, I imagine?"

"Dad—" Jimmy wanted to tell him about keeping Matt in his bedroom and giving him the tracker but closed his mouth when everyone in the kitchen stopped talking to stare at him.

His mother crossed the space to give him a hug. "Isn't it wonderful news? Matt's been found, and he's well."

Guilt surged through him. How was he going to tell his secrets without being grounded for the rest of his life? Would they believe he couldn't be trusted ever again? He nodded before she dropped her arms and stepped back.

Mrs. Johannson smiled at him and then looked at his mother. "We're going to meet Nelly for lunch. She's the one who called this morning and told us to check the news. Would you like to join us?"

"Why, thank you, Miriam, but you and Everett go ahead. Lanny needs to work in the barn, and I'm in the middle of cleaning the house." His mom winked at Jimmy as if they were sharing a joke. He had no doubt he'd find her curled up on the couch in the living room reading with a cup of tea after they left.

Mr. Johannson motioned for his wife to open the back door. "Let's get moving, Miriam. You're holding everyone up." He looked at Jimmy's dad. "She had to hightail it over here. A phone call simply wouldn't do."

"And we appreciate it," Jimmy's mom said firmly. "This is a bit of good news in a terrible week."

Mr. Johannson grimaced. "The boy could have been in on it. Nobody's ruled that out. I mean, where's he been these last few days? Seems to me he and this man could be like that army guy and the kid who were working together and shot and killed all those people in the States." He looked at his wife. "Whaaat? You think I'm blowing smoke?"

"That's not kind, Everett, in addition to being highly unlikely." Mrs. Johannson bowed her head and pulled on the door handle. She turned back to face them. "Whatever did Stu and Devina do that could lead to their murders? Because if their deaths were random in this sleepy middle of nowhere — well, then, nobody on Earth is safe. And I pray Matt Clark had nothing to do with it, because that is too hard even to contemplate."

Jimmy watched his parents exchange a glance before both looked away. Everett poked his head back inside the door. "Looks like you got visitors. That reporter from *The Capital*. We'll be at the pub if you find out anything new. Feel free to come fill us in. The wife hates to be the last one in line spreading the gossip." He grinned before disappearing from sight.

"Well, that was awkward," Jimmy's mom said. "Sometimes I wonder how those two remain married."

"After Devina left town and moved to the States, Everett was heartbroken. He finally settle—" Dad glanced back at Jimmy and stopped what he was about to say. "Well, let's see if the reporter has more to tell us before I get to work in the barn."

CHAPTER 36

The doctor advised that Matt Clark should spend the night in the Children's Hospital to monitor his health, both mental and physical, before the police questioning. Quade agreed, as long as an officer was allowed to keep watch outside his room. She decided Matt would stay separate from his mother until after he'd been interviewed, although Glynnis had been informed that her son was safe. She was currently with the FBI, hidden away in a safe location, waiting for Matt to join her. Blaine Dumas was in custody, and it turned out that he was well known to the FBI. His grilling would start as soon as his lawyer arrived on the red-eye from New York City. Liam used the delays to catch a nap at the station before going through the background on Dumas that Thorburn had compiled in the wee hours.

Liam lifted his eyes from the computer screen. Thorburn had entered the office with two large coffees. She crossed the room and set one in front of him before plunking onto the visitor chair. Liam thanked her and finished rereading Dumas's bio. He was a decorated army vet, having served three tours of duty in Afghanistan. Born and raised in New York City, he'd left his unit five years earlier and opened a business specializing in security and protection for high-profile persons. He'd hired several of his army alum, and before long, the rich and famous were beating down the door for his company's services. A staunch member of the National Rifle Association and linked to white supremacy groups, albeit not a vocal participant in any particular one, he often handled cases himself while coordinating teams wherever needed. Twice married and twice divorced, he lived at an unknown address and conducted business through a secure website.

Thorburn waited for him to look up. "Not a lot to go on." She sipped from her cup. "My main question is why would a man with his credentials take on an assignment to kill two old people and abduct a kid?"

Liam studied her face while he thought. Auger and Quade had obviously not told her this morning that she was being transferred. The knowledge of what was coming weighed heavily, but he forced himself not to dwell on it. He held out a slim hope that her work on this case would buy a reprieve. He'd use her input today and yesterday as leverage when arguing again to keep her as his partner whenever he got a chance to be alone with Quade. He considered Thorburn's question. "Somebody desperate with deep pockets paid him. It's appalling what people will do for money."

"A case of greed over ethics?"

"He could have been convinced that he was supporting a cause. He has several affiliations linked to the far-right agenda."

"Maybe." She'd chosen not to contradict him, but he could see by her body language that she wasn't convinced. He had his doubts too.

His cell rang, and he checked call display. "The hospital," he said before answering. He nodded at Thorburn and held up a finger as he listened. "We're on our way," he said into the receiver. "Yeah, keep him safely stowed away until we get there. Should be thirty minutes, tops."

"Showtime," he said to Thorburn as he set the phone on his desk and reached for a jacket slung over the back of his chair. "Matt Clark is ready to talk."

"Let's hope he has some answers. What about Dumas?"

"Auger, Boots, and Jingles are on standby. I'll send them a message to get the interview started if his lawyer shows up before we get back."

———

A NURSE DIRECTED them to a room at the end of the hallway, guarded by a police officer sitting on a chair. She nodded at Liam and let them enter without asking for ID. They'd worked other cases together, and her smile seemed an open invitation as he passed by. She'd suggested drinks after hours the last time they'd crossed paths. He couldn't recall now why he'd turned her down. Matt Clark sat fully dressed in a chair near the windows. A social worker who would act as his adult stood nearby. His mother had given her consent to this arrangement. As soon as Matt saw them, he leapt to his feet and faced them.

"When can I see my mom?"

"Soon. We need to talk with you about what happened first." Liam motioned for Matt to sit down before carrying a chair over from the other side of the bed and placing it a few feet in front of him. Thorburn positioned herself behind him and took out a notebook and pen, although Liam knew she was also recording the interview. The social worker introduced herself as Sally before a nod of her head signalled to Liam that he was running the show. "Matt's mom didn't want a lawyer present, but I will ask for one on Matt's behalf if I see a need."

"Of course," Liam said.

Matt's eyes darted from Thorburn to Liam. He was a good-looking boy, but his face was pale and anxious, and the effects of his ordeal were evident. He'd lost weight and appeared frail in a loose-fitting t-shirt. "I don't know who that guy was that put me in his car."

"We're sorting that out, Matt. He's in custody, and we have other detectives questioning him. You don't have to worry that he'll try anything again. Are you feeling up to answering some questions?"

"I'm okay."

"Good. I'd like to go back to the day Stu and Devina died. Could you take me through what happened as best you can remember? Take your time. I know this isn't easy."

Matt nodded. "Me and Jimmy had been fishing at the river, and we were late starting back. It was getting dark, and Devina liked me to be home while it was still light. I was halfway up the driveway when I saw light shine off the windshield of a car behind the woodpile. It looked like somebody was trying to hide it."

"Did you see what kind of car?"

"Well, maybe it was a truck. I never got a good look."

"Okay. What happened next?"

"I got off my bike and waited. Someone came out the front door, got in the vehicle, and drove off. I never saw them either. The porch light was off, and I ducked behind some bushes. Something felt weird."

"So it could have been either a man or a woman?"

Matt nodded. "I was surprised they used the front door. Most people go around back, but I think whoever it was wanted to get away fast." He dropped his eyes and stared at a spot on the floor. "I went in by the back door. Devina and Stu were in the living room on the floor. The blood — I knew they were dead. I was scared because my mom told me I had to hide out here for the summer while Dad testified against his boss. Mom and Dad were fighting a lot and I thought that might be why they wanted me out of the way, you know, to patch things up. Until I saw Stu and Devina lying there, I didn't believe anybody was really out to hurt us. I knew it wasn't safe there anymore, so I went into my bedroom to get my knapsack, but someone drove up and came into the house by the front door. I thought it was the killer coming back, and I got out through my bedroom window and ran to the chicken coop. I hid behind it."

So he'd been right thinking Matt had escaped out the window. "Did you see who came into the house?"

Matt stared straight ahead. "It was the guy who picked me up on the highway. From where I was hiding, I saw him standing on the back steps looking toward the garden and the trees. The porch light was off but his size and shape and that ball cap are hard to miss." Matt stopped talking for a moment and swiped at his eye. "He must have heard me … he walked all around the yard and checked inside the chicken coop. He used his phone as a flashlight. I kept moving along the back wall, and he never saw me. It felt like forever. He finally got in his car and left. Then I hid in the woods."

"The entire time?"

Matt fidgeted in the chair and nodded but with little enthusiasm.

"How did Jimmy get the tracker to you?"

"I don't want to get him in trouble. I … kind of kept a lot from him anyway. I thought the less he knew the better."

"I know you're friends. It's natural he'd want to help you." Liam waited.

Matt was quiet for a long while. Sally leaned closer to him and asked if he thought he could answer. He nodded and took a deep breath before looking Liam squarely in the eyes. "I got to his house the next day and hid in the barn, but Jimmy saw me and said I could stay in his bedroom. There was room in his closet during the day."

"Did anybody know?"

"Not at first, but his sister Theo saw me Friday morning. Jimmy swore her to secrecy. His parents never found out, and we want to keep it that way."

"The story will be difficult to keep from them now, Matt. I'll try to help them understand."

"Jimmy only stayed quiet because I begged him. That guy came to the house twice looking for me. The first time, he left without coming inside. Jimmy distracted him the second time while I went out the back door." Matt shrugged. "Last night, the man found me on the highway, hitching to Ottawa. I recognized him and tried to run, but he caught me and put this rag over my mouth. I woke up tied to the bed in that motel room."

And Tony and Ella tracked you down. Liam realized Ella had been unusually quiet. He'd send a text after this interview and ask her to check in. Find out what she knew. He looked back at Thorburn, but she signalled that she had nothing to add. He was now convinced that Matt had zero to do with the murders. Everything he said added up in the timeline. He certainly hadn't been travelling with Dumas voluntarily. "We need to get you out of here and over to your mom. You'll be in safe hands, and hopefully we'll wrap up our investigation soon so you can leave Ottawa."

"Can I see Jimmy again?"

"No promises, but if there's any possible way, I'll try to make that happen."

"Don't let him get into trouble because of me. Everything was my fault. Jimmy only lied because I asked him to."

CHAPTER 37

Auger was standing in Quade's office with the door open when Liam and Thorburn made it back to HQ. Boots spotted them first and waved them over to his desk.

"Dumas's lawyer showed, and we did the preliminary interview. Dumas says he played concerned citizen and gave Matt a ride but has no idea how the boy ended up tied to the bed in a motel room. He insists he went for food, and Matt was fine when he left."

"Did he try to sell you some land in Florida too?" Liam asked.

"Believe me, I wasn't buying anything that thug was selling."

Liam looked toward Quade's office. "So what's going on with them?"

Boots smile faded. "They haven't got enough to charge Dumas with murder. The kidnapping is more certain, but not ironclad. Prosecutor was not convinced, anyway. The two of them are deciding whether to hold Dumas or let him go. Dumas admitted he dropped by the Petrie house on that Saturday evening but said they were already dead. Insists he didn't kill them. Wanted us to know that's not how he operates."

"Did he say what he was doing in Ashton exactly?"

"Surprise, no surprise, he's a resident of New York City, and ZTMeds hired him to locate Matt and Glynnis Clark, but his assignment did not include harming anybody."

"And yet he didn't come forward when he found the bodies."

"He admitted that was poor form but not criminal on his part. The shock disoriented him." Boots let out a sharp laugh. "If you saw Dumas up close, you'd know not much unnerves the man. He has fish eyes, pale blue and cold as my uncle's wife."

Liam focused on a loose end that bothered him. "How in the world did he find Matt Clark? He was keeping a low profile, and this out-of-the-way village is nowhere near his home in the U.S."

"Apparently, there's a public Instagram page. Theodora Dooley has a site under the name CuteKitty-Girl and posted photos of Matt and updates all summer. Once anyone found the page, it was like she lit up a neon arrow pointing to his location. They were running searches and her feed came up, apparently. Then they found the Petrie farm website."

"And the circle closes." Liam glanced at Thorburn, who was reading a text. She raised her eyes to his. "I'm to go into Quade's office. Did you get a text as well?"

"No."

"I'll find out what she wants."

He should have warned her, said something to ward off the blow that was coming, but she was gone before he found the words. *Damn it.* He'd wanted to plead her case with Quade one more time, and now... He watched Thorburn enter her office and close the door. This was turning out to be a terrible day and getting worse. A message dinged on his phone: Ella Tate agreeing to meet. He looked toward the office door. Would it be better to wait around and try to lift Thorburn's spirits or give her space to accept her transfer without him hovering? He thought which of the two options he'd prefer. No way he'd want to speak with anyone after getting this news. He'd give her space and catch up with her in good time after he connected with Ella.

———

ELLA CAUGHT Daisy's eye from where she stood in the doorway to the diner before crossing to her regular booth with a good view of the entrance. Sherry had dropped her at the café upon their arrival from Ashton, where Ella had managed to return the phone to Jimmy without his parents noticing. The morning had slipped away, and the breakfast crowd was gone, with the exception of a white-haired man drinking coffee at the counter. Daisy finished chatting with him and picked up the coffee pot. She sauntered over to Ella and poured a cup without asking. "Been a while," she said. "Your gentleman friend coming by, or you want to order?"

"I've been hibernating. Yes, he's on his way, so I'll wait. Thanks, Daisy. You're looking well."

Daisy patted her beehive, and her eyes darted to the man at the counter. "My own gentleman friend has a way of putting some sparkle in my day."

"You been dating long?"

Daisy smiled. "Forty-five years and counting. We got married when I was seventeen."

"That's … amazing."

"Isn't it? We divorced when I turned forty, but the separation only lasted five years." She gave a coy smile. "Dating suits us more than marriage. More action in the bedroom, if you get my drift. Anyway, glad you and your fella patched things up."

Ella watched her return to the counter and slide onto the stool next to him. Daisy continued to surprise. They moved their heads close together like a couple of magnets. Their obvious attraction made Ella happy but wistful at the same time. What must it be like to have a soul mate with whom to travel through life into old age? Someone you wanted to have sex with after forty-some years? She gave her head a shake. What was wrong with her, first dreaming about a simpler life in the country and now this? She was spending too much time around Lena.

She'd nearly finished sipping her coffee when the door opened and Hunter stepped inside. He stood for a moment as his eyes swept the room, finally landing on her. He smiled, and his face lightened before he started toward her. Ella's breath caught at the sight of him, and she realized how much she'd missed him. The feeling was unsettling. He sat across from her, and Daisy appeared with the coffee pot and took their orders.

Hunter's jaw tightened as he took in Ella's arm in a sling and the bruise on the left side of her face. She'd kept both turned away from Daisy, not wanting her to fuss. "What happened? Was this from last night? Why didn't Tony tell me?"

"It's nothing."

"Doesn't look like nothing. That guy you tracked down do this?"

She shrugged with her good shoulder. "He tossed me over the side of the embankment. Cracked my head and a couple of ribs. Dislocated my shoulder. Good news is I'm on the mend. I told Tony not to say anything, because I felt stupid putting myself in that situation. Plus, what happened to me isn't important. Getting Matt back is all that matters."

"Jesus, Tate. Are you pressing charges?"

"He's going down for abducting Matt Clark and those murders, isn't he? My push over the cliff seems anticlimactic."

"We might not have enough to hold him. His name is Blaine Dumas by the way, and he's working for the generic drug company ZTMeds in New York, which is currently before the grand jury for fraud, racketeering, and lord knows what else. Unfortunately, he wasn't caught with Matt in the motel room, and Matt doesn't remember anything because he was drugged. There's no proof Dumas killed the Petries, a charge he vehemently denies. Says he showed up and they were already dead. He also has a savvy lawyer from New York who's working to get him released as I speak. Paints Dumas as a do-gooder patriot, from what Auger said."

"Well, it will be my word against his, and sounds like he has an answer for everything. He'll probably insist I tripped and threw myself down the ravine. So, if he didn't kill the Petries, then who?"

"The million-dollar question. For now, can you tell me how you came to be in possession of the phone with the tracker app?"

She kept her face neutral. "I had a source."

"Matt Clark has already told us that he hid out in Jimmy's bedroom, and Jimmy gave the tracker to him."

"Then why ask me?"

"Covering bases. So?"

She weighed sharing against saying nothing and couldn't come up with a good reason not to confirm what Matt had already told him. "Yeah, all right. Jimmy gave me the phone when I saw him and his sister hovering over it in the Ashton Pub yesterday evening. His parents don't know about Jimmy's part in hiding Matt, and I promised to keep his confidence if I could. Earlier today, Sherry and I drove to the Dooley house, and I slipped the phone to Jimmy."

"Odd that his mother didn't miss it."

"Apparently, she owns two phones. So why is this important?"

"It gives us a timeline. Matt said somebody was in the house when he came home the night of the murders. He waited for them to drive off, went inside, and found the bodies. Another person, or possibly the same one returning to find Matt, drove up and entered the house. Matt escaped through his bedroom window."

"You've ruled him out for the killings?"

"There's no forensic evidence pointing to Matt. After interviewing him in the hospital, I'm ninety-nine point nine percent convinced he didn't have any part in what happened to them. He's frankly traumatized and frightened."

"It could be someone from Devina's or Stu's pasts who came to collect on a debt. Matt might not have been the only one hiding out in the Ashton countryside."

"Worth considering. We've also pretty much ruled out a murder-suicide."

"Is there any evidence of that?"

"Forensics says no. The fact somebody was in the house when Matt arrived home confirms their conclusion in my mind. Unfortunately, he got no details of the person or vehicle, since dusk had settled in, and he was staying out of sight."

"Well, by all accounts Stu Petrie liked to socialize and Devina was reclusive. She kept to the farm for the most part, almost as if she was in hiding, although this could simply be me making appearances fit a theory. She met regularly with Everett Johannson, whom she dated in high school, but didn't appear to go out much otherwise. Some thought she was the love of his life. Their friendship or whatever they had going on could have been a sign the Petries' marriage was in trouble, yet the neighbours say Devina adored her husband." Ella leaned forward, one elbow on the table, her hand cupping her chin. She stared out the window as she thought over possibilities.

Daisy arrived with their food order, and they paused their conversation while they ate. Ella pushed the eggs and bacon around on her plate without raising the fork to her lips more than a couple of times. Hunter watched her with growing concern in his eyes but stayed silent. She avoided meeting his gaze. Luckily, his phone buzzed as she was reaching the limit of feeling uncomfortable.

"Excuse me a sec," he said. He listened for a moment and thanked Boots for the heads-up before setting his phone on the table.

"Anything important?" Ella asked, dropping her fork on the plate and giving up all pretence of eating.

"Internal matter." He signalled to Daisy for the bill. "I've got to track down Rosie Thorburn. She's been transferred out of Major Crimes and didn't take the news well."

"That's awful. Why was she moved?"

"Lack of experience. I argued to keep her but was outvoted." He picked up his jacket from the seat next to him and stood. "Thanks for meeting. Let's keep in touch."

"Yeah, let's do it again soon." She wasn't sure he'd heard her. She pushed away the plate of food and waited a moment until he'd gone before standing. She had no doubt Auger was behind Rosie's transfer and that Rosie was too scared about his power in the force to take him on. The idea that he could get away with such monstrous behaviour didn't sit well. Ella grabbed her bag and hurried toward the door, eager to get back to her apartment to start digging into Auger's past. Rosie might be unwilling to confront the man, but she person-ally liked a challenge, especially if it meant exposing — pun intended — a man who had no right being in the business of serving and protecting.

CHAPTER 38

osie sat in her car, staring straight ahead. She'd fled HQ as fast as her feet would take her, flung herself into her car in the underground parking, and driven to this side street, where she'd slammed the stick shift into park under the branches of an oak tree. She'd repeatedly pounded on the steering wheel with the palm of her hand until the pain vibrated up her arm and into her shoulder. A minute of hyperventilating with a couple of screams thrown in for good measure and she had gained control of her emotions — rage at Auger, sadness at the loss of a job she loved, and fear at what was next. How was a stint in patrol going to make her a better detective? She took a deep breath and told herself to see the good. All experience was valuable. She had to remember that. *But not like this.*

She thumped the steering wheel one last time and silently chastised herself. Why hadn't she taken on Auger before he had time to make her pay for rebuffing him?

How had she let him gain the upper hand without doing anything to stop him? Of course, he'd force her out of Major Crimes. He didn't want her in his orbit once she was no longer of use to him. Had she learned nothing from living with her father? Men like these always had to flex their power and control the narrative. He might believe she was too weak to pose a threat, but he'd want her gone.

She pulled out her phone. Several unopened messages. She scrolled through the list and opened the one from Carlos, inviting her to meet for a drink after work, no matter how late. He was on a day off and free. She stared out the window again and thought before sending her response. It would be a relief to drink away her troubles with a man obviously interested in her who knew nothing about her life. Mindless, easy ... but there'd be no turning back. Once she crossed that line, she'd be giving up on Brad and whatever future they had together. *This isn't a good day,* she typed with more reluctance than she should have allowed herself, *but thanks for thinking of me.*

The second message she opened was from Hunter, looking for her and wanting to talk about her transfer. She deleted it without answering. She didn't want his pep talk or his pity. She tossed the phone onto the seat and thought about going to a bar and drinking away the evening alone. It was a long time since she'd gotten hammered. The last drunken spree had probably been with her high school girlfriends when they'd all gathered for the summer on a trip home from various universities. Appealing as oblivion might be, she decided to give it a pass too. There was a better way to deal with losing the job she loved. She reached for the phone and typed a quick message to Brad before starting the car and putting on her seatbelt.

Finn was working with a client when Rosie entered the gym, but he came over to welcome her, and some of the tightness in her chest began to ease. She'd kept a gym bag in her car and carried it into the change room, dressing quickly and exiting a moment later. Beginning with stretches and progressing to sit ups and lunges, she kept moving to keep herself from thinking. Once on the treadmill, her eyes roved around the gym. It was a busy evening. Two women sparred in the boxing ring set up near the back of the room. A couple of bulked-up young men lifted weights, and three stationary bikes were in use. Everybody was a stranger. Rosie relaxed and concentrated on her breathing, happy to be alone without feeling any need to interact.

Once she was sweaty and tired and the others had changed and left, she entered the change room and showered, closing her eyes and letting the water stream onto her face before getting back into her work clothes. She sat on the bench after pulling on her shoes, and only then did she let the demotion — for there was no other word for it — overwhelm her. She'd followed Auger here from Toronto because of the position in Major Crimes. She'd clung to it like a life raft as Brad angled to have her return to Collingwood with him to start a quieter life with a house and children. What was wrong with her that she didn't want the same future as he did? Once he found out about her ousting from Major Crimes, he'd up the pressure to move back. How much more could she take before giving in? The very idea of standing up

to Brad left her weary. He was on days off, and she had
no desire to drive home and face him with her news, to
watch the silent hope on his face that she'd given up on
her dream of becoming a detective.

She stood and angrily stuffed clothes into her bag.
This was her damn life, and she hated everything about
it. But the gym would be closing in twenty minutes, and
the time to linger was over. She strode across the room
toward the main entrance. Halfway there, her steps
faltered. Brad stood in the doorway to the office and
turned to smile at her. A mix of emotions filled her chest
as she slowly covered the last of the distance between
them.

"I'll see you later, Finn. Great meeting you," Brad
said. "Hey, Rosie. I got your text and thought I'd
surprise you. Feel like going for a drink? Finn says
there's a pub a block from here."

"I'm tired—"

"One drink, okay? We need to talk."

"All right, but I warn you. I'm not in a great
mood."

She detoured to lock the gym bag in her car, and
they walked side by side in silence until they reached the
pub. Brad pulled the door open and waited for her to
enter ahead of him. "Pick a table, and I'll get a couple
of drinks from the bar. Red wine okay?"

"Sure, why not."

He returned with two glasses and pulled his chair
around so that he sat close to her before raising his glass
and tapping hers.

"To us," he said.

She clinked glasses and eyed him warily as he took a
long drink. He was up to something, and she dreaded

another confrontation. "Did you have a good day?" she asked.

"I did." He pulled a piece of folded paper out of his pocket, smiling like he'd won a lottery. "Remember that house we looked at a few months back in Centrepointe? The three-bedroom you liked with the big backyard?"

"You weren't keen on it, and while we debated the logic of home ownership, it was sold."

"Well, the real estate agent called, and the financing fell through for the other couple. I spent yesterday getting ducks in a row, and our offer was accepted a few hours ago. We own the house!"

She sat stunned. This was not even close to anything she considered he'd be raising when he said it was time they talked. Yet the day's heaviness didn't allow for hope. "But what about moving to Collingwood to be closer to our families?"

He shrugged. "We can always visit, or they can come here. We have plenty of room for the first time."

"Why buy the house, Brad? Why now?"

"You want to live here, and I want to support you while you build your career. It makes sense to own property."

She swallowed hard and worked to keep her voice steady. "I got moved out of Major Crimes today. Shuffled to patrol."

"I know."

"How—"

"Liam Hunter came by the house. He was worried about you."

"Is it too late to rescind the offer on the property?"

"Why would I do that?"

"Because the reason we came to Ottawa, my job, it's

gone." Her voice couldn't have sounded any more miserable. "I might never have another chance."

He reached over and grabbed her hand resting on the table with both of his. "This is simply a setback. You are a detective to your core, and you'll earn that job again. Hell, they'll be begging you to return. Hunter has faith in your skills and instincts, and so do I. You never ask for anything, Rosie, and I know this is what you want. If at some point in time we decide to leave Ottawa, we can sell, probably even make a tidy profit. For now, though, I'm all in."

"But what about your dreams? You're tired of shift work, you told me that last week. I hate that you're sacrificing for me."

"Making you happy is no sacrifice." He let go of her hand and unfolded the paper. "Have another look at our house, drink up, and let's do a drive-by on our way home."

She gulped some wine and set her glass on the table. "I love you, Brad."

"I sure hope so." He grinned and hunched forward, his expression turning serious. "I know we've been like ships passing in the night, but I promise you things are going to get better. One of the paramedics on days is leaving, and I put in for their job. I'll know by end of the week, but signs are good that I'll get it. It'll be something we can count on. We can spend more time together, and I won't be as exhausted as I've been."

She ducked her head so that he couldn't see the tears threatening. She never cried. Prided herself on it, in fact. Today and the last few months had been a roller coaster, but she'd never let herself give in to the emotion before now. She and Brad weren't repeating her parents' marriage, as she'd feared for so long, and the knowledge gave her the hope to dream again, even if her career had veered out of Major Crimes into patrol. She smiled as Brad squeezed her hand and pulled her up from the chair and into a hug that reminded her of days gone by and all the reasons they were still together.

CHAPTER 39

Murky light filtered through the gap of open window beneath the slatted blind, and Liam groaned softly as his eyes adjusted to the gloom. The air gusted warm and muggy across his face, promising an unsettled and close day, as the weather sometimes turned in late September. He wondered if the rain would hold off until evening.

Lucky leapt onto his chest from the floor, purring like a lawn mower. Liam scratched under the cat's chin while thinking over the day ahead. First, he'd ask to speak with Quade about Thorburn and see if he could get that decision reversed. Then he'd seek an interview with Dumas to take his own stock of the man. The last message from Boots indicated no charges had been laid. Worrisome.

After a quick breakfast of coffee and cereal, he made it downtown to HQ by eight o'clock. Auger hadn't arrived yet, but the light was on in Quade's office. Liam rapped on her partially open door, and she called for him to enter. Her smile beamed warmly, but everything else about her hinted at weariness, from her dark eyes to her sloped shoulders and hunched back. "Have a seat," she said, turning from her computer and resting her elbows on the desk. "I imagine this is about Rosie Thorburn."

Liam sat on the edge of the chair and leaned toward her. "There's no good reason to move her out of the unit. I'd like to keep her as my partner."

"I wish it were that easy. Auger made a solid case, and HR acquired the final approvals for her transfer. She starts in patrol a week from today."

"You bought Auger's argument?"

"It's not a question of me buying anything. He had proof that she'd messed up in her previous job as well as when she worked for him here. I agree that more experience on a lower-profile team will give her the skills she's lacking. She can always apply again to return to Major Crimes down the road once she proves herself. Auger admitted that he erred in giving her too much responsibility so soon but agrees she has potential."

"I never saw any signs of ineptness or mistakes. Quite the opposite." He paused, running through his mind how to word his mistrust of Auger. "Could Auger be grinding an axe? By their recent interactions, the two of them appear to have had a falling-out."

Quade took a moment to consider his not-so-veiled accusation. "I can't very well go suggesting Auger is acting in bad faith without proof. We are both applying for this position, and if I make a charge that he got rid of Thorburn out of spite, and he denies it — as he will — I'll come out the loser. Surely, you can see that?"

"I understand you're in a bind because of the career situation."

"And neither of us has to like it." A tightly controlled anger flashed in her eyes for the briefest of moments and was gone as quickly. She offered him a wide, tired smile. "Let's set this aside for now. Where are we with the Petrie murders?"

"I believed we had the killer when we took Dumas into custody. Boots told me he denied it."

"Yes, and we didn't have enough to charge him."

"What about Matt's drugging and abduction?"

"Again, not enough evidence to hold him, especially with the hotshot lawyer Dumas hired. The woman may not be Canadian, but she certainly knows our law inside out and upside down. Matt doesn't remember seeing whoever tied him to the bed, and Tony didn't actually witness Dumas in the motel room with Matt. It's a shame Tony removed the boy before the police arrived."

"But the photos Tony took—"

"Prove Matt was tied to the bed but not who put him there. Dumas admits he gave Matt a lift but claims he dropped him off outside the motel because he said somebody was picking him up. Dumas said he had a rest before driving back to the highway truck stop to buy food and had no idea how Matt got into his room. He claims Tony might have set him up."

"Has the world gone insane? Ella Tate saw Dumas shoving Matt into the back seat of his car before he pushed her over the side of the embankment. She's suffered injuries."

Quade frowned. "Ella hasn't come forward."

"I only spoke with her late yesterday. She believed you had Dumas on other more serious charges."

"Well, get her statement on record and maybe it will be enough." Quade's doubtful expression belied her words. "We ran everything by a Crown prosecutor, and they were skeptical that we have enough to hold Dumas with what we presented. We released him close to midnight."

"He's likely returned to the States with his lawyer."

"That would be my guess."

Quade was the first to break eye contact. She partially turned away from him. "I have to prepare for a meeting and need some time." Her eyes flicked back to his. "Dumas might very well have killed the Petries, but we require solid evidence, especially if we have to extradite him from New York. Alternatively, if someone else is responsible, you'll need to run through motives and opportunity. The one good thing that has come out of the last few days is that Matt and his mother are reunited and safe. We've got them stashed away with the FBI in an unknown location. They've agreed to stay put while you collect evidence. It'll be tough telling them Dumas got off scot-free if that's the outcome."

"And my partner?"

"Thorburn has a few more days. Then, we'll see. HR has a long list of applicants who'd like to transfer into Major Crimes, so I don't anticipate you'll be on your own for long."

"I'd rather keep the partner I have."

"Duly noted." Quade shook her head. "But my advice is not to hold your breath."

―――――

ELLA HADN'T MADE it to bed until 3:00 a.m. and woke later than she'd intended. She double-checked the time, not believing at first that she'd slept six straight hours. A knocking at her apartment door appeared to have served as her alarm clock. She climbed slowly out of bed and eased into a bathrobe. Her headache had all but disappeared, and the throbbing in her shoulder and ribs had eased into manageable. She might just make it through the day without any painkillers. Tony stood in the hallway when she yanked the door open, and Luvy scooted past her and scampered out of sight. Tony held a squirming Lena in his arms. He was wearing a jacket and cap, ready to head out. He frowned at her. "Did you forget Piper had the day off and you volunteered a few hours to mind the baby?"

"Mama," Lena cried and held her arms toward Ella so that Tony stumbled forward.

"Don't call me that," Ella said wrapping her good arm around the girl's chubby stomach. "My name is Ella. Ella, not … well, not what you said."

"We could all start calling you little baby mama," Tony said before following her down the hall and into the cramped living room. He took a look around and headed into the kitchen. A moment later, Ella heard him running water and making coffee in the machine he'd bought her a month earlier. She still hadn't taken the time to figure out how it worked.

"I'd forgotten about my offer," Ella said when he returned with a steaming, frothy latte. She gave Lena a squeeze before placing her on a mat on the floor laden with stuffed animals and toys. Even though the pain in her ribs had dropped from sharp to ache level, she took a moment to catch her breath after straightening. Lena tucked a stuffed bear under her arm and picked up the wooden puzzle. She'd keep herself occupied a long while, content to be left alone to figure it out. Ella wondered if this was normal behaviour and thought probably not. Still, Lena seemed happy enough.

Tony glanced down at her as she held a wooden puzzle piece with a cow painted on its surface close to her face. "She kind of reminds me of you. I can't put my finger on it."

"Don't go there, Tony. No good can come of comparing me to a needy, helpless baby whose main activities are eating, pooping, and sleeping."

"No, I suppose not. Well, I'm off and home at one thirty to take over. Don't get busy and forget you have a child relying on you. One that crawls faster than a sand crab."

"I'm on it."

She listened to Tony's footsteps clatter down the stairs before checking on Lena, taking a sip of coffee, and opening a file on her computer. She gave herself fifteen minutes before she'd get dressed and take Lena for a walk in her stroller. They could both use some fresh air, which would also help make the baby sleepy. Ella made a list of phone numbers and jotted notes, organizing her time for when Lena would go down for her nap after lunch.

She'd finished getting dressed when her cell phone rang. Liam Hunter's name popped up, and she lowered herself onto the floor next to Lena as she swiped up on the screen to receive his call. "This will only take a minute," she said, handing Lena a teething ring. "Hey, Hunter. What's going on?"

She heard street noises while he filled her in on the latest developments. He ended by asking her to drop by HQ to file a complaint against Dumas about the injuries she sustained.

"I'm kind of busy——" She listened. His request had morphed into a demand. "All right, twenty minutes. Yeah, twenty minutes, give or take. I'll be there." She signed off and ran her hand through Lena's curls. "This might work out in our favour, kid," she said. "We're going to enter the lion's den, and the big bad beast has no idea we're coming for him."

———

HUNTER SEEMED THROWN AT FIRST that Ella showed up pushing a baby in a stroller, but he quickly recovered. She was pleased to see Rosie with him in the office and thought for a brief moment that she wasn't being transferred. Rosie didn't look as devastated as Ella would have thought she'd be. Ella waited until Hunter was leading the way into a meeting room to turn to her. "Everything okay?"

"The same as yesterday. I'm being moved to patrol next week. I'll adjust." A weak smile didn't reach Rosie's eyes.

They all crowded into a small, windowless room. Lena agreeably slept in her stroller throughout the half hour of questions as Ella replayed the evening when Dumas had picked up Matt Clark on the side of the highway. After Hunter left them to join Boots in a second meeting room, Ella turned to Rosie. "Would you mind watching Lena for a few minutes while I go to the washroom?"

"Of course not. Take your time." She smiled at the baby in a way that gave Ella pause. Did all women of child-bearing age get this same dreamy look in their eyes? It had to be hormonal.

Instead of turning left toward the washrooms, Ella headed into the main office area. She scanned the room until her eyes landed on Kurt Auger's desk. He had his head down, typing on the keyboard and barely acknowledged her as she approached.

"Excuse me. I'm here giving a statement but thought I'd pop in to tell you about the story I'm writing."

He looked up. His eyes regarded her coldly, without any sign of interest.

"My name's Ella Tate, and I'm a freelance reporter as well as true crime podcaster."

"I know who you are. So?"

"I'm doing an in-depth story about sexual harassment within police services and abuse of power."

"Sounds like you're trying to get on the Me Too bandwagon. Good luck with that."

"Yeah, well seems there's been some of that allegedly going on with you at the centre. I've done some digging and found two women officers in Toronto who made complaints against you."

Auger blinked; his expression became less disinterested and more calculating. He tilted back in his chair and crossed his hands over his stomach. "Accusations that went nowhere."

"Granted, but not because you were proven innocent. In both cases, the women withdrew their allegations after receiving transfers. I'm sensing a pattern here."

"Officers change units all the time. I had nothing whatsoever to do with their choices."

"Well, fair warning to let you know I'm still digging. If there's a story the public should know, I'll get it out there."

His eyes narrowed. "That sounds like a threat. Well, here's a warning back at you, honey. Print one line of slander, and my lawyer will have you and your two-bit paper in court so fast, all your heads will be spinning. You'll be mighty sorry you ever started down this path. That's not a threat; it's a fact."

She didn't bother with a reply, instead holding his stare without flinching, even though a ripple of unease coursed through her. Auger wielded a degree of power and had few if any scruples. A man like this wouldn't hesitate to crush anybody in his way. She had to hand it to him. The family man, purveyor of law and order, was a brilliant front for a predator. Ella broke eye contact first, turned, and sauntered out of the office, aware of his gaze on her as she attempted to keep her shoulders back and not let him see any sign of weakness. Once in the hallway and out of his sightline, she slumped against the wall for a moment while she collected herself. Rosie Thorburn picked that moment to leave the meeting room, pushing the carriage ahead of her.

"Everything okay?" she asked as she hurried toward Ella.

"Fine. I was just running an idea for a story past Auger."

"Really? Why ask him?"

"Because the topic is abuse of power and sexual intimidation in the police force." She lowered her voice. "I didn't mention you, although I brought up two women officers in Toronto who brought allegations against him. Both moved into new positions after dropping the charges."

"Wow. So I wasn't the first."

"Most predators hone their tactics over time. If

you're ever alone with him, turn on your phone recorder, although be careful. There's something about the guy that makes me wary."

"You felt it too. He wasn't like this in Toronto when he recruited me. I foolishly considered him a mentor."

"Nothing foolish about giving someone the benefit of the doubt. These people are pros at secretly manipulating their prey. Are you out of the unit for certain?"

"Patrol next week. I'm okay with it, though. Things are going better with Brad, and we bought a house. I'm looking forward to the future and putting Auger in my rear view. This transfer will become a blip but not the defining moment in my career." She touched Ella's shoulder. "I appreciate what you're trying to do for me, even if Auger has won this round. I can't … I just can't take him on. Don't put yourself in any danger."

"I hate to see him get away with the sexual blackmail and what he's done to your career. He has to be stopped."

"He's been careful to keep his secrets. You need to be careful too. Auger's not going to take your threat lightly, so watch your back."

Ella nodded and took a few steps away from Rosie in case Auger left the office and found them together. She said over her shoulder, "If you want to connect again, text me and we can meet up at Finn's gym, where it's private. Until then, keep the faith and stay safe. I'll let you know when I come up with something concrete that we can use to bring the bastard down."

CHAPTER 40

Ella thought about driving to Ashton, but the morning had worked its way into early afternoon, and aches and fatigue convinced her to veto the idea. Instead, she picked up some fast food on the way home, navigating the stairs with Lena and a bag of take out, relieved to make it to the second floor without dropping either. Tony opened his door, and Celine Dion's voice filled the hallway, promising that her heart would go on. He leapt forward and reached for Lena, raising his voice to speak over the music.

"You look a sight, girl. Come in and take a load off."

"No thanks, Tony. I'm heading upstairs for a nap, if you're ready to look after Lena. My ribs and shoulder could do with another painkiller."

"Of course. I'll even turn down the volume on my stereo. Sweet dreams."

Once in her apartment, Ella put the burger and fries on a plate before pouring a glass of orange juice and popping a couple of pills. She carried her meal to the desk in the living room and sat in front of her blank computer screen. As she munched on the food, she thought over the encounter with Auger. She'd expected him to deny her accusations, so that was no surprise. Had she jumped the gun? Gone after Auger without enough concrete evidence? The idea that she'd let her anger override common sense and somehow blown her chance to corner him kept her from relaxing. Add to that Rosie Thorburn's dismissive attitude toward exposing him, and Ella wondered about continuing. Yet she hated to let him get away with intimidating Thorburn and derailing her career. She'd seen men like Auger grow bolder if they weren't confronted or brought to task.

The night before, she'd tracked down the two women officers in Toronto who'd made complaints against him and sent each an email with a brief message and her cell phone number. Neither had responded by the time she went to give her statement. Granted, she'd sent the messages after 2:00 a.m., and the women might not have opened them yet. Ella's eyes jumped over to the urn with her brother Danny's ashes on the window ledge. She knew that she had to be careful not to confuse their own tragic experiences with that of these women. She needed to stay objective. Giving in to frustration, she smacked the palm of her hand against the desk. *Damn it all. He's already gotten away with harassing three young women. He needs to be stopped before there are more victims.*

Ella downed the last of the orange juice and stood without turning on the computer. She'd believed the night before that Hunter had the man who killed the Petries under arrest. To find out Dumas hadn't been charged and had instead been set free reeked of police incompetence. Somebody higher up than Hunter must have pulled strings and given in to pressure. She couldn't imagine where this left the investigation. She'd need to make another trip to Ashton, maybe bring Tony along and spend some time chatting to the locals in the pub. Canard wanted a story with more background on Devina and Stu. He'd told her to keep digging regardless of who ended up getting arrested. Maybe the answers lay in the tightly knit little community.

She made her way to the bedroom, discarding her clothes on the floor as she went. The pain in her head was back, thrumming behind her eyes. Every square inch of her body ached, and fatigue made her movements sluggish. All the questions would need to wait until she'd slept and her body had a chance to recover. As she slipped under the covers, her mind landed on Stefan and his unusual silence. She realized in an uncomfortable moment of self-awareness that she hadn't given him a thought for a couple of days. He was likely ghosting her, and she'd been too wrapped up in her own stuff even to realize. They'd been dating a couple of months. She should have been more upset than she was about his silence. At the very least, she should have noticed. "Alone again," she muttered as the pills she'd taken earlier began to take effect." Her eyes closed, and she let out a soft moan, whether from the discomfort in her shoulder or a sudden flash of insight. *I'm simply not cut out for the long haul. Stefan is better off finding someone else.* The idea brought relief but no comfort as she drifted into a dreamless sleep.

———

LIAM HESITATED before pushing open the door to Churchills, a popular pub in Westboro a short drive from HQ. He knew that he should be looking forward to meeting the woman his sister Hannah had set him up with, but it felt like one more obligation to get through. He'd called Hannah as the go-between earlier in the day to move this evening's get-together from seven to nine thirty, and she'd assured him that Georgina wasn't put off by the later time.

Once inside, he gazed around the seats, trying to locate a woman sitting alone. The space was long and narrow, bar to his left, dark wooden tables and chairs, booths toward the back. There was a good crowd, and the place hummed with conversation. An attractive woman with long brown hair sat watching him from a table to his right. She smiled and waved when he looked her way. He waited for a server to pass by with a tray of food before approaching her.

"Georgina?"

"I am. And you must be Liam."

She held out a hand that he shook before sitting in the seat opposite her. "You work with Hannah, I understand."

"Yes, your sister is great. I figured someone that warm and lovely must have decent relatives." Georgina smiled.

A server arrived and took their order, and Liam felt himself relaxing. Georgina proved to be an easy conversationalist who didn't ask too much of him. She seemed to sense he was tired and kept the mood light.

"Listen," she said forty minutes in. "I can see you've had a long day, so why don't we wrap up and perhaps get together for a meal when your load is lighter at work?"

"I'm sorry, is it that obvious I need some sleep?"

"It is." She pointed to his phone on the table. "Do you mind? I can enter my number, and you can text when you'd like to meet up next?"

"I'd like that."

He paid the bill and walked her to her car a block away. She kissed him on the cheek before climbing into the front seat. She pulled into traffic while he walked in the opposite direction to retrieve his vehicle. Georgina had been a breath of fresh air and a pleasant surprise. He hadn't felt a crazy attraction, but maybe this was a good thing. They could take it slowly and see where things led.

He checked his phone before opening his car door. All seemed quiet. Nothing pressing on the investigation, so he could go directly home with a clear conscience. He experienced a mild disappointment that Ella hadn't texted with any updates. He held his regret to just that, not wanting to think any more deeply about his feelings for her or the reason why she had replaced Georgina in his thoughts so soon after their first meeting.

CHAPTER 41

Ella and Tony decided to make the Ashton Brew Pub their first stop for a bite to eat late the following morning. The solid night's sleep had done wonders for Ella's body, and a renewed energy replaced the previous day's fatigue. Tony insisted on driving, and she agreed. Today, she'd take things easy and not overtax herself as she'd been doing.

They arrived at the pub shortly after one o'clock and hurried inside as the first drops of rain began to fall. She could have sworn that three sets of guilty eyes stared in her direction as she stood in the doorway to the back room. She half-turned to Tony waiting behind her and said under her breath, "Let's go see what's preoccupying the happy trio."

She plunked down at the table immediately next to Miriam and Everett Johannson and Everett's sister Nelly, whom Ella guessed was on her lunch break from the corner store. The anxiety level punched in at high with discomfort evident on their faces. Reba arrived a few moments later with plates of burgers and fries that she set in front of the three of them before she took Ella's and Tony's orders.

"You city folk can't stay away," she said.

"Love us some back country," Tony agreed. He'd put on a red and white checked shirt, blue jeans, and cowboy boots that Ella could have sworn were brand new. He pointed at Nelly's burger. "We'll order food in a minute, but for now a couple of coffees, little lady." He'd slowed his speech so that he sounded like John Wayne in an old Western movie and winked at Reba. Ella wanted to clock him on the side of the head but relaxed when she saw everyone else chuckling. He'd effectively broken the tension.

"Is it true the police let the man who took Matt Clark go?" Nelly asked, jabbing her fork in Ella's direction.

"Yes. Apparently they didn't have enough to charge him."

Nelly exchanged a look with Everett. "Insanity, if you ask me. What do the cops need before they put him away? A signed confession? Sheesh." She looked back at Ella and aimed her fork at the sling. "What happened to you?"

"I fell. It looks worse than it is."

"I hope you aren't covering up for an abusive partner. I've been guilty of protecting a man's sorry ass in my day, and the only answer is to break it off."

Miriam cleared her throat. "So the police believe this man who took Matt is guilty of the murders, and they're still digging for proof?"

"That would be my guess." Ella straightened as Reba slid a cup of coffee in front of her. She scanned the three at the next table, her stare coming to rest on

Everett. "So, what's brought you all together this morning?"

"We were reminiscing about Devina, having a cuppa in her honour."

"You and Devina used to meet here most mornings. Was she worried at all about someone from her past or, I don't know, business or personal issues?"

Everett held her gaze, but his fingers toyed with the coffee mug, tapping and twisting it back and forth in his bear of a hand. "I'm not giving up her confidences, if that's what you're after. She's allowed her privacy, even in death."

"But what if some detail she told you could lead to her killer?"

Ella watched to see if this shot hit a nerve, but Everett remained calm, fully in control. "Devina never told me about anyone threatening her. Doesn't mean she didn't have secrets. She led a vagabond life in the States until she met Stu."

"What did you think of Stu?"

The two women at Everett's table had gone still, heads down, neither looking at Everett. He took a moment to consider his answer. "Stu struck me as a user. Devina had this childlike trust in people, and he knew how to get what he needed."

"Can you give an example?"

Nelly reached over and put her hand on Everett's wrist as if to warn him to stop talking. He shook her off in a quick motion, dropping his hand into his lap. He continued without acknowledging her. "Devina had a lot of money when she met Stu. She'd been saving for some time and had won a couple of jackpots in Vegas. She was also in line to inherit the farm, which happened five years ago. The police might be better advised to look at people in his past, as opposed to Devina's."

"She adored Stu," Nelly said. "He couldn't have been all bad, or she wouldn't have brought him with her to the farm. She was no dummy."

"I'm not sure intelligence has anything to do with women sticking by lousy partners." Everett's jaw tightened. "But you're right. Devina had a thing for the man. He doled out enough crumbs for her to stay committed to their marriage."

"Not our business to sling mud at dead people," Miriam said. "We should get on home, Everett. That delivery is coming in half an hour."

"And I'm due back at the store," Nelly said, pushing away her empty plate.

Ella and Tony remained seated while all three filed out of the room without a backward glance.

"Was it something you said?" Tony asked. "Because they couldn't get out of here fast enough."

Ella replayed her conversation with Everett before answering. "It's the first time anyone spoke ill of Stu. Everett had a thing for Devina in high school. She was the love of his life, by all accounts. His opinion could come out of a deep well of jealousy."

"Does that still happen?" Tony asked.

"Does what still happen?"

"Romantic obsessions spanning fifty years. I'd have thought a rough country man like Everett would be the last one to keep a flame burning."

"Passion doesn't belong exclusively to the cultured, as you well know, my friend. Sure, Everett never left this village, and his worldly experience appears limited, but he might have built up a fantasy about Devina that rekindled his infatuation upon her return."

"Not sure Stu or Miriam would have been comfortable with their partners' renewed friendship, if that's true. Certainly looks like Nelly's siding with or covering up for her brother. You said Everett met Devina for coffee every morning?"

"Yup.

"I'm smelling a fish. Might be a rotting red herring but sure makes one wonder."

"Yeah, even if the two of them were discreet, meeting out in the open like that, tongues were a-wagging. I'd be gobsmacked if Stu and Miriam didn't secretly worry about their spouses' daily rendezvous." Ella looked around the bar but didn't spot anyone else who looked familiar. "You up for a bowl of chowder? We can linger and maybe somebody else will come in who knew the Petries."

"I got nothing but time, little lady. Let's giddy up to the trough and fill our boots."

"Good lord, Tony. Stop talking before I lasso you to a post in the other room and go in search of a horse whip."

———

Rosie smiled in relief at Hunter when he suggested they take a run out to Ashton before lunch. She'd avoided looking in Auger's direction since he entered the office but didn't know how she'd survive the entire day with her stomach churning and head aching. Ella Tate had wanted her to take him on, but flight always won out over fight in her confrontations. She felt physically ill at the thought of standing up to him.

She drove while Hunter read reports on his laptop. He recited key points from the interviews to refresh both their memories. "Where should we go first?" Rosie asked as they exited the Queensway.

"Devina's uncle, Terrence Garnett, arrived last night. Let's pull into the Petries' driveway and see if he has anything new to add. I've already called to let him know we're on our way."

"He's the sole person to inherit, is that right?"

"Correct. I spoke with him on the phone early on, so meeting him in person should close off this thread."

The rain had started when they left Ottawa, a light pattering on the roof of the car that gained in intensity as she drove. Rosie parked close to the Petrie house, and they made a dash for the open front door. Terrence stood behind the screen, watching their approach.

"Coffee's brewing," he said after introductions. "Let's sit in the kitchen. The cleaners have begun in the living room, but I'd prefer not to talk in there. They'll be returning later this afternoon."

They followed him down the hall, his grey ponytail bobbing as he walked. He'd made a start on the kitchen, filling boxes with dishes and pots, but he'd left three mugs on the counter. He filled the cups without asking and pulled a carton of milk out of the fridge, telling them to help themselves. They took up positions leaning against counters and the stove.

Rosie read '60s hippy in Terrence's leather sandals, loose jeans, and tie-dyed shirt. His head was a bald dome except for the circle of hair halfway down that he'd secured at the nape of his neck with an elastic band. He began speaking before Hunter had time to ask his first question.

"Glad we can have another chat. I was in shock when you phoned last week and might have omitted a few details about Devina and Stu now that I've had a chance to think things through."

Rosie detected a shift in Hunter's expression and knew Terrence had his full attention. Hunter had told her once that often the breakthrough in a case arrived when least expected. She realized how much she was going to miss him as her partner. "Anything you can tell us would be appreciated," he said.

"I guess I forgot to mention that my stepdaughter Linny gelled with Devina when they were in high school. They're the same age, and Devina even came to live with us for the better part of a year when she moved out of this house."

Rosie interjected after Hunter gave her a nod to go ahead, "I'd heard from her friends that Devina went to the States when she left Ashton."

"That's what she told people. A boy she'd been dating wanted to chase after her, so she kept her location vague."

"Was his name Everett Johannson?"

"Sorry, I can't remember. We're talking a lot of years under the bridge. Anyhow, Linny was in touch yesterday and was as shocked as I was to hear about the deaths."

"I'd like to speak with your stepdaughter. How can I get ahold of her?" Hunter had his phone out to record her contact info.

"Sorry, she's travelling in India and out of reach the next few weeks. She's at one of those meditation centres that takes away electronics at the door. Maybe I can fill you in anyway."

Hunter slipped the phone into his pocket and nodded. "We're wondering if someone from Devina's or Stu's pasts might be responsible for their murders."

"Yeah, I remember you raising that idea when you called. I asked Linny if she knew of anybody, but she couldn't come up with a name or a reason. Devina was into drugs at one time, but not heavily and never dealt. Stu wasn't dealing when she took up with him. I only met Stu twice, the one time when they drove up to Vancouver and stayed for a week and the second when they stopped in five years ago on the way to move in here. They'd been married a year the first time, and Devina was crazy about him. He treated her fine, and we were all pleased for her, finding a man who made her happy."

"Was this the case on their second visit?"

"I didn't notice any animosity or tension. The opposite, in fact."

"Had Stu ever been involved in anything illegal?"

"I'm inclined to say no. He claimed never to deal drugs or get sucked into anything criminal. He worked at different jobs. Construction, landscaping, that kind of thing. Maybe some under-the-table work, but that was common back then. Still is, for all I know. The man was a talker, would have made a terrific salesman. I told him that, and he laughed. Found the idea humorous. He was from Seattle originally and has a sister, Margaret, still living in the city. His mom is there too but is in assisted living. Dementia. I called to let Margaret know about the deaths and am keeping her updated. She's in a wheelchair and never travels due to multiple sclerosis.

I'm going to take Stu's and Devina's ashes to her when Linny gets back, and we'll scatter them in the ocean. I know Devina would like that."

He spoke quickly, and Rosie struggled to keep up as she took notes. Everything he said sounded positive, but she sensed he was sugar-coating his observations. Hunter must have felt the same. He asked, "What was Linny's opinion of Stu?"

"Good. She said he was charming. Kind to Devina."

"Is there a but in there?"

"Not really. Just we both worried he had no money or stable job, but Devina said that didn't matter to her. She was a free spirit and generous. Not all that taken with material things."

"So the marriage was a good one?"

"That I wouldn't know firsthand, but Linny said Devina was always upbeat when they spoke. Stu encouraged her to move home to Ashton, and she didn't like to deny him anything. He was keen for her to claim the farm and for them to put down roots."

Terrence had an odd expression on his face, and Rosie thought he was leaving something unsaid. She glanced at Hunter to see if he'd caught it too, but he was reading a message on his cell phone. Going on intuition, she said, "Devina didn't come back here often after she left at the end of high school."

"No." His eyes skimmed over her and landed on a spot above her right shoulder. He seemed uncomfortable for the first time. "My sister, Devina's mother, was a hard woman."

"Hard? How so?"

"Hard to get along with, hard to like, hard on Devina. Gail was as rigid as they come. Loved her Bible above all else. She had no idea how to deal with a teenage daughter in the '70s, especially one as pretty and popular as Devina. I used to tell Gail she'd drive the girl away. Sadly, my warning came to pass. Devina was strong enough to leave as soon as she was able, but that first year when she lived with us, I could tell her mother's attitude had left its mark. Devina had a sadness about her, a need to be liked. Linny confided in me years later that Devina slept around quite a bit, even for that era. She was searching for a deep connection is my guess. Stu was that for her. She'd have walked on nails for the man. Strange, really, how she ended up back here. I can't imagine it was easy, even after all that time."

Hunter waited for Terrence to finish speaking and checked with Rosie in case she had more questions. She shook her head. Devina had sharpened into focus for the first time, and her sorrow for the woman deepened.

"What do you plan to do with the farm?" Hunter asked, setting his empty coffee cup on the counter.

"I've had an offer, and lawyers and real estate agents are working on the sale as I speak."

"Who's made the offer?"

He hesitated before shrugging. "Guess it can't hurt to tell you. Calvin Frisk owns the neighbouring farm, and this gives him room to expand. I guess if we can't keep the land in the family, he's the next best thing."

They wrapped up the interview, and Rosie followed Hunter out the front door. He stopped on the top step and surveyed the property until she moved in next to him. The rain had lessened to a drizzle, but puddles filled the crevices, and water pooled in the lower-lying sections. The air smelled damp and clean, pleasing after the mustiness inside the house and the strong smell of cleaning products.

"Frisk didn't wait long to put in his offer," Hunter said. "This piece of land has to be worth a fair penny."

"He was one of the two who found the Petries." Rosie pulled her hood up over her hair. "Do you think Devina moving back here stirred up something that led to her and Stu's deaths? Maybe Matt Clark wasn't the reason at all. Calvin was in her circle back in high school and could have had a thing for her, like all the other boys seemed to. He could easily have started something up with her when Stu was off playing darts or doing charity work."

Hunter turned his head and shot her a wry grin. "As in we've been chasing the wrong trail? I agree we need to look at all options besides the obvious one. Let's visit Frisk and the other neighbours with that in mind and see what else we can dig out of them. While we can't definitively rule out the New York connection, we need to keep open minds and cross off people from the community."

Rosie turned her face toward the side window and lifted a finger to trace a raindrop streaking down the glass. The conifer trees beyond the driveway swayed in the gusty wind, storm clouds, swollen and grey, lining the ridge of sky above. "I'm going to miss your mentorship," she said. "I wish this had worked out."

"I'll be waiting for you to reapply to Major Crimes, because you honestly are cut out to be a detective. Don't be discouraged, Rosie. Think of this transfer as being sent down to the minors for a stint to fine-tune before you join the major-league team again."

She wanted to believe him, but as long as Auger was

around, he'd make certain she never made detective. Hunter had no idea. She turned back. "Yeah, that's a good way to look at it. Thanks … for everything."

"This isn't goodbye, Thorburn. I promise you our paths will cross again, and we'll take up right where we've left off."

CHAPTER 42

Jimmy knew he shouldn't be eavesdropping on his sister and her friends, but he was bored and they'd left the door to her room open. This might be a new low, confirmation that he was a loser. Theo had more friends and fit in better than he did by a long shot. He wished he'd been born with some of her sunny outlook, the knack of being easy with people. Matt was the first person who'd made him look forward to getting up in the morning. Of all the kids living in and around Ashton, Matt had chosen him to go fishing with, to hang out. *Well, not anymore.*

The three girls didn't do more than whisper secrets and giggle until Jimmy couldn't stand it another second. He returned to his room and lay on the bed with his arms crossed behind his head. Before long, Theo's friends giggled their way downstairs, reminding him of a flock of gobbling turkeys. He heard their moms speaking with his in the front door hallway, and soon they collected their daughters and their tires crunched on the driveway as they returned to their own homes. Jimmy stayed where he was, watching the curtains billow and twist in the breeze coming through the open window.

Theo's footsteps climbed the stairs and stopped in front of his door. "Why are you in bed?"

"I'm tired."

"We haven't even eaten lunch, silly."

She crossed the room and jumped onto the mattress next to him. She was holding her iPad, her constant companion.

"Did you delete that Instagram page?" he asked.

"Yup."

"For real?"

"I stopped posting photos."

"Theo, if Mom finds out…"

"But she won't. She has secrets too, Jimmy. Big ones."

"Oh yeah? Like what?" He rolled his head sideways to study her, quite certain she was making something up to distract him. She was wearing a pink tutu with a sparkly crinoline skirt, matching tights and bright red lipstick, slightly smeared. One of her friends had tied clumps of her hair into ponytails that stuck out at odd angles, fastened with scrunchies.

"Like not staying for my dance classes." She put a finger to her lips. "I'm not supposed to tell Daddy."

Jimmy saw a gap opening in front of him that he instinctively knew would lead to trouble if he continued probing. It was unlike his mother to ask Theo or him to keep something from their dad. His mind scrambled for an innocent explanation. Perhaps she was working on a surprise gift for their father or going to a gym to get in better shape and feel better about living on the farm. She'd hide that from his dad because he'd have considered joining a gym wasteful when work on the farm was more than enough to keep her in shape. While Jimmy wanted to believe she wouldn't deliberately lie to their dad for a bad reason, part of him remained worried. Theo waited, her vivid blue eyes staring at him while she plucked at a loose sequin on her skirt. He hesitated. But if he didn't find out more, the worry would only blossom into a bigger lump in his chest. "Where did she go?" he finally asked.

"Jimmy! Theo!" their mom called to them from the bottom of the stairs.

"Coming, Mom!" Jimmy yelled back. "Tell me later," he hissed as Theo leapt toward the door, clutching her iPad.

She stopped and turned. Her eyes danced with mischief. "She met that man." Theo twirled until she faced him again. "And you can't tell Mom, but I told Daddy."

————

LUNCH — actually an early dinner — took on new meaning. His mom had rallied and cooked a chicken in the oven with bread stuffing, roast potatoes, and crisp green beans, just like Jimmy liked them. Theo bubbled with stories about Amelia, Becka, and dance class. He caught her eye once as she spoke about her ballet teacher, but she managed not to let any secrets spill out. Jimmy hadn't really noticed how quiet his parents were at the table lately with Theo filling in the spaces, but this time, he sat still and listened. He realized that his mom encouraged Theo's chatter while his dad kept his head lowered over his plate, only looking up now and then to grunt or reach for a bowl. Had his parents always been this distant, and if so, why hadn't he noticed? The air in the kitchen felt heavy. Nobody laughed or smiled except when his mom absentmindedly reacted to Theo's stories. None of them noticed his silence.

His mom announced that dessert would be big bowls of cherry ice cream with sprinkles on top to celebrate their return to school the following day. Theo's dance classes would settle back into their regular schedule after school on Thursdays and Saturday mornings. Their dad said he'd have his dessert after a while. He excused himself and went out to the barn to check on a cow that he expected to give birth later in the week, and the mood in the kitchen lightened. Even the rain had stopped momentarily, and the sun had moved into a position where shafts of golden beams poured through the window over the sink. The three of them took their full bowls into the living room, and their mom put a record on the old stereo. Taylor Swift. Theo and his mom began dancing and lip-syncing, using their spoons as microphones. Jimmy sat on the couch and watched his mother. She seemed less herself somehow. Thinner and more tired. She'd been on edge since the Petries died. He wondered why she was keeping a secret from their dad. Were they going to split up? He knew other kids whose parents had divorced. They lived in two houses and shuttled back and forth for holidays and weekends. He'd hate if that happened to his family. He couldn't imagine his father looking after him and Theo.

The music stopped, and his mom and Theo flopped onto the couch beside him. He sat quietly until he felt like his head would burst. Anger was growing inside him like a balloon inflating. For once, Theo's smiling, innocent face made him want to lash out. She'd been keeping a secret Instagram account, posting pictures of Matt that probably brought that man to Ashton to find him. She'd told his dad something his mom hadn't wanted him to know. His parents thought she was this cute little doll who lit up their lives with sunshine while he was either ignored or blamed for anything that went wrong. It killed him that she got away with so much.

"So where did you go when Theo was at her dance classes, Mom? She said that you never stuck around." He recoiled at the sight of his mother's shocked face.

"What has Theo told you?" Her eyes darted from his to focus on his sister. "Tell me now." Her voice was dangerously quiet.

He wished he could take back his question and fumbled for an answer. "Just that you didn't stay to watch her dance and you met someone. A man."

"Theo."

"I know it was a secret, Mama. I shouldn't have told." Theo's voice rose in a plaintive wail.

"Who else did you tell?"

Theo was crying now, but their mom didn't relent. "Who else?"

"Just Daddy."

"Oh, my god." His mom flopped back on the couch and put a hand over her eyes. "When, Theo? When did you tell your father?"

"I don't remember."

"You have to. Think hard. Was it before the Petries—"

Theo's face lit up. "Yes, just before. Your suitcase was packed and inside your closet. I knew you were going on a trip, and I asked Daddy."

"What did he say? How did he react?" His mom grabbed Theo's arm and shook it until she moaned in fear.

"He asked me if I saw you together with that man. I said sometimes, and I saw you kissing in the car once. Daddy got very quiet and told me I wasn't to share this with anyone else. It was private. I never told anybody else. Never, never." Theo was rubbing her arm and shaking her head. "I wouldn't. No. No. No. I wouldn't."

Jimmy watched his mom work out something in her head. Her eyes scanned the far wall before she looked toward the entrance to the living room. The hand that was holding Theo's arm let go and made a fist that she lifted to cover her mouth. Jimmy shifted to follow his mom's sightline. Their father stood in the shadows of the hallway, holding a melting bowl of ice cream. He must have come into the house while the music was playing, and they hadn't heard him enter. His eyes held their mother's gaze, but he stayed where he was, staring at them without moving. Fear rose up in Jimmy like a burning flame. His mom was the first one to break the silence.

"Go upstairs, children," she said without looking at them. After Jimmy stood and moved in front of her, she said in a voice so low he could barely hear, "Take Theo into the bathroom and lock the door. Don't come out until I say."

CHAPTER 43

Calvin Frisk's driveway extended in a long, straight line up an incline to a vinyl-sided, two-storey box house. Farm machinery and tires littered the side yard in front of a barn covered in faded, peeling red paint while cornfields stretched beyond the house as far as the eye could see. Cows and sheep grazed in a penned-off field to the right of the property.

"Not to be sexist, but this place lacks a woman's touch," Thorburn said, her head twisting back and forth. "Even the curtains on the living room window are hung crooked."

Liam peered through the windshield. "Are you saying that men are the slob half of the species?"

"Not at all, but I'll wager Calvin Frisk lives alone."

"I won't bet against you."

"Do you think he'd kill his neighbours to get their land?"

"The Petries owned a nicely situated, lush bit of property. Their farmhouse with the wraparound porch has this place beat hands-down. I'd say people have killed for less, but that doesn't mean he did. It's simply an avenue of enquiry to cross off the list. He had motive and opportunity, living so close by. He also stayed in the truck and let Lanny find the bodies. I'm not sure that means anything—"

"But we need to make certain it doesn't." Thorburn grinned. "You've made me a fan of setting one theory aside to look at the entire picture, Hunter. Not sure how useful it'll be on patrol, but I'll always keep an open mind."

"You'll do us proud."

They found Calvin in the barn, working on a tractor. He stopped what he was doing and stepped outside, wiping his greasy hands on a rag stained with motor oil. "I've already been interviewed, but if you have more questions, go ahead and ask. I was finishing up here anyway."

"We do have a few more questions. Thanks for being so accommodating." Liam paused, organizing his thoughts. "As I recall, you said that you worked late Saturday evening when Stu and Devina died and went to bed after a quick supper. You didn't speak with anyone, and nobody can confirm your whereabouts that night. Is this accurate?"

"S'about right, yeah. It's not as if I expected to need an alibi."

"I believe you're not married?"

"Nope. Never had the urge to settle down with one woman. I enjoy going to the pub unhindered."

"Do you date?" Thorburn asked and smiled at him as if she already knew the answer. Liam tried to see Frisk through her lens. He was early-fifties, broad-shouldered and fit, with an easy manner, eyes the colour of dark chocolate and a full beard that suited him. Liam imagined many would find him attractive enough. He appeared to take her smile as a compliment.

"There are lots of ladies who enjoy male company without strings attached."

"Even married ones?"

"On occasion. If they feel the need for some variety, I'm up for the challenge." He grinned at her, his stare never leaving her face.

"How about Devina Petrie? Did you ever have a relationship with her?"

"She was a friend, my neighbour, nothing more." He tilted his head as if remembering. "We talked once about fidelity. She believed in it, and I didn't."

Thorburn's brow furrowed. "What about her nearly daily meetings with Everett Johannson? Had they rekindled their high school romance?"

"I'd be surprised. She loved Stu, rightly or wrongly, through thick and thin. Even Everett got the message eventually. For Devina coffee was just coffee. A break in her day."

Liam nodded at Thorburn and drew Calvin's attention and gaze. "What did you think of Stu? I'm curious."

"He was good company on dart night at the pub. A talker and self-proclaimed expert on lots of subjects. He liked his beer and had ample capacity. I'm not convinced he wanted to farm, though. I figured the two of them would sell and move before long, if he had his way."

"We heard that he encouraged her to move back here."

"He probably had his reasons, none of which had to do with farming."

"You've put in an offer on the Petrie property." Liam said the sentence mildly, without judgement.

"Is that what this is about? I was under the impression that you arrested the killer." Calvin rolled his eyes before staring down Liam. "Yeah, I put in an offer. I want to control who moves in next to me. Not a crime, as far as I know."

"It's a nice piece of land to farm," Liam said before turning away and squinting into the sun.

"Terrence gave me a fair price, but even then, I had to take out a second mortgage. I'm probably going to rent the land, maybe turn it into a co-op. I'm simply preventing a development from going in. So any more questions, Detective? It's been a long day, I missed lunch, and I'm hungry."

Liam sent Thorburn a questioning look, and she shook her head. "No, that's it for now. We may be back."

"I'd expect nothing less." Calvin tossed the rag onto the ground and left them without another word. Thorburn was the first to break the silence.

"He might have put the moves on Devina. It wouldn't be difficult for them to meet, living so close to each other."

"Killed for their farm or for passion?" Liam took one last look around and started walking back to their car. "It'll be hard to prove either way but is definitely worth considering. Let's go to the pub and mull things

over. Talk of lunch and all this fresh air have given me
an appetite."

———

"THE ASHTON PUB's half-full or half-empty, whichever
way you see the world," Liam mused. "Looks like we've
missed the worst of the lunchtime rush." Most patrons
had a beer or glass of wine in front of them, along with
half-eaten plates of fish and chips, burgers and poutine,
nachos. "Man that smells good," he said, looking around
for anyone he knew and coming up disappointed. "Let's
try the back room with a view of the river.

Thorburn led the way and tilted her head in the
direction of Ella Tate and Tony at a table off by themselves at the end of the line of windows.

"Let's go sit with them," Liam said, experiencing a
buzz of pleasure at the sight of Ella. Thorburn never
commented on his cozy relationship with a reporter, and
he took her silence as acceptance of this odd alliance.
He wondered if his new partner would turn the same
blind eye.

Ella looked up from her bowl of soup at their
approach. Tony set down his spoon and said, "Well, if it
isn't. How are you two fine detectives doing this Ashton
afternoon?"

"Better once we eat. Mind if we join you?"

"Belly up," Tony said, pushing out the chair next to
him. "Take a load off, pard'ners."

"You're looking very Calgary Stampede today,
Tony," Liam said, taking the proffered seat. "Any particular reason?"

Tony made a point of looking around. "*This* is back country, is it not? I'm merely fitting in with the locals."

"We're twenty minutes out of Ottawa and five minutes from Carleton Place. *This* is not exactly *Rawhide* country," Ella said, giving him a fond yet exasperated look. "Maybe stop calling our server 'little lady.' She seems affronted every time you say it."

"I believe my John Wayne drawl suits the setting and gives a fitting nod to the inhabitants' settler roots."

"If you can't tell whether Tony is serious or not, accept that most of what he says is in jest," Ella said before pointing at the menu. "Try the chowder. It's delicious." She set the spoon down next to her empty bowl. Thorburn and Ella grinned at each other, and Liam sensed a deeper connection between the two women than he'd witnessed before. Had they come to a mutual understanding, much like he'd fostered with Ella? He wasn't sure how he felt about that.

After the server arrived and he and Thorburn had placed their orders, Ella turned to Rosie. "Any change of heart on the matter we discussed?"

Thorburn shot Liam an apologetic glance before looking back at Ella. "I'm good. So, have you uncovered anything we should know about the Petrie case? I'm guessing that's why you drove all the way out to the western fringe."

"Adept change of subject, but okay." Ella broke eye contact with Thorburn and looked across the table at Liam. "If the murders have nothing to do with Matt Clark staying at their house for the summer, then who else? It takes examining the neighbours through a new lens."

"Exactly," he said. "The murders don't have the feel

of stranger randomness. We're going back through time-lines — who was where when — and relationships, both past and present. The answer has to be somewhere in the tangle."

Their server arrived with two glasses of draft and two chowders, and the discussion paused. Liam and Thorburn dug in while Tony and Ella watched them eat.

"You two cowboys be chowing down," Tony said. He slapped the table with his palm. "Giddy up, giddy up."

"I seriously can't take you anywhere," Ella said, "and I really can't take you anymore."

Liam's cell phone rang in his pocket, and he groaned. He fumbled around until he pulled it out and flipped it over to see call display. "Unexpected," he said, glancing at Thorburn before swiping up. "Detective Hunter here."

He listened. "Can you speak up, Jimmy?" The boy's voice rose in his ear. "Okay, Jimmy. Stay calm. We're on our way." He listened again. Someone was wailing in the background. "Stay where you are. We'll be there in a few minutes and will get this sorted."

"What is it?" Ella asked.

Liam stood, still holding the phone to his ear. "Something ugly is going on at the Dooley farm. Thorburn, we need to get there right away."

Ella started to rise. "Can we be of any help?"

Liam motioned for her to remain seated. "Stay put for now. I'll let you know when things are settled. Thorburn, you ready?"

"Of course."

"Might be a domestic," he said as they hurried out

the front door of the pub after he paid their tab. "Jimmy sounded terrified. Said his parents are having an argument."

"Should I call for backup?"

"Let's hold off until we find out what we're dealing with. Call Dispatch, though, to let them know where we're going. Let's hope Lanny and Hope have their disagreement settled by the time we arrive."

CHAPTER 44

The yelling seemed to go on forever. Theo had covered her ears and curled up, whimpering in a corner of the bathroom, knees tight against her chest. Jimmy leaned against the door and tried to hear what his parents were saying. He'd left Theo's phone on the stool next to the tub after calling the detective. The cop had promised to be here soon, and then his parents would return to normal. They'd stop fighting, put on their "we-have-company" faces, and his mother would serve coffee and cake, or at least that's how Jimmy imagined it.

His parents never argued, not like this. Silence was their usual method of dealing with anger, and Jimmy would gladly trade that now in place of this screaming. He heard a loud crash followed by a thump and jumped back. Theo lifted her head and stared at him, eyes wide and scared. "Why are they fighting, Jimmy? Make it stop."

"I wish I could."

"Is this my fault?"

"No, definitely not."

He turned the door handle and looked into the hall-way. The lights were off, and shadows criss-crossed the carpet. Another smash from downstairs, and he knew he had to get down there, no matter what their mother had said. He looked back at Theo, who had gotten out of her crouch and was standing still, close to the far wall. "You stay here, and I'll go make them stop. Be sure not to leave the bathroom. Promise me, Theo?"

She put her thumb into her mouth and bobbed her head up and down. He tried to smile at her. "It'll be all right. I'll be back to get you soon."

He closed the door behind him, walked as silently as he could to the head of the stairs, and leaned over the banister. His parents were in the living room. His father was speaking, not as loudly as before, and Jimmy took this as a good sign. Maybe they'd gotten the anger out and were now talking things through. He thought about returning to Theo, even took a step backward. Then he remembered phoning the detective. He'd be here soon, and somebody had to let him in, to explain that the call was a misunderstanding. He hoped his parents would forgive him. Maybe they wouldn't have to know. He'd gotten away with hiding Matt in the house for a few days and making a phone call to the cops wasn't nearly as bad as that. He crept down the stairs, avoiding the creaky spots and stopping at the bottom to listen. His dad's voice rose for a moment, and then silence. Jimmy moved closer to the doorway but stayed out of sight.

"You knew I wasn't happy living here." His mother. She sounded as if she was pleading for his dad to under-stand. "I said many, many times that I needed more."

"What about the kids? Were you planning on leaving them too?"

"I can't — this is too hard." Jimmy could hear her sobbing and froze as her sadness filled him. He wanted to run to her but hesitated.

"I can't lose you, Hope. I'll do whatever you want. Sell the farm, move into the city."

"How can I live with you now? Your jealousy has ruined us. No, I'm not ... let go of me. I said let go of me!"

Jimmy could hear them struggling, and fear propelled him forward. He skidded into the living room and yelled, "Stop it! Stop it, Daddy!"

His mother looked so small and terrified, her face streaked with tears and blood smeared across her mouth. Her favourite lamp and a vase of flowers lay smashed on the floor next to the couch. Cold fear pumped through Jimmy's veins. His mother was no match for his father, who stood holding her shoulders with both his hands. The veins on his neck stood out taut with the strain of keeping her in place. Jimmy lunged and wrapped an arm around his father's neck, trying to pull him away from his mother. She began screaming and twisting. His father let go of one of her shoulders and reached across to knock Jimmy off his back. Jimmy's grip loosened, and he fell with a violent jolt onto the hardwood floor, his head barely missing the coffee table. He stared up at his father, who scowled with the cold, blank expression of a stranger. His mother stepped away from his dad, whose gaze remained focused on Jimmy. She held out a hand toward him, beckoning for him to get off the floor and come to her. His dad's head turned in her direction.

"You shouldn't be here, Jimmy. Lanny, let him up. This has nothing to do with the children."

Jimmy scrambled to his feet and backed up until he was next to her. His dad ground the palms of his hands into his eyes and moaned. "I didn't mean it. I only wanted to stop him from taking you away."

"I'm not a possession. You had no right——"

He dropped his hands and glared. "I had every right. *You* are my wife. *We* signed a contract."

"Well, this life isn't what I signed on for. I want out."

"You can't mean that. Give me another chance. I can make it work."

Jimmy held his breath. *Please give him another chance. Please, please keep our family together.*

His mom met Jimmy's eyes, and her face crumpled for a split-second. She inhaled a long, shaky breath and let the air out slowly. He couldn't read what she was trying to tell him. She looked over at his dad and whispered, "You know that's not possible. Not after what you've done."

Two things happened almost simultaneously. Someone thumped on the front door as Jimmy's dad took a step toward his mother with one fist raised at shoulder level. His mom jumped back, raising an arm to protect her face. Before Jimmy could think, he threw himself in between them, yelling at his dad to stop. He took the blow from his father's fist on his collarbone, and pain seared across his chest and down his arm. His mother screamed as he fell back and his head cracked against the arm of a chair. He could hear the front door smash open and heard running feet as his eyes closed and the world began to spin. Movement all around him and a hand on his forehead. His parents had stopped yelling at each other, for which he was grateful. The detective, Hunter, kept saying close to his ear that everything was going to be okay. He wasn't sure if this was true but closed his eyes and tried to keep the world from spinning. He wondered why he didn't hurt more than he did. His mother's hand held on to his but the rest of him felt cold and numb. He couldn't hear anything beyond his own heart pounding in his ears. He wondered if this was what it felt like to die.

————

LIAM HANDCUFFED Lanny Dooley and escorted him to the back seat of a waiting police car after the ambulance sped away with red light flashing and siren blaring to the nearest hospital with Jimmy and Thorburn in the back. Lanny sat silently, like a deflated balloon, shoulders hunched and chin resting on his chest, staring straight ahead, all fight gone as Liam gave instructions to the officers to take him to HQ on Elgin Street.

Hope was sitting on the boot rack in the front hallway, rocking her daughter in her arms, when Liam returned inside. She'd agreed to stay back and drive with him to the hospital so that she had time to find Theo upstairs and comfort her as best she could. It had taken a while to locate and draw the girl out of the closet where she'd taken refuge, and that had only been accomplished with the help of her favourite doll. Hope's entire body was trembling as Liam stood looking down at her. She attempted to regain her composure, standing and setting Theo on the floor while keeping a firm hold of her hand. "We should go to the hospital," she said.

"Do you have everything you need?" he asked. "You could be gone a while."

"I'll get my purse. Would it be okay if we dropped Theo off at a friend's on the way? She's had enough upset for one day."

"Of course."

"I want to stay with you, Mommy. I want to see Jimmy."

"You'll have more fun at Amelia's house, and I won't be long. We can read your favourite storybook when I come home."

They set off, and Hope arranged by text for Theo to visit her friend. Theo was sombre when Hope walked her to their door, but her tears had dried, and she went inside the house without a fuss. Hope climbed into the front passenger seat on her return, and Liam backed out of the driveway onto the highway. They had a half hour ride ahead of them, and he intended to draw out her story by the time they reached the hospital.

"The cut on your cheek—"

"Is nothing." She dabbed at the crusted blood with her fingertips. "A shard of glass from the vase." She looked out the side window for a moment, composing herself. "This is all my fault. I should have thought of a better way."

"A better way?"

She turned her head to stare at him then. Her large eyes glistened with gathering tears. "A better way to leave my husband. I believed Stu Petrie was my ticket out of here. My chance at the life I wanted." She was silent a moment, and Liam gave her the space to tell the story in her own time. She began speaking after a long pause. "It started innocently enough. I went for a walk while Theo was in dance class and it began raining. I stopped in at Tim Hortons to wait out the worst of it, and Stu was sitting at a table. He invited me to join him. I hadn't spoken with him before that morning and was pleasantly surprised by his sense of humour and his interest in so many subjects. We talked for almost an hour. It was as if he really saw me and empathized with my struggle to live this small life on a farm in the middle of nowhere. I came to learn that he felt much the same way. He suggested we meet for coffee again during Theo's next dance class two days from then."

She shot Liam a quick glance, perhaps to check his reaction. He gave an encouraging nod before turning back to the road. She resumed her narration, her voice less unsure. "We met once a week for the rest of the month. I found myself looking forward to seeing him. I began planning what to wear, putting on makeup. It felt as if I was alive again. Then one morning, he wasn't in the coffee shop and I was upset. The strength of my disappointment surprised me. I bought a coffee and stood in the parking lot when I spotted him in his car. He called me over and invited me inside. We drove to a nearby park. That was when our relationship turned … intimate. At first, I felt such guilt, but Lanny was oblivious. He spent almost every waking hour working and fell asleep soon after dinner. I rationalized that he didn't care, that he'd stopped trying to make me happy, but deep down I knew I was lying to myself. Working and struggling to keep us afloat were his way of showing how much he loved us. It just wasn't enough for me anymore."

"Did Devina know about the affair?"

Hope shook her head and stared down at her hands

folded in her lap. "Stu said it was best she didn't find out. He said she was possessive. I was happy enough to keep things a secret, since I also worried about how Lanny would react. As you've witnessed today, my husband has a temper. Stu and I met all spring and summer, finding more places and times to get together. Theo began to ask why I never stayed to watch her dance classes, or why I dropped her off at her friends' homes and never went in for coffee like I used to. I had no idea she had started watching and taking pictures of me with Stu in my car."

"That's how Lanny found out?"

"Theo cannot keep a secret. She found my suitcase, packed to go away with Stu. Neither of us had told our spouses, even on the eve of our departure. I was ... I was going to leave a letter for Lanny and text him when we were a distance away. I believe Stu planned the same with Devina. You see, besides detesting life on farms in the middle of nowhere, Stu and I share another thing in common: jealous partners."

"Did Lanny shoot the Petries?"

Hope's body stiffened, her stare straight ahead, focused on the line of highway. "I didn't know until today. He didn't act any differently or let on that he knew I was leaving with Stu. He told me when I confronted him today that Theo had let the truth slip out, and he went over to tell Stu that Saturday evening to call it off. He doesn't remember picking up the gun from where it sat by the back door. He only intended to scare Stu, to make him know that he meant business. He believed when he entered the house that Devina was visiting Miriam or working in the barn."

Hunter remembered where the bodies had fallen

and tried to place how the scene had played out. Lanny would have been standing under the beam that separated the dining room from the living room, yelling at Stu, who was standing next to the couch, where he'd been sitting moments before. Lanny fired a warning shot that embedded in the wall behind the couch. Devina heard the noise of the gun going off from outside and rushed into the house through the back door and into dining room. The image blurred. "Did he tell you how events unfolded?"

"No, our conversation escalated. He kept saying nothing mattered but us staying together. He said he'd only done what he did for me and the kids."

"I'm sorry. You appear to have been unhappy for a long time."

"I'm not cut out for this life. Jimmy has no friends, and he's as lonely as I am in his own way. I worry that my depression has affected him the most. Theo's fine. She'd be happy anywhere, really." She stopped as if knowing that she'd never be able to justify her plan to leave her two children behind.

In profile, the angles of Hope's face, softened by a tumble of wavy hair, lent her a beauty that he imagined would become more interesting with age. She was cultured and intelligent, a woman who lit up any room she entered. Lanny must have believed he'd punched above his weight when she agreed to marry him. How must he have felt to realize that he was losing her, not only on the day when he found out her bag was packed, but all the days leading up to that moment? To realize that no matter how hard he worked, the life he provided for her and his children would never be enough; that trying to keep her tied to him was only driving her farther away?

Hope kept her silence until Liam pulled into the hospital parking lot and they were walking toward the main entrance. She touched his arm at the crosswalk, and he turned toward her. "Lanny and I stopped talking about anything important a long time ago. If I lose Jimmy too—" She looked away to compose herself, taking a deep breath and wiping her eyes. Her face was resolute when she faced Liam again. "If I lose Jimmy too, I don't know that I'm going to survive."

CHAPTER 45

Jimmy hadn't regained consciousness by the time Hunter and Hope Dooley made it to intensive care. Rosie stayed with Jimmy until they arrived, but Hunter asked her to return to HQ in his car and help take Lanny's statement. "I've spoken with Quade, and one of us should be there, since we know the case better than anyone."

"Wouldn't you prefer to handle this?" Rosie asked.

"I have every faith in you leading the questioning." He briefly filled her in on what Hope had told him on the drive to the hospital. He'd recorded their conversation on his phone and sent her the file so that she could replay it on her way to the station. "I'll keep you updated on Jimmy's condition," he said as she was leaving.

Rosie listened to the tape once she'd left the parking lot and found Hope's words heartbreaking. She could relate to much of her story and realized how fortunate she'd been with her own relationship. She'd also been tempted to find comfort with another man but had taken a different path. There were no guarantees, though. Every journey depended on the individuals involved and who was willing to bend when necessary. The give-and-take of commitment could save or sink a marriage.

Quade met her as she entered the office. "You and I are going to interview Lanny Dooley, but I want you to lead the questioning."

"Auger—"

"Is busy elsewhere." Quade clamped her mouth shut and strode past Rosie on the way to the stairwell to take them to the basement and the interview room. Rosie followed, nearly running to keep up.

"From what I hear, Lanny hasn't spoken since he was arrested," Quade said, looking over her shoulder as she pushed the door open. "Do your best to get his statement."

Lanny was already seated at a table when they entered the small, windowless room. His handcuffs had been removed, and he was still wearing his street clothes. He'd turned down the offer of a lawyer, but Rosie asked him again if he would like one present. He took a moment to respond with the shake of his head. Rosie told him that their conversation was being recorded and videotaped. "Can you tell us what led up to the argument with your wife today, Lanny?" she asked.

Lanny dropped his head. He kicked at the table leg but stayed silent.

"Hope told us that she'd been having an affair with Stu Petrie and was planning to leave Ashton with him. Theo told you enough that you figured out what was going on. Is this accurate, Lanny?" She worked to make her voice sympathetic. "I can only imagine what you must have been feeling, how hard that must have been to hear."

He raised his eyes to hers. "Really? I doubt that. How's my boy?"

"He's getting the best of care. We'll tell you as soon as we have an update."

"I'd appreciate that."

"When did you find out about your wife and Stu?" For a moment, she thought she'd blown it asking him so soon into the interview. He appeared on the cusp of shutting down. He took a breath and looked at his hands. After a brief silence, he began speaking in a low monotone.

"Theo spilled the news that Saturday morning. I hid out in the barn all afternoon so Hope wouldn't figure out I knew about her and Stu. Jimmy was off fishing with Matt Clark, the boy staying with Stu and Devina for the summer. Hope took Theo to town before dinner, so I had time to talk to Stu and make him see reason. Hope would have been livid if she found out I interfered, but I felt I had no choice. She wasn't acting rationally. I drove to the Petrie farm and half-hid the truck behind a woodpile in case Hope drove by and looked up the driveway. When I went in by the back door, Devina wasn't in the kitchen like she normally would be, so I figured she'd gone out or was working in the garden or the chicken coop. Stu asked who was there, and I said it was me, Lanny. He was quiet for a few seconds but then called me to come on through in this fake, hearty voice that made me madder than hell, knowing how he was screwing my wife. I don't remember picking up the gun or loading it but must have because it was in my hands when I went in through the dining room. Stu stood up when he saw me and told me not to do anything crazy. I said that I knew he'd been sleeping with my wife, and he had to leave her alone. 'I wondered how long it would take you to figure it out,' he said like I was stupid and their affair was a test or something. I saw red."

"What did you do next?"

"I fired a shot into the wall to let him know I was through being jerked around. The sound of the gun going off must have brought Devina in from outdoors because the next thing I knew, she was standing next to me, asking what was going on. I told her Stu had been cheating on her with my wife and they were planning on leaving us. Up until then, I wasn't sure they were going away for good, but Stu didn't deny it. Devina looked at him for what felt like a long time and must have read the truth in his face, because all of a sudden she lunged for the rifle and got it pointed in his direction. Next thing I know, the gun's gone off and he's dropped like a bag of cement onto the floor."

"Did Devina shoot him?"

"We both had our hands on the gun. I tried to get it away from her after the bullet hit Stu, and we struggled and it went off again. This time, Devina took it in the chest, and she crumpled on the floor. All I could do was stand there with my mouth hanging open in total shock. It felt like a few minutes passed before I started thinking properly, and even then—"

"It must have been horrifying."

"Yeah, it was like a bad movie. I couldn't believe this was happening to me. I'd only come over to talk to Stu, and now he and Devina were lying dead on the floor. I knew Matt would be home soon, and I had to get out of there. I wiped off the gun, set it next to Devina, and pressed her hand on the shaft and trigger. Then I took off through the front door and got in my truck. Thankfully, I didn't see Matt and made it home before Hope. I think I might have passed Jimmy on the road, but he didn't see me. It was getting really dark by then."

"Hope never suspected?"

"No, I acted like everything was normal while I waited all night and the next day for the police to come pick me up, or word to get around about the deaths, but nothing. It didn't add up. Matt should have called somebody. I was shocked to hear he'd gone missing."

"Were you concerned about him?"

"Yeah. I thought the fear of finding the bodies might be the reason he took off."

"Did you believe he saw you in the house?"

"I was quite certain he hadn't." Lanny shrugged. "If he witnessed anything and told the police, I was okay with that. It felt like my chances improved of somehow escaping detection the longer he was away. Still, I can't tell you how sick I felt, knowing my part in all that went down. My main concern was keeping Hope from finding out I'd gone over there, as irrational as that now seems. Anyway, I went with Calvin Frisk to pick up Stu for darts Sunday night, and the Petrie house was quiet. Completely in darkness. I began to think I'd imagined the whole thing but knew I hadn't. We both commented on how strange it was that Devina hadn't turned on the porch light, but Calvin didn't appear overly concerned. I told him to wait in the truck while I went inside for Stu. I thought if my DNA was found in the room, that would give a reason." He rubbed his forehead. "I never meant any of this to happen. I only wanted Hope — I wanted to go back to the way things were.'"

"What happened today?"

"I don't know. Theo must have said something that tipped Hope off. She acted terrified of me and told the kids to hide. I couldn't make her see reason. I guess I grabbed her and tried to shake sense into her. Things went flying and crashing. The more scared she acted, the madder I got. Then Jimmy ran into the room like I was this monster hurting his mother. I … I couldn't believe how out of control it had gotten. I swear I never meant to hurt them." He covered his eyes with a hand.

Rosie looked sideways at Quade, who'd been studying Lanny the entire time. Quade nodded and said, "I'm afraid we're going to have to charge you with causing two deaths and covering them up, Mr. Dooley, and I suggest now is a good time for you to speak with a lawyer. More charges are likely pending, so you need to have representation."

Lanny lowered his hand onto the table and nodded. "Believe it or not, I'm glad to have this out in the open, and I'll accept blame for my part. I feel bad about Devina, who didn't deserve any of this. Stu is another matter, but even he didn't deserve to die that way. I've lost my family, so anything the courts decide to do to me can't hurt any more than this already does."

Quade stood and signalled for an officer to take Lanny to a location where he could call a lawyer. She led Rosie from the room while reading her cell phone, stopping at the door to the stairs and lifting her head to look at her. "You did great work in there, Rosie. I agree with Hunter that you're cut out for Major Crimes. Don't give up if this is where you want to work. Gain experience and apply again. I'll leave you here."

Quade motioned for Rosie to go on without her and

resumed reading her phone screen. Rosie opened the door and started up the steps, more hopeful than she'd been in a while. The office was quiet when she entered. Boots sat in his usual place with Jingles standing next to him, leaning in to watch something on the computer monitor. Auger was nowhere in sight, so Rosie ambled over to see what had captured their interest. Both looked at her like guilty schoolboys caught playing hooky.

"What's going on guys? Don't tell me you've discovered Pornhub."

"Ha, I wish it was only that." Boots turned up the volume and angled the screen so she could see.

"Is that Auger with the top brass?" she asked.

"It is, and they've announced him as the new head of Homicide and Major Crimes."

"No." Rosie grabbed on to the desk to keep herself from falling. "How could that be? Quade is doing a fantastic job. I just left her."

"No idea," Jingles said, "but he was next in line when Greta was staff sergeant. That must have factored in."

"Shit. I can't believe he wrangled the job away from Quade. She must be devastated."

"At least you get a break from this unit," Boots said. "We're all thinking about transferring to patrol."

Rosie made it to her desk without stumbling and dropped into her seat. It was time to pack up her things and leave before a triumphant Auger returned from the news conference to gloat. She hoped he'd choke on a fat old piece of crow. She checked her phone. Nothing from Hunter and no word about Jimmy. Hunter was going to be blindsided by Auger's news. She was happy now to be leaving the unit, uncomfortable with her decision not to take on Auger when Ella had offered her support. She couldn't have stopped him, though, could she? His power kept growing, and he'd have completely destroyed her career. She believed this to be true, even though the ugly seed of self-doubt had begun to take root. She had to hope Auger would be satisfied with winning this promotion, and he'd decide she wasn't worth his time. Now that he was staff sergeant, he'd have to believe she wasn't a threat to smear his reputation, because his ego was all-consuming and he considered himself omnipotent. She would be less than nothing to him once she was out of his sight — but why did she have this sick feeling that nothing when it came to Auger was ever going to be over?

CHAPTER 46

E lla hit *Send*, stood, and backed away from her desk. Canard would be pleased. He'd asked for an update article on the Petrie murders for the morning paper, and she'd come through with an exclusive. She checked the time. Nine o'clock and plenty of evening left. Classical music swirled up through the floorboards from Tony's apartment, a reminder that he was holding dinner for her. She changed her top and washed her face before descending the short flight to his apartment door, which he'd left unlocked. Tony and Finn both stood to embrace her. Their faces glowed in the candles Tony had lit around the living room. She counted at least twenty in her sweep of the space.

"We thought you'd never finish. Sit, sit while I pour you a glass of vino." Tony checked on Lena sleeping in the playpen as he moved over to the drinks cart. "So, any news on young Jimmy?"

"No." Ella struggled to control the sadness she felt for the boy. His own father had put him into intensive care, and the last report was that Jimmy might not recover. How could one make sense of that? She'd been fortunate Hunter had called her at the pub and offered the scoop. Kurt Auger's promotion had filtered through the team, and Hunter had been rightly disgusted enough not to let Auger grab the glory as he surely would have. She regretted even more not having been able to convince Rosie Thorburn or the other two women in Toronto to make an accusation against the man. He needed to be stopped, but perhaps now was not the time. She'd continue to watch him in his new position, and wait for him to slip up.

Finn raised his glass after Ella accepted hers from Tony. "I want to thank you both for helping out with Lena these past few months. I don't know how we would have managed without you."

They clinked glasses. "Have you any word from Adele?" Ella asked. She'd put off questioning Finn, and he hadn't volunteered any information. However, he seemed relaxed tonight, and there might never be an optimal time to raise the issue of his missing wife.

"Not for the past month. Her mother believes she's in the area but not certain where."

"And I've advised Finn to hire a lawyer," Tony said.

"Whatever for?" Ella asked.

"To protect his parental rights and to make sure Lena doesn't get in the middle of a tug of war."

"But I want Adele to be involved in her life." Finn's eyes blazed with conviction in the candlelight.

Ella considered Adele's erratic behaviour before weighing in. "Finn, Tony might have a point. Why don't you talk with a lawyer and explain the situation? It can't hurt."

"I have just the person lined up," Tony said. "I can

put you in contact with her whenever you give the word. Her specialty is family law."

"Let me sleep on it." Finn stood abruptly and walked over to look at Lena.

Tony and Ella exchanged glances. Tony leaned in to whisper into her ear. "He still believes she's coming home." He straightened and spoke in a louder voice. "So, what's the news on Stefan? I haven't noticed him around."

"And we stagger from one awkward subject to another." Ella drank from her glass and set it on the coffee table. "He appears to have ghosted me."

"And you are naturally devastated."

"It doesn't make me happy, but—" She shrugged. "To be honest, it doesn't bother me that much either. I liked him well enough, but I've hardly noticed his absence."

"Jeesuz, girl. Your dating record is a marvel."

"Thanks." She scowled. "I don't need a man to complete me."

"An admirable quality, if I didn't believe you'd be happier with someone in your life who cares for you."

"But I have that."

He returned her smile before getting to his feet. "That shrimp creole isn't getting any fresher. What say we eat and set aside our troubles for an hour? Come sit, Ella, and we'll wait on you. Your poor face still resembles a prizefighter's breakfast."

"Good by me," Finn said.

"And me." Ella sat at the table and watched her two friends serve the meal. She'd known Finn the longest, but Tony had fast become as dear to her. She liked her life now, regardless of how much Tony believed she needed a mate. In the final analysis, Stefan hadn't held her interest or captured the part of her she kept hidden. He hadn't entered her thoughts in quiet moments, like Liam Hunter did, a realization she dared not linger on.

Her cell phone pinged a message, and she pulled it from her pocket. *Speak of the devil,* she thought as she read Hunter's name on the screen.

Jimmy Dooley awake was all he'd written, but it was enough for the tightness in her chest to ease and the night to feel less overwhelming. The entire case had been tragic, but the boy's recovery was a ray of hope for better days to come. "I have good news," she said as Tony set a heaping plate in front of her. "It turns out not all is lost."

———

JIMMY WAITED in the wheelchair outside the hospital main entrance for his mother to pull up in their van. He was chilled in his sweatshirt, but it didn't take long for his mom to arrive. The nurse helped him climb into the front passenger seat.

"Where's Theo?" he asked, looking behind him.

"At a friend's. We'll pick her up on the way home."

He settled back in the seat. So far, he hadn't talked to anybody about his father and that terrible afternoon. His mom had tried, and the police, but he couldn't answer their questions. His mind had blocked that day, and when he tried to remember, panic welled up, and he'd have trouble catching his breath. His mom said not to worry; they could talk about things when he was ready.

They started driving, and he closed his eyes.

"Does your head hurt, honey?"

She had rarely called him that before, and his closed eyelids held back tears. *Big fat baby. Hiding behind your retard sister. Stupid fat goof.* He turned his head to look out the side window. "I'm just kinda tired," he said.

They drove for what felt like a long time, and he thought they must be close to Ashton. He didn't want to return to their house, and his stomach tightened at the thought of going inside. He faced forward and made sure no tears slipped out before closing his eyes again. "Where are we going?" he asked when he finally looked at the road. Nothing was familiar. They were in the country but not anywhere close to their house.

"A detour." She turned her head and smiled at him. "A nice surprise."

Half an hour later, she drove into a driveway and stopped in from of a tall metal gate. Someone asked who she was through a two-way microphone, and a moment later, the gate swung open and they continued down the tree-lined drive to a bungalow surrounded by woods. A man opened the front door and ushered them inside. The front hallway was empty; there was a camera above them on the ceiling. They crossed into a front room with curtains drawn across the windows. Two lamps provided pools of light on either side of a couch. Matt Clark and a woman both stood, and Jimmy's eyes widened at the sight of his friend. Matt jumped across the space and gave him a careful hug.

"This is my mom and my soon-to-be little sister." He grinned and turned to put his hand on his mother's belly.

"Pleased to meet you at last, Jimmy." Matt's mom bent forward and wrapped her arms around his shoulders. "Thank you for looking after Matt and keeping him safe. You're a very brave boy."

"Matt's my best friend."

"So he told me. We'll leave you to catch up. Lunch will be ready soon. I hope you like hamburgers."

"I do." The despair and anxiety of moments before lifted, and he watched her and his mom smile at each other before leaving the two of them alone. He and Matt sat sideways at each end of the couch, facing each other.

"They wanted to take us to the States, but I wouldn't leave until I knew you were okay. Your mom is nice. She said you've had a tough time."

Jimmy swallowed hard. He could feel his face turning red and knew tears weren't far off. He couldn't let himself cry in front of Matt. He kept his mouth shut and looked down at his feet.

"It's okay," Matt said. "I was freaked out when we found out my dad was involved in bad things too."

"And how did you get over it?"

"I'm learning to take it a day at a time. Helping my mom keeps me from thinking about him as much."

"My dad tried to hurt my mom. He killed the Petries." The misery threatened to spill out of him, and he lowered his head to hide his face from Matt.

"You should talk to your mom about those things, Jimmy. Don't keep what happened bottled up. It's a lot to handle."

Jimmy nodded but kept his face averted. He took a few moments to steady himself. "When are you leaving?"

"Tomorrow. I don't know where we're headed. We'll be going into witness protection, I guess."

"Then I won't see you."

"Mom says we can be in touch once we're settled, but we'll have to work things out. We could meet at summer camp or somewhere in the summers."

Jimmy straightened. "That'd be great." He'd have something to look forward to. "Mom says we're moving too. Away from the country and into the city so we can meet new people. Theo doesn't want to leave her friends, but Mom says it'll be a fresh start."

"Well, don't throw out your fishing rod, 'cause you'll need it next summer when we get together." Matt prodded Jimmy's foot with his own. "When I heard how you protected your mom, well, you're the best friend to have, Jimmy Dooley, and you're the only good thing to come out of this summer."

For the first time in a long while, Jimmy could imagine himself fitting in somewhere, maybe in the new life his mom was promising. He never had to face the bullies at his old school. He didn't have to tell anybody about his dad if he didn't want to. Maybe the fresh start his mom talked about could happen.

"Wanna get something to eat?" he asked, hungry for the first time in a while. He didn't want to talk anymore about his dad or remember waking up in the hospital. He'd keep those thoughts to himself for another day, maybe longer if he felt like it.

Matt grinned. "Yeah, I could eat." They stood, he slung his arm around Jimmy's shoulders, and they walked into the kitchen, where their moms were having a glass of wine and waiting for them to spend one final afternoon together, trying to be kids again before they went their separate ways.

ACKNOWLEDGMENTS

Each book begins with the nugget of an idea. For me, this story began when my husband and I were driving on the highway through Ashton on our way home to Ottawa. The well spaced farms and homes, woods and fields seemed a perfect backdrop for murder. I've taken liberties with the locations, (the Petrie farm is pure fabrication, for example), although I highly recommend visiting the very real Ashton Brew Pub and General Store if you're ever out that way.

Thank you to my editor, Allister Thompson, and cover designer, Laura Boyle. Again, I owe my beta readers my thanks for their initial feedback - Carol Gage, Derek Nighbor, Darlene Cole - your insights have helped to improve the manuscript as always. Another huge thank you to Susan Rothery for such a careful copy edit, and to Lisa Weagle for her final read-through. So, so much appreciated!

And I owe a debt of gratitude to you, my readers who have supported me and kept me motivated these many years. This is my 25th book, published 20 years after my first release, and I am aging along with each publication. I recently told my husband that this might be my last effort, but then I got a new idea, and I'm well into the fourth in the series. Without question, your emails and enthusiasm keep me at the keyboard.

Booksellers and librarians are some of my favourite

people. Thank you for your support with each of my books. I've been fortunate this year to be invited to several book clubs and can't say enough good things about all the lovely readers I've met. Another shout out to local media, who continue to review my books and keep me in the public eye.

And last but not least, I'm indebted to my family for your continued love and support as I spend hours at this book business. I truly am loved and blessed.

ABOUT THE AUTHOR

Brenda Chapman is a crime writer who has published twenty-five books, including the lauded Stonechild and Rouleau series, the Anna Sweet mysteries for adult literacy, and the Jennifer Bannon mysteries for middle grade readers. Brenda's work has been short-listed for several awards, including four Crime Writers of Canada Awards of Excellence. A former teacher and senior communications advisor in the federal government, she makes her home in Ottawa.

Manufactured by Amazon.ca
Bolton, ON